ALLEN COUNTY PUBL
Y0-ACF-332
3 1833 03598 8937

FICTION
ROSENBERGER, JOSEPH.
CARIBBEAN BLOOD MOON

on had
rm. He
felt a microsecond of pain, ... into un-
consciousness. McKenna's right hand, formed into a *mao shou,* streaked toward the mobster's throat. Three fingers stabbed into the jugular notch, the "soft spot" in front of the neck just above the top of the breastbone. With the speed of a blinking eye, the man's tracheal cartilages were crushed and he was choking and drowning—deluged in his own blood—at the same time singing his own discordant requiem, a rapid series of gasping and gurgling sounds that could have been coming from a half-clogged water pipe. Or the death rattle of a man being hanged slowly by piano wire.

QUANTITY SALES

Most Dell books are available at special quantity discounts when purchased in bulk by corporations, organizations, and special-interest groups. Custom imprinting or excerpting can also be done to fit special needs. For details write: Dell Publishing, 666 Fifth Avenue, New York, NY 10103. Attn.: Special Sales Department.

INDIVIDUAL SALES

Are there any Dell books you want but cannot find in your local stores? If so, you can order them directly from us. You can get any Dell book in print. Simply include the book's title, author, and ISBN number if you have it, along with a check or money order (no cash can be accepted) for the full retail price plus $1.50 to cover shipping and handling. Mail to: Dell Readers Service, P.O. Box 5057, Des Plaines, IL 60017.

CARIBBEAN
BLOOD
MOON

Joseph Rosenberger

A DELL BOOK

Allen County Public Library
Ft. Wayne, Indiana

*This book is dedicated to
Perry, Pema, and Brian Browne*

Published by
Dell Publishing
a division of
The Bantam Doubleday Dell Publishing Group, Inc.
666 Fifth Avenue
New York, New York 10103

Copyright © 1988 by Joseph R. Rosenberger

All rights reserved. No part of this book may be reproduced or transmitted in any form or by any means, electronic or mechanical, including photocopying, recording, or by any information storage and retrieval system, without the written permission of the Publisher, except where permitted by law.

The trademark Dell ® is registered in the U. S. Patent and Trademark Office.
a division of the Bantam Doubleday Dell Publishing Group, Inc.

ISBN: 0-440-20016-4

Printed in the United States of America
Published simultaneously in Canada

August 1988

10 9 8 7 6 5 4 3 2 1

KRI

There is a thing inherent and natural,
Which existed before heaven and earth.
Motionless and fathomless,
It stands alone and never changes;
It pervades everywhere and never becomes exhausted.
It may be regarded as the Mother of the Universe.
I do not know its name.
I call it Tao, and I name it as supreme. . . .

Tao-te Ching
by Lao Tzu

CHAPTER 1

Scott McKenna was in a happy, relaxed mood when Raymond Dearl Gordel met his 8:30 P.M. TWA flight from Boston at Tampa's International Airport. McKenna had not seen Gordel in eleven years, since they had attended high school together in Boston, Massachusetts. The two had been good friends ever since the fifth grade. The friendship, however, had been interrupted when Albert William McKenna, Scott's father, had been appointed United States ambassador to Japan, and the family—including Wayne and Mary-Elspeth, Scott's older brother and sister—had gone to live in the Land of the Rising Sun.

McKenna had spent ten years in Japan, eight of them in Master Yoshiaki Nawa's *kodokan,* a ninja school, or "the place to learn the way." In the meanwhile, Ray Gordel had obtained a degree in oceanography and, in 1986, had gone into partnership with Victor Felix Jorges in Tampa, Florida. A professional diver and salvage expert, Jorges, a Cuban expatriate, was the owner and operator of the Dolphin Salvage Company. After Gordel had bought into the business, the name had been changed to the J & G Salvage Company.

After the two picked up McKenna's luggage, the first thing Ray wanted to know was if it was true what he had heard about Scott's becoming a Master Ninja while he had been in Japan. Yes, it was true, admitted McKenna, who then, as he and Gordel walked toward the parking lot, had a question of his own.

"Ray, how sure are you and Jorges that you've found the *Santa Francesca*?" McKenna asked. "In one of your letters to me when I was in Japan, you mentioned that treasure hunters have been looking for that Spanish wreck for the past hundred years."

Carrying one of McKenna's suitcases, Gordel turned and took
a route through several long rows of cars. As blond as a Swede, he
had long sideburns, a thick mustache, and sky-blue eyes. At an
even six feet, he weighed 187 pounds, none of it fat. There were
two unusual features about him: half the little finger of his right
hand was missing. He had been born without it. He was also very
tan. Most blue-eyed blond people only sunburn, or tan only
slightly.

"We're ninety-five percent certain that the *Santa Francesca* is
where we think it is," Gordel replied, his tone firm and confident.
"If we're right, the three of us are sitting on top of a treasure worth
three hundred million dollars, based on the price of gold today—
and that's not any kind of buildup because we need your eighty-five
thousand. We want you to see maps and hear the evidence before
making up your mind. Actually, Cotton knows more about the
Santa Francesca than I do."

"By 'Cotton' I assume you mean Mr. Jorges," said McKenna,
who didn't look like a ninja. Then again, what are ninja supposed
to look like? They're supposed to be Oriental. They're supposed to
be Japanese. Scott McKenna was the exception. He was the only
Caucasian in history to learn *ninjutsu* in Japan and, in only eight
years, become a Master Ninja with the rank of *jonin,* order of Men
T'u Shen Mi—Disciple of Mysteries.

He didn't look like a millionaire, either. Scott's maternal
grandmother had left him millions. After the trust fund had re-
verted to his control, he had invested much of it wisely, and those
millions were increasing each day. But no one would have known it
to look at him. He was dressed in an off-the-rack Holland blue suit,
light-blue shirt, a navy-blue tie, and Carmel kiltie mocs on his feet.

"Yeah, I mean Vic," replied Gordel. "When he was twelve
years old, he had some kind of fever. He and his family were in
Havana then. Whatever the fever was, it turned his hair snow-
white. He's been 'Cotton' ever since. He refuses to dye his hair. He
says he's not going to hide from the world who or what he is."

"He sounds like a good person."

"He is. And does he hate Castro—communists in general and
Fidel Castro in particular. The Fidelistas murdered his father and
two of his uncles."

They came to Ray's Dodge minivan and in a short time had
left the airport and were on the highway driving west. McKenna
sensed that something was troubling his old friend, and Gordel

debated whether he should tell Scott now about Charles Lombardo or wait until Scott had seen the maps. Scott had a right to have all the facts. He might not want to risk getting his head blown off.

McKenna rolled down the window and let the breeze blow in his face. Far in the distance were the lights of Tampa, a city about which McKenna knew next to nothing, other than the fact that it was a center of cigar making and was connected to St. Petersburg, southwest across the bay, by the fifteen-mile Gandy Bridge.

Gordel and Jorges didn't have their salvage vessel, *Little Big Man,* docked in Tampa's harbor. They did have *Slick Sister,* a Chris-Craft used to take tourists sport-fishing. That part of the business was operated by Alfredo Jorges, Cotton's younger brother. J & G Salvage was headquartered in a warehouse on a mile-long peninsula two miles southwest of Sweetwater Creek, a little blob of spit on the highway a mile west of the northwest city limits of Tampa. *Little Big Man* was docked in front of the warehouse.

Gordel was soon driving through the business section of Sweetwater Creek—a half block of buildings whose architecture was out of the nineteenth century, with a lot of decorative fretting and frieze work. Fifteen minutes later, Gordel was parking the minivan in front of the office of the salvage company at the west end of the warehouse. Getting out of the van, McKenna saw that the building was one large rectangle of corrugated iron painted white. He could hear the two air-conditioners on the roof doing their job.

"The apartment is in the rear, in back of the office," said Gordel, pulling one of the suitcases from the van. He glanced at McKenna and grinned. "Cotton is anxious to meet you. But I wonder why he only has the lamps burning?"

The two men crossed the tiny porch and its overhang and entered the office. McKenna, trained in sweep vision, took in the interior in seconds. Victor Jorges was seated at a desk in the northwest corner of the office. In the center of the rear wall was the doorway to the apartment. The door was open, the room beyond dark. East of the door were shelves filled with used sextants, used outboard motors of various sizes, and scores of Aqua-Meter small-boat compasses. Other shelves were filled with smaller marine items—Barlow winch handles, Rangematic distance finders, nautical clocks, wind vanes, stainless-steel top fitting, and more.

On the floor in another corner were stacked six long crates

filled with unassembled aluminum fly-bridge outriggers and outrigger holders. The double doors to the warehouse section were between the stacked crates and the shelves on the other side of the big room. One of the doors was half open. An old couch—the lower front showed the results of a cat manicuring its claws—three wooden filing cabinets, and a short table (on which was a Mr. Coffee maker) were against the south wall. Against the west wall were four bookcases filled with nautical books and volumes on treasure hunting.

Several battered chairs, each with a leather seat and back, were in front of the green metal desk. One of the lit lamps was toward the front center of the desk. Another lamp was on top of one of the bookcases. The third lamp was on the table with Mr. Coffee. Because of their large shades, the lamps cast a downward glow, leaving the upper portion of the office shrouded in twilight.

"What's wrong with the other lights, Cotton?" Gordel put down the suitcase and looked questioningly at Jorges, whose face he couldn't see clearly. Although the light from the lamp on the desk was at Jorges's level, his face was hidden partially by the lampshade.

In reply to Gordel's question a man stepped from the darkness of the first room of the apartment with a .357 Colt Python revolver in his right hand, its long barrel pointed in the direction of Gordel and McKenna.

"We'll give you plenty of light," sneered Jody Karl, advancing into the room. He motioned toward Jorges with the Colt Python magnum. "Go ahead, spic. Turn on the lights."

Ray Gordel and Scott McKenna, realizing they had walked into a trap, remained silent and motionless as another man came into the office through the apartment entrance and four more hoods moved into the room from the warehouse. All five had guns in their hands.

Jorges came around the desk, went over to the west wall, and flipped a light switch. Immediately, two banks of fluorescent lights suspended from the ceiling flooded the room with brightness. It was then that Gordel and McKenna saw that Jorges's left eye was blackened and that the left side of his face was swollen.

Seeing that McKenna and Gordel had noticed his beat-up condition, Jorges shrugged. "They jumped me before I knew what was happening," he explained with only a slight accent, moving over to them in the center of the room. "I was in the bathroom.

When I came out, there they were. They think we have a treasure map with a big red X on it!"

"Yeah, and here we are, and you dumb jokers know what we want," growled Jody Karl. By then, he and the other five gunsels were surrounding Jorges, Gordel, and McKenna.

"Your boss has gone too far this time," Gordel snapped defiantly, thrusting out his square jaw. "You've broken in here, beat up Cotton, and now you're pointing guns at us. All of you and Lombardo are going to have some explaining to do to the police."

"Ha! This guy's a riot!" jeered Nick Flipps, one of the men who had been in the warehouse. A 9mm Browning DA autoloader was in his left hand. "He's so fuckin' dumb he thinks the cops can help him!"

Karl nodded. A cruel-looking, sharp-featured man of about thirty-five, he had thick, wavy hair the color of mahogany and was wearing an expensive tan suit that didn't entirely conceal bulging muscles. He was the eldest of the group. The youngest was Vito Gallucci, the tall, perpetually smiling dirt-bag who had followed Karl from the apartment into the office.

"You two fools have a lot to learn," Karl said coldly, a warning in his voice. His eyes jumped to McKenna. "You, too, 'ninja boy'! Tomorrow, you're going to catch the first plane back to Boston—unless you want to commit suicide." He smiled mockingly at Gordel and Jorges. "For all we care, you can call the police commissioner of Tampa! What are you going to tell him—some wild tale about sunken treasure and that we were here trying to find some maps? We're not even here! There are a score of very respectable people who will swear we were someplace else—different places, since there are six of us!"

"The police won't ignore three murders," Jorges said. "Sooner or later the police will connect Chuckie Lombardo with us and start asking questions."

Karl laughed. "You yahoos have been watching too many late-night movies on TV. We're not going to knock you off. We don't have to. But if we don't find what we're looking for, you're going to wish you were dead by the time we're finished with you."

"I told you, we don't have any map," insisted Jorges, folding his arms across his broad chest, "and all your threats aren't going to make one miraculously appear."

Karl's eyes narrowed and his mouth twisted in anger. "I suppose you bastards are going to deny that you're looking for the *Santa Francesca*?" he said contemptuously.

"Sure we're looking for the vessel—who isn't?" admitted Gordel. "But we don't have a map. What the hell do you think we did—go out and buy some phony map that hucksters sell to dumb tourists? As far as we know, the *Santa Francesca* sank in 1649, somewhere between the southeast coast of Florida and Andros I, one of the larger islands of the Bahamas."

"Yeah, you believe that like I believe in the Easter bunny!" Karl said roughly, the corners of his wide mouth twisting upward.

"Fuck! Let's stop all this crap and work 'em over," growled Virgil Dudenbossle. A hood with a large, wide face, a skinny neck, and such a thin body that his silk suit looked too big for him, he was armed with a 9mm Astra-80 DA autopistol held loosely in his right hand.

"Hey, whoever you guys are! I just came here on a visit," McKenna said suddenly. "I don't know anything about any treasure." There was such fear and timidity in his voice that both Gordel and Jorges glanced at him with surprise and disappointment in their eyes. They had expected better from McKenna, especially Gordel.

"You were still going to give them eighty-five grand," Karl said imperiously. "Let me tell you, stupid! You'd be tossing your dough into a lost cause. If you have any sense, you'll keep your money—and remember what I said about grabbin' a plane back to Boston! Unless you want your kneecaps worked over with a sledge-hammer."

"And both arms broken!" warned Pete Ratta, another goon, with a savage, shaggy look about him.

"Handcuff the three of them," Karl said, looking around the office. "We'll tear this motherfuckin' place apart."

"Why waste time, Jody?" Ellis Joost said impatiently. "Hell, why not beat the truth out of them? That goddamn map could be anywhere around here or in the back rooms."

"Because Chuckie doesn't want them roughed up unless we have to, dummy!" growled Karl, looking at fat-boy Joost as though he had just crawled out from the inside of an outdoor toilet. "We do it the way Chuckie wants. First we search the office and the apartment."

"What about the salvage boat?" asked Pete Ratta.

"We search that too."

Flipps, Dudenbossle, and Ratta jerked the arms of Gordel, Jorges, and McKenna behind their backs and snapped handcuffs on their wrists. The sadistic Dudenbossle snapped the jaws of the cuffs extra tight around Gordel's wrists. The three hoods shoved them over to the wooden cases of outriggers on the floor in the corner of the office.

"Sit down and keep your traps shut," Flipps said. "Get cute and you'll lose a lot of teeth—with this!" He held up the Browning DA pistol.

Gordel, Jorges, and the Ninja Master sat down side by side on one of the long wooden cases and watched as five of the mobsters started to search the office, first pulling out drawers from the filing cabinets and the desk.

"Scott, you have certainly changed," muttered Ray Gordel, glancing in disgust at McKenna. "I thought you were going to get down and kiss his feet."

McKenna did not reply.

"Keep your damned mouth shut," warned Flipps, who had sat down on a chair close by. The hood snickered, "It ain't no secret about your friend here. He's a fuckin' coward."

Gordel and Jorges said nothing. What could they say? Flipps had only put into words what they were both thinking.

Scott McKenna, taking short but deep breaths, tested the handcuffs. Made of stainless steel, with welded chain-and-cheek construction, the cuffs were of a rotary swing-through design that allowed them to be closed quickly. Two stainless-steel links held the cuffs together.

The question was—could he do it? There was only one answer: *I had better!*

Closing his eyes, McKenna began to inhale slowly, taking long and very deep breaths and mentally concentrating on an invisible spot in the center of his forehead. He was not only invoking the Absolute, he was very rapidly increasing his Chi and using self-hypnosis to open the reserves of energy stored by the pineal gland. In the parlance of the ninja, he was Stroking the Death Bird.

He was ready in three minutes and fifty-one seconds. The fifth and final stage of the Hsi Men Jitsu, the Way of the Mind Gate, rushed to the front of his consciousness as he tested the two links holding the handcuffs together. Once this fifth stage of *tensui* had fully established itself, McKenna was pure strength, total energy. He was one with the Tao. With supreme confidence he exerted steady pressure on the links, moving his wrists opposite to each other. One of the links snapped. McKenna continued the pressure. In a few more seconds his wrists were free.

Much in the manner of a mongoose preparing its strike against a cobra, McKenna noted the positions of the six gunmen. Jody Karl and Vito Gallucci had piled the contents of the desk drawers onto the top of the desk and were absorbed in going through papers and other items. Vito Gallucci was by the side of the desk and Karl stood in front of it.

Ellis Joost—he had a freak face that only a blind mother could love—had pulled several dozen books from one of the bookcases and was thumbing through them while Pete Ratta and Virgil Dudenbossle continued to pull files, booklets, charts, and advertising material from the wooden filing cabinets.

Nick Flipps was only seven feet from McKenna, rocking the chair back and forth on its two rear legs. His eyes were on Karl and Gallucci across the room.

McKenna's attack was so fantastically fast that Raymond Gordel and Victor Jorges never saw him leave the crate. Neither did Nick Flipps. The goon had time only to turn his head and see the Ninja Master's descending arm. He felt only a microsecond of pain; then he was sinking into unconsciousness and dying from the terrible sword-ridge hand that had chopped him in the left side of the neck and ruptured his jugular vein and carotid artery. Flipps's body hadn't even begun to slide from the chair before the Ninja Master had turned his attention to Pete Ratta and Virgil Dudenbossle.

Both men had caught sight of McKenna from the corner of their eyes and, still in a state of surprise, were swinging around to face him, the stick-thin Dudenbossle reaching for the 9mm Astra he had shoved into his belt.

Pete Ratta—pimp, second-story man, and strong-arm goon—was also wasting his time. His hand was reaching for a 9mm Arminex Trifire autoloader under his coat when McKenna reached him and the now worried Dudenbossle, who almost succeeded in lining up his weapon with McKenna's stomach. Dudenbossle was still thirteen inches short of his goal when the Ninja Master's right arm shot out and his fingers tightened around the right wrist, pushing the Astra pistol to one side. Simultaneously, McKenna slammed his right knee into Dudenbossle's sex machine, the savage uplift crushing his testicles. The hood uttered a loud, choked cry as the Astra slipped from his limp fingers and fell to the floor. At the moment, Dudenbossle was in such agony that he couldn't have defended himself against a six-year-old boy.

Neither could Pete Ratta defend himself. The Arminex Trifire autoloader was half out from underneath his coat, but it was too late. McKenna's left hand chopped against the right side of his head, the *shuto* sword-ridge blow as effective as a hammer hitting his jaw.

McKenna had killed Flipps and taken out Dudenbossle and Ratta in only ten seconds—a very short time, yet long enough to alert the three other hoods, all three of whom lost five or six seconds in surprise with the sudden turn of events.

By the desk, Vito Gallucci and Jody Karl stopped going through the papers they had piled on the desk and reached for their weapons. The only other persons more astonished by McKenna's action were Raymond Gordel and Victor Jorges.

The bucket-headed Ellis Joost had a lot of courage but little common sense. He was not fast, being overweight by twenty pounds. He charged McKenna, who had picked up Dudenbossle's Astra, and snapped off a shot with his 9mm large-frame Llama pistol, firing only a micromoment after the Ninja Master threw the Astra pistol.

A ninja is trained not only in the use of conventional weapons, but in how to use conventional weapons in an unconventional manner. Much of this involves Ugokasu Jitsu, the art of "moving" or throwing, whether the object be a brick, a stone, or a bottle. Or a semiautomatic pistol.

The butt end of the Llama autoloader struck Ellis Joost just above the bridge of the nose and instantly switched off his consciousness. His 9mm full-metal-jacket bullet cut through McKenna's coat and shirt on the right side, the chunk of metal coming within .79 millimeters of touching his flesh. The slug ripped through the back of his coat and hit the east wall.

As Joost started to sink to the floor, Jody Karl yelled, "KILL THE SON OF A BITCH!" and fired wildly at the Ninja Master. McKenna charged toward them with great speed, ducking and dodging from side to side with incredible agility. Karl's big magnum revolver boomed, the .357 flat-nosed bullet cutting air an inch below McKenna's left armpit and only half an inch from his upper-left rib cage.

Karl did his best to step back and trigger off another round,

but he had hesitated a fraction of a second too long—and so had
the terrified Vito Gallucci. Jumping several feet into the air, Mc-
Kenna twisted his body and executed a perfect right-legged spin-
ning dragon kick. The sole of his foot shot into Karl's midsection
like a battering ram, the dynamite blow knocking the hood off his
feet and giving him the worst stomachache of his life.

Pete Ratta might have succeeded in wasting the Ninja Master
if he had been an experienced gunsel. Instead he made a fatal
mistake by waiting to be absolutely certain that his bullet would hit
the target. At the same time that his finger was squeezing the
trigger of his Arminex Trifire pistol, McKenna grabbed his right
wrist and pushed the revolver to one side, the magnum exploding
when the muzzle was pointed toward the ceiling.

No longer smiling, Gallucci tried to free his wrist from Mc-
Kenna's left hand and at the same time let the Ninja Master have a
left uppercut. He failed in both attempts, although he didn't have
time to dwell on his failure, not even for a few moments.

McKenna's right hand, formed into a *mao shou,* the eighth of
the nine hand forms, streaked straight toward Gallucci's throat.
Three fingers stabbed into the jugular notch, the "soft spot" in
front of the neck just above the top of the breastbone. Within the
speed of an eye blink, Gallucci's tracheal cartilages were crushed
and he was choking to death and drowning—deluged in his own
blood—at the same time supplying his own discordant requiem, a
rapid series of gasping and gurgling sounds that could have been
coming from half-clogged water pipe. Or the death rattle of a man
being hanged slowly by piano wire.

Gordel and Jorges, still sitting on the wooden crates, stared at
the quivering and dying hood with all the awe most people would
reserve for a newly arrived alien stepping out of a flying saucer.
Most of their wonderment had been generated by the sudden lightning action McKenna had taken. Not only had he freed himself
from his handcuffs, but in minutes he had slammed all six hoods,
moving so fast they had not been able to keep track of him—and
they had thought he was a coward! But why had he pretended to
be afraid? Why had he acted so subservient in front of Jody Karl?
McKenna had a handcuff around each wrist, and it was plain that
he had actually broken—*broken*—one of the links! What kind of
man had Scott McKenna become?

The Ninja Master picked up the handguns and deposited
them on one of the wooden outrigger crates.

"Scott, how did you do it?" asked Gordel in a small voice. "How could you pull those links apart—some kind of ninja trick?"

McKenna moved over to the stone-dead Nick Flipps and took the key to the handcuffs from the right side coat pocket of the corpse.

"It wasn't a trick," McKenna told Gordel and Jorges, both of whom had gotten to their feet. "Let's just say it was 'mind over matter.' Turn around so I can remove the handcuffs."

McKenna freed Gordel, and as he removed the handcuffs from Cotton Jorges, the Cuban said, "I must apologize to you, Mr. McKenna. From the way you were talking a little while ago, I had assumed you were a coward. I was wrong."

"I don't get it. Why did you pretend to be afraid, Scott?" Gordel rubbed first one wrist, then the other. Both wrists were very red, the skin deeply indented from the tight handcuffs.

"To keep them off guard," McKenna told him. He turned the key in the cuff on his left wrist. "By the time the wolf realizes the rabbit is really a tiger, it is too late—for the wolf. Keep them covered. The two I only knocked out will be able to take their wounded friends out of here, after I am finished with them." He pointed to Pete Ratta, who was still unconscious on his back, then at Ellis Joost, who was lying face down.

The four other hoods were in far worse condition. In fact, Nicholas Flipps and Vito Gallucci could not have been worse off: they were dead. Jody Karl, kicked in the stomach, and Virgil Dudenbossle, kneed in the testicles, were in a world of agony. Moaning, Dudenbossle lay on his left side, his hands clutching his crushed balls, his knees drawn up. Flat on his belly, Karl had his hands pressed into his stomach and low "Uh, Uh, Uh, Uhs" were jumping from his mouth. Now and then his hips and buttocks moved up and down, as though he were trying to have some strange kind of intercourse with the floor.

Ray Gordel picked up Pete Ratta's Arminex Trifire autopistol.

"What are you going to do with them, Scott?" he asked. "God Almighty, I think two of them are already dead."

"They are," replied McKenna. "I meant to kill them. We're in no danger from the authorities. The others can't tell what happened here, not without incriminating themselves."

"They must have parked a short distance from here," Jorges said, checking the 9mm Browning DA that Nick Flipps had carried, "or I would have heard them drive up. They sneaked up on me."

"Who is Lombardo?" asked McKenna.

"I was going to tell you about him." Gordel sounded embarrassed. "We weren't going to accept your money without letting you know what we're up against. Charles Lombardo is a big-shot attorney in Tampa. He's also looking for the *Santa Francesca*. His father is Vincent 'The Crusher' Lombardo, the semiretired Chicago mobster. You've heard of him. He's supposed to control 'the Outfit' in Chicago."

"One of you get some ice water." McKenna looked down dispassionately at Pete Ratta, then turned to Gordel. "You can give me the details about Lombardo later."

"I'll get it," said Jorges. He shoved the Browning pistol into his belt and headed into the apartment north of the office and warehouse.

"Scott, somehow Lombardo knew you were going to come to Tampa," Gordel said, sounding worried. "Remember how that one scumbag called you 'ninja boy'?"

McKenna put a finger to his lips. Quickly, he walked over to a surprised Gordel and whispered in his ear. "Watch what you say. I think this office or your apartment has been bugged. We'll check for a transmitter after we get rid of these cruds. In the meanwhile, don't say anything about the *Santa Francesca*. Warn Cotton when he gets back. Whisper it to him."

Concern etched on his face, Gordel nodded.

After Jorges returned with a pitcher half filled with water and half filled with ice cubes, McKenna dragged Ellis Joost across the floor and let him sag next to Peter Ratta. It didn't take long to awaken both men with the ice water. Slightly dazed, they sat up and looked at the Ninja Master in fear. The rabbit had indeed turned into a tiger.

"Where are your cars parked?" McKenna asked in a pleasant voice.

Ellis Joost, who had a red lump above the bridge of his nose, glared at McKenna. Ratta, rubbing the side of his head, said nothing.

"I asked a question; I want an answer—or would you prefer I break your fingers, one by one?" He looked at Joost, who had recovered more quickly than Ratta.

"A quarter of a mile to the northeast," Joost muttered, cautiously feeling the lump on his forehead. "We parked under some palm trees."

"I knew the son of a bitches crept in," Jorges said with a satisfied grin. Of medium height, he was brawny, with a wide face and a great mane of thick white hair, sprinkled with some gray and rising from a lofty brow. There was usually a fierce, lyric look in his black eyes. At one time he had been religious and had even thought about becoming a priest. That seemed like a million years ago. . . .

McKenna said to Gordel and Jorges, "Keep your guns trained on these two. If either one tries to run—kill him." He turned back to Joost and Ratta. "Pick this creep up"—he pushed at Dudenbossle with the tip of his foot— "and the one in front of the desk and sit them on the couch. Don't concern yourselves with the other two. They're dead. *Move!*"

Joost and Ratta managed to lift Dudenbossle to his feet and get him to the couch. All the while, Dudenbossle kept muttering, "OH . . . OH . . . OH . . . OH," and, once he was on the couch—"G-G-Get m-me to a-a doc-c-tor. . . ." With his legs spread as wide as possible, he acted as if he had a red-hot football between his thighs. He leaned back, resting his head on the top part of the couch.

It was easier for Joost and Ratta to get Jody Karl to the couch. While the kick in the stomach was painful, it could not be compared to a slam in the testicles. By the time Karl was seated on the couch, the pain in his stomach was bearable. He was fully aware of what was going on around him and of the danger he and his men were facing. What could he possibly tell Chuckie Lombardo—that Scott McKenna had pulled his handcuffs apart and then slammed out all of them, killing Nick and Vito in the process! But that's what had happened!

"We—we only follow orders," Karl mumbled to McKenna, hoping to get on his good side. "We don't have anything against you guys personally."

"He's tellin' the truth," Pete Ratta said quickly. He, too, sensed that McKenna was actually the leader, even if Gordel and Jorges didn't realize it yet. Ratta was seated next to Karl. Joost sat at the end of the couch next to Ratta.

The Ninja Master's move was extremely fast. His right hand, formed into a *seiken* forefist, struck Joost in the solar plexus. The blow was light, and Joost, surprised but not hurt in the least, drew back and braced himself for the real attack, which did not come. All he received was a slight smile from McKenna, who had just given him a *hsin chuan* heart punch, one of the nine fatal blows of the *dim mak way,* commonly known as the "ninja death touch."

Peter Ratta also assumed that McKenna was toying with them, the way a cat toys with a mouse before it kills. He didn't even flinch when McKenna struck him lightly in the center of the chest. The blow had been so light that he had hardly felt it. Ratta didn't know it, but he had just received a fatal *fei chuan* lung punch and had only two days to live. Nervously, he wondered what McKenna would do next.

Ray Gordel and Cotton Jorges, standing back with their guns trained on the hoodlums, exchanged glances. Would Jody Karl be next? But why? What was Scott trying to prove?

The Ninja Master skipped over Jody Karl and, with a left *seiken* forefist, punched Virgil Dudenbossle in front, just below his right rib cage, twisting his wrist slightly as he delivered the *kan chuan* liver punch. The blow was no more powerful than a playful punch to the shoulder by a friend. Nonetheless, Dudenbossle let out a low cry of pain. It wasn't the punch that had caused his discomfort. He had been startled and had jumped in surprise; it was the jerking that shook his testicles that had caused the pain.

McKenna's eyes—two orbs of ice—moved to Jody Karl. "I believe you are the leader of these men?"

Karl hesitated a moment, mentally kicking himself for misjudging McKenna. The motherfucker was a one-man army. . . .

"Y-yes," Karl finally admitted.

"And your boss is Charles Lombardo?"

"Yes."

"I have a message that you can give to Mr. Lombardo," McKenna said. He pointed at Ellis Joost. "He will die tomorrow afternoon before five o'clock. And he"—his finger moved to an openmouthed Peter Ratta—"will die the day after tomorrow, before noon."

"Hey! Wait a minute! I—" began a frightened Ratta.

"And he will leave this world"—McKenna turned his head toward Dudenbossle—"in three days, between noon and four in the afternoon, and no power on earth can stop it!"

Karl and Ratta and Joost looked up in stark amazement and disbelief at McKenna. Jody Karl, tasting bile in his mouth, didn't feel like laughing because he knew McKenna wasn't joking. That was it! He was using psychological warfare. How could he make any man die the next day, or the day after? It had to be nonsense. Yet McKenna had freed himself from the handcuffs. Karl didn't know what to say. Neither did Ratta and Joost, both of whom were terrified. Who really knew what that son of a bitch McKenna had learned in Japan? Shit! Everyone knew the Japs were tricky bastards who knew all kinds of strange ways to waste a guy. All they could do was stare at McKenna, a cold fear spreading along their spines.

"Ray. Cotton. Take these two to where they have their cars parked," the Shadow Warrior said, pointing at Joost and Ratta. "Don't take any chances with them. Kill them if they give you any trouble."

It was forty-five minutes before Gordel and Jorges returned with the two mobsters. Ratta drove a Chrysler Le Baron, with Ray Gordel in the seat next to him. Ellis Joost was behind the wheel of a four-door silver Buick Park Avenue. Cotton Jorges was in the rear seat, holding a Browning DA pistol against the back of Joost's head.

McKenna first had Ratta and Joost carry the bodies of Nick Flipps and Vito Gallucci to the two cars and dump the corpses in the rear seats. Before the two mobsters helped Virgil Dudenbossle and Jody Karl into the cars, the Ninja Master said to Karl, "Tell your boss Lombardo not to bother my two friends again. Tell him that if he does, he will have me to deal with. I will come after him, and I'll kill him. Do you understand?"

Karl nodded quickly. He hesitated, but finally his curiosity got the better of him. "About the others dying," he said. "You were only trying to frighten them, weren't you?"

"All the flowers of tomorrow are in the seeds of today," Mc-Kenna said, smiling slightly. "All the graves of tomorrow will be filled with the life that existed today. The three will die. I am permitting you to live so that you will remember my words. Now go—and never come back. All you will find here from now on is swift death."

McKenna, Gordel, and Jorges watched the beaten mobsters drive off, and when the taillights of the two cars were no longer visible, the three started back toward the office. Gordel and Jorges at once wanted wanted McKenna to explain his strange behavior

toward the hoods, why he had punched three of the thugs so
lightly and then said they would die?

"What was the purpose, Scott?" said Ray Gordel, frowning
deeply. "We're going to look stupid when they don't die."

"It was a poor bluff to use against that *hideputa* Lombardo,"
observed Jorges, glancing at McKenna, who did not appear to be
the least bit disturbed.

"I was not bluffing," McKenna said matter-of-factly. "I said
the three would die and I meant it. They will die."

Gordel stopped and turned to McKenna, new respect in his
eyes. "A ninja technique. You used a secret ninja technique? Was
part of it those soft blows you gave them?"

"Yes, it was a ninja technique," McKenna admitted. "But I
am not at liberty to discuss it. We have more important things to
talk about—and what I learned in Japan is not one of them. . . ."

*(What I used on the three gangsters is only a part of Nien Jih
Ssu Ch'u Chueh, the fine art of killing without leaving a trace.)*

Only three qualities are needed to successfully execute the
"ninja death touch": The *Will,* the *Knowledge,* the *Silence.* A lot of
people in the West have heard about the "mysterious" Dim Mak,
the special technique of killing by interfering with the body's normal flow of Chi. This is accomplished by striking the Points of
Alarm of the same system that is used in the ancient medical art of
acupuncture. The force of the blows and the manner in which they
are delivered determine the time of death. But only an expert can
accomplish this feat.

Nien Jih Ssu Ch'u Chueh is actually a triangle. Dim Mak is
the base. The left side is Dim Haueh, in which a ninja strikes the
blood vessels and causes blood clots to form. The right side is Dim
Ching, the technique used in causing death by working against the
nerve plexes of the body. Scott McKenna was an expert in Dim
Mak. He was also proficient in Dim Ching. He would not become
adept in Dim Haueh until he had reached the Order of Men T'u
Tao—Disciple of the Way.

Ray Gordel glanced up at the star-studded sky and shifted his
feet uncomfortably. "Scott, you mentioned the possibility of
Lombardo's having a bug planted in the office. Even—"

"Or in the apartment, or in *Little Big Man!*" interjected Mc-
Kenna.

"Anyplace! Even if you're right, how can we be certain? We
don't have any antibugging equipment," pointed out Gordel.

"You do, up to a point, if you have a portable television set with rabbit ears for an antenna," McKenna said. "A TV set will detect a hidden mike, unless the padder or the oscillator in the transmitter has been adjusted to receive slightly above or slightly below the standard band."

Jorges lit a Vantage cigarette with a four-for-a-dollar K mart throwaway lighter. "Scott, you seem to know a lot about bugging. Don't tell me they taught electronics at that ninja school in Japan!"

McKenna laughed lightly. "They did—and I am telling you. The ninja of today is an expert in many fields. That's what it's all about—survival."

"But who could have planted a bug, if one is there?" It was clear that the Cuban was skeptical. "After all, you can't just drop the damned thing on the floor. It takes time to hide it."

"You and Ray have a crew, don't you?"

"Yes and no," Jorges said. "We have six or seven men who go with us on a large salvage job. We don't keep the men on a steady payroll; we can't afford it. And I've known those men for several years. I'm sure that none of them could have planted a transmitter."

"First we have to find a bug." Gordel looked at McKenna. "Until we do, it's useless to speculate who might have planted it."

"Until we're sure, don't discuss the treasure," warned McKenna.

"We already have," Gordel said in a sad voice. "For months! At least, we've mentioned the general vicinity of where we think the *Santa Francesca* sank. Of course, that means a hundred-square-mile area."

McKenna resumed walking toward the door of the office. "Once we're inside, don't discuss the treasure or the possibility of a bug. Talk about how we beat the hell out of the hoods. We don't want to let Lombardo know we suspect we're being monitored."

Now it was Gordel and Jorges's turn to stop, both glancing uncertainly at the Ninja Master. "What do you mean, not letting him know we suspect? He'll know we've found the bug when we destroy it and it stops broadcasting!"

"Why destroy it? Why not leave it in place?" offered McKenna. "We'll have an advantage over Lombardo. We can tell him what he hopes to hear, and then some."

"But he already knows that the *Santa Francesca* sank only a short distance southwest of the Dry Tortugas!" Gordel responded tersely, giving McKenna a challenging stare.

"And the *cagada* probably is keeping an eye on us," Jorges amplified, "and will follow us when we go after the galleon."

"All the more reason for us to keep the bug in place, should we find one," McKenna said quickly. "First, we have to locate it. It will be where one would least expect it. By the way, who cleans your office and apartment?"

"We do," Gordel said. "We clean the rooms ourselves."

"I don't see how a TV set can help us," Jorges added skeptically.

Scott McKenna resumed walking toward the office. "Once we're inside, get the TV set and the rabbit ears," he said brusquely. "While I'm looking for the transmitter, don't ask me to explain what I'm doing. Just watch and think twice before speaking. If we don't find a transmitter in the office, we'll search the apartment, then the boat. One more thing: if we find a bug and have to search for it, don't make any noise moving furniture. And speak in a normal tone of voice."

"You're the boss," conceded Gordel. "I suppose you know what you're doing."

"I do—count on it."

Their curiosity raised, Gordel and Jorges watched the Ninja Master switch on the television set and turn the volume all the way to zero. As soon as the set was warmed up, McKenna turned to Channel 2. Then—while Gorden and Jorges carried on a conversation about imaginary repairs of one of the engines of *Little Big Man*—McKenna turned the fine-tuning knob to its extreme counterclockwise position, which brought the frequency to about 54 MHz. Picking up the rabbit ears, at the end of a twenty-foot antenna wire, he motioned to Jorges and indicated that he wanted him very slowly to rotate the fine-tuning knob clockwise so that the frequency would be advanced to approximately 60 MHz.

Jorges nodded to McKenna, who had moved to the middle of the office with the rabbit ears. "I think we'll have to get at least three new pistons for the starboard engine," Jorges replied to Gordel, keeping up his end of the cover-up conversation. He moved in front of the television set and reached for the fine-tuning knob.

"We'll begin repairs in a few days," Gordel said. He peered

intently at McKenna, who had raised the rabbit ears up to shoulder height and was moving them from side to side and up and down. Now and then the Ninja Master would glance at the TV screen as Jorges turned the fine-tuning knob and the 6 MHz band was swept.

After the 6 MHz band had been swept and Jorges looked questioningly at McKenna, Scott placed the rabbit ears on the floor, walked over to the Cuban, whispered in his ear, and told him what to do. McKenna then went back to the rabbit ears, picked them up, and nodded to Jorges.

Cotton Jorges turned to Channel 3, whose low end is 60 MHz, and turned the fine-tuning knob back to its full counterclockwise position. The entire process was then repeated.

All U.S. television channels are 6 MHz in width. Thus, repeating the process through Channel 6, the spectrum between 54 and 88 MHz can be investigated. Beginning with Channel 7 the frequency jumps to 174 MHz. Repeating the process now through Channel 13, the 174-to-216 MHz spectrum can be scanned. From this point on, the ultrahigh-frequency band can be covered. Beginning with Channel 14, the low end of which is 470 MHz, the spectrum can be covered in 6 MHz increments to Channel 83, which is 890 MHz.

The scan continued. The slow search for the hidden transmitter continued . . . and continued. It was not until UHF Channel 74 had been reached—almost an hour later—that McKenna saw what he hoped he would see, a herringbone pattern on the television screen. There was proof! A broadcasting transmitter was hidden somewhere in the office.

McKenna pointed to the screen and smiled. He put down the rabbit ears, walked over to the TV, and shut it off.

All this time, McKenna, Gordel, and Jorges had carried on a conversation about repairing and painting *Little Big Man*. McKenna also initiated a conversation involving "twenty-five degrees longitude and eighty-four degrees latitude," and "a possible thirteen minutes, if the old records are correct."

Jorges proved he was quick thinking by instantly responding with "It was difficult putting together those six old pieces of the map."

McKenna hurried to the desk, leaned down, and, with Jorges to his left and Gordel to his right, printed on a pad—THERE IS A BUG IN THIS OFFICE. START LOOKING FOR IT AND

CONTINUE TO TALK. LOOK BEHIND PHOTOGRAPHS ON THE WALL, INSIDE DRAWERS, AND BEHIND AND UNDERNEATH FURNITURE. DO NOT MAKE ANY NOISE. GET SOME FLASHLIGHTS AND TAKE YOUR TIME. I'M POSITIVE A BUG IS HIDDEN IN HERE.

"I wonder if Charlie Lombardo suspects that we talked to the police about him weeks ago?" Gordel said, winking at McKenna.

The three men went to work. Gordel began looking behind pictures on the walls and knicknacks on shelves. Jorges gently pulled out the couch.

McKenna studied the wooden mahogany desk. An old piece, it might have belonged to a grade-school teacher. It was that kind of desk, plain and unpretentious. The front was one long panel of wood, the rear composed of a wide center drawer and three drawers on each side—a large bottom drawer and two smaller drawers above it.

McKenna pulled out the three drawers on the left side, piled them one on top of the other, and looked inside the open space with a flashlight. There wasn't a transmitter inside the space. Mc-Kenna hadn't expected to find one. If a transmitter had been attached to the rear of the front panel, one of the drawers would not have closed all the way.

How many people take out their desk drawers, hold them up, and look underneath them? Almost no one. McKenna held up the top drawer and looked underneath it. These drawers were on concealed metal runners. Because of the runners, there was a fifth of an inch space between the bottom of a drawer and the open space of the one beneath it.

There wasn't any mike under the three drawers on the left side. There also wasn't one hidden under the center drawer—nor the two smaller drawers on the right-hand side. The Ninja Master hit the jackpot when he looked under the large drawer. There it was, toward the rear—a transmitter. No larger than a quarter, but perhaps a fraction of an inch thicker, the round transmitter appeared to be a VOR device—it was activated only when voices were present. It had to be powered by a tiny battery similar to the battery of a modern hearing aid. Range? McKenna had no way of knowing without inspecting it, but to do that, he would have to remove and open the bug. That would be far too risky. He would guess the maximum range to be four miles. Lombardo probably had a listening post in Sweetwater Creek!

McKenna stood up and signaled Gordel and Jorges. Once they were at the desk, he put his finger to his lips, held up the drawer, and showed them the transmitter. Anger flashed over the faces of both men. The possibility of a bug was one thing. Finding and confirming it was quite another. It was the same as looking at an exposed cancer.

Cotton Jorges cleared his throat and reached for his cigarettes. He had to let off steam without mentioning the bug.

"For what those sons of whores did tonight, coming in here and handcuffing us, I'd like to beat the shit out of Lombardo," he growled. "I'd prefer to blow the son of a bitch away with a shotgun, but I have a horror of jails." He gave a chuckle that sounded obscene. "Come to think of it, if I were put in jail for anything, I'd never get out." In response to McKenna's look of inquiry, he added, "After all, in these modern times who wants to bail Cotton?"

The Ninja Master smiled. He liked a man with a sense of humor.

CHAPTER 2

Major Emilio Calleja's face did not reveal any emotion, nor indicate in the slightest the tenseness he was feeling over being in General Rolando Ramiro Dorticos's office. Any agent was always on guard when in the presence of the feared Dorticos, who was called by his subordinates El Tiburón—"The Shark"—and for good reason. As director of Cuba's Directorate of General Intelligence, Dorticos demanded perfection not only in his own DGI, but also in the DSE, the Department of State Security, which was under the control of the DGI. It was the Department of State Security that handled spying and sabotage and sent intelligence officers into the field, principally into the United States.

Colonel Calixto Bernardo Hevia, looking respectfully at General Dorticos, said in a steady voice, "Our special cell in Florida will know when the Americans put out to sea. They have set up a station in a beach house close to an area known as Rocky Point. The vessel of the Americans will have to pass Rocky Point. Our people will then follow at a distance, discreetly, in their own vessel, the *Laughing Lady.* I do not anticipate any problems with the operation, at least none that can't be rapidly overcome."

Immaculate in his brown uniform, General Dorticos nodded and glanced again at an uncomfortable Major Calleja. He took another sip of *aguardiente,* the strong cane brandy.

"There cannot be any mistakes, not a single one," Dorticos said peremptorily. "Castro wants all the gold aboard the sunken galleon. He will not accept excuses; he will not accept failure. Keep that in mind, both of you. The *Independencia.* The arrangements have been made?"

"*Sí, mi General,*" Hevia replied promptly. "The *In-*

dependencia is an ordinary freighter. She will not generate any interest by *americano* authorities, since she will never be north of the twenty-fourth parallel. This will still enable her to serve as a supply base for the *Laughing Lady* and the submarine."

Not commenting, General Dorticos placed his glass on a silver tray on the small table next to the armchair in which he was sitting, then gazed speculatively at Colonel Hevia. Heavy lidded, heavyset, and balding in front, the fifty-four-year-old Dorticos had slight jowls and was an authority on Afro-Cuban religions, especially Santería, whose main feature was the honoring of "dead great people." Many black Cubans regarded Roman Catholicism as the Spanish version of Santería.

"An earlier report I read stated that the vessel of the Americans, the *Little Big Man,* is extremely fast," Dorticos said at length, his tone indicating he wanted an explanation.

"That is true, General," admitted Hevia. "The American boat used to be a Venezuelan attack patrol craft. It can reach a speed of nineteen knots. The British built six of the craft, but the Venezuelans replaced them in 1985 for even faster ships. However, the engines of *Laughing Lady* have been modified. She can reach the same speed. Besides, once the American vessel leaves port, our station at Rocky Point will alert our submarine by shortwave. The submarine is currently in the Gulf of Mexico, two hundred kilometers west of the Florida Keys."

General Dorticos picked up a small blue rubber ball from the silver tray and began squeezing it with his left hand. For several years, he had suffered from arthritis in his left arm and shoulder, and squeezing a rubber ball gave him some relief from the almost constant ache.

Knowing that General Dorticos was mentally weighing the various factors of the operation, Hevia and Calleja waited—Calleja impatiently and Hevia relaxedly. Unlike Calleja, Colonel Hevia was not in awe of El Tiburón, even though General Dorticos was his boss. For one thing, Hevia was very good at his job as chief of DSE, the Department of State Security. For another, he had an "in" with Fidel Castro. Calixto Hevia was a confidential friend of Raúl Castro, Fidel's brother and the head of the Cuban armed forces.

Major Emilio Calleja—deeply tanned and with wavy obsidian hair and a long mustache that merged into curved, narrow sideburns—cleared his throat and wished he could smoke. He didn't even dare show a pack of cigarettes. General Dorticos, a non-smoker, couldn't stand the stink of tobacco smoke.

General Dorticos finally fixed his eyes on Calleja, his expression one of amusement. Even so, Calleja shifted uncomfortably on the sofa and wished he could be elsewhere.

"Tell me, Major, did you mug a clown before you came into the DGI building?" Dorticos asked, his question bringing a slight smile to the face of the thin-lipped, cold-eyed Colonel Hevia, but making Calleja flinch.

"Perdón, Excelencia. I do not understand," responded Calleja with some hesitation.

Dorticos's mouth curled into a smile. "The way you are dressed. You look like a flag for some Third World country!"

For only a micromoment, Calleja appeared uneasy. Then, realizing that the Shark was joking, he relaxed. He couldn't deny that his mode of dress was—at least for Cuba—unconventional, and without any color coordination. He was wearing a Chinese red sportcoat, light-green trousers, and black-and-white open-toed shoes. His slipover cotton shirt was yellow with bright green, red, and blue horizontal chest stripes.

Interposed Colonel Hevia, "I was thinking he reminded me more of an Easter egg, General. Those colorful clothes will be normal in the Estados Unidos, especially in the Tampa area."

"I'll be leaving for the United States in four hours," Major Calleja said. "Naturally I shall not be wearing these clothes on the flight to Mexico. I was only trying them on when Colonel Hevia picked me up. I didn't have time to change."

Dorticos's gaze swung to Hevia. "You are sure his 'in-route' will be secure? The American ONI and the CIA are very active in the Florida area."

"As secure as it can be under the circumstances, *mi General,"* declared Hevia. "Major Calleja will fly from Havana to Mexico City as Señor José Valdez. His passport and other papers will prove he is a Mexican businessman. In Mexico City, he will go to our Z-station and resurface as Jesús Ramírez, a Mexican-American who owns a pecan farm in Casa Grande, Arizona. With a forged *pasaporte americano,* he will then fly from Mexico City to Tampa, Florida."

Dorticos's expression was faintly tolerant. "Hmmmmm, in Arizona. Why a pecan farm?"

Neither Hevia nor Calleja was surprised at Dorticos's question. Dorticos was a man who considered and analyzed every detail to make sure each tiny part fit perfectly into the overall picture.

"General, more pecans are grown in Arizona then in any other American state," explained Colonel Hevia, getting up from the couch. "A Mexican-American growing pecans in Arizona will not raise any suspicions. Actually, sir, my only real concern is with Señor Lombardo. He could cause us some slight trouble. As you know from earlier reports, he is the son of an *americano* Mafia boss and has some tough people in his employ. He, too, is determined to obtain the treasure."

"We'll be able to handle his men," Major Calleja said with complete confidence, a certainty acquired from three years of fighting in Angola and two years organizing Cuban penetration units within the revolutionary Farabundo Martí Liberation Front in El Salvador. He had also played a role in helping the FMLN set up bases in Honduras. "From the reports of our agent in Tampa, we can be sure that Señor Lombardo's men will follow the Americans when they put out to sea. Captain Penzula will sink their ship if they become too annoying."

"Major, if the Americans have put to sea before you arrive in Tampa, what arrangements have been made for you to join the unit you will command?" Dorticos's words sounded as if they had been punched out from a machine press.

"I would make use of a helicopter to fly to the *Laughing Lady,*" replied Calleja. "One of our people has been in America for ten years. He works for a helicopter service at the St. Petersburg–Clearwater International Airport. As you know, sir, Clearwater and St. Petersburg are across the bay from Tampa."

Nodding, Dorticos looked from Major Calleja to Colonel Hevia, who had sat down in a chair next to him. "Do you have anything else of value to tell me about the operation?"

"Only that if the Americans find the wreck, our Maximum Leader will have his gold," Hevia assured his superior. "Every detail of the plan has been well thought out."

Major Calleja, now feeling more self-assurance in front of Dorticos, added, "We will not be able to get in close to the Americans' vessel. They would see us. But it will be easy for Captain Penzula to watch them with the submarine. Should señores Gordel and Jorges and their friend find the treasure, we will wait until they have it aboard their vessel. All we will have to do is take it away from them. Should they not have the equipment to bring the gold to the surface, we have everything we need on the *Independencia*. The American government couldn't take any action against us, even if it wanted to. The area is in international waters."

"This friend of Gordel and Jorges," Dorticos said briskly, "—Colonel Hevia, has your department developed any more information about him?"

"The first report covered everything," Hevia said. "Scott McKenna is the son of a wealthy and prominent family. He spent years in Japan and is supposed to be a ninja, one of those Japanese karate experts."

"A lot of good that will do him against machine-gun slugs," murmured Calleja. "One bullet in the right place and all his ninja nonsense will be over forever."

"It is McKenna's money that is making it possible for Gordel and Jorges to go after the *Santa Francesca*," explained Hevia. "He's paying for the diving equipment and everything else that is necessary."

General Dorticos stood up, indicating that the meeting had been completed. "Very well, gentlemen. Both of you have done well. I gave you permission to complete the plan." He peered closely at Calixto Hevia and Emilio Calleja, both of whom had gotten to their feet. "Whatever you do, do not involve the government of Cuba in any way with the operation. The Russians want better relations between our country and the United States, and Fidel himself would prefer that the Americans view us in a different light. Any serious difficulty with the Americans now would be disastrous."

"*Sí*, we understand," Hevia said while Calleja nodded. "The only danger would be from American intelligence. That is not likely. We have operated our special Y-cells in the Florida area for many years. We have even penetrated several 'anti-Castro councils' in Miami. No, my General, this operation will not fail."

"*Buena suerte*, Major. Bring back the treasure from the *Santa Francesca*." Giving Calleja a long look, Dorticos walked to the door of his office and opened it. It was time for Hevia and Calleja to leave.

After the two intelligence officers had left Dorticos's office, he strode to the wide, covered window behind his desk, pulled back the drapes, and looked out over the Plaza de la Revolución, Havana's main square. For a moment, his eyes wandered over the gigantic sign—five stories tall—on the south side of the Vivarel

Building. VIVA EL PARTIDO UNIDO DE LA REVOLUCIÓN SOCIAL-ISTA!

Dorticos turned from the window, closed the drapes over the special glass, sat down at his desk, and did some hard thinking. Colonel Hevia and Major Calleja had planned well; yet there were always variables, those unforeseen factors tossed in by fate. But Dorticos knew there wasn't anything he could do now except wait for reports from Florida.

And hope, along with Fidel Castro, that the Russians in Cuba did not become aware of what was going on. . . .

CHAPTER 3

Better to sit up all night than go to bed with a dragon! This meant that Scott McKenna, Raymond Gordel, and Victor Jorges had to maintain a constant vigilance and expect more trouble from Charles Lombardo and his dirt bags. Yet there was only peace and tranquility during the three weeks following Lombardo's first attempt to force Ray and Victor to reveal the location of the *Santa Francesca.*

At first, McKenna thought that Lombardo's knowing about the vast treasure trove had been due to poor security on the part of his friends. The Ninja Master had soon learned otherwise. Only by a grim twist of fate had Lombardo learned that Gordel and Jorges were very close to finding the *Santa Francesca,* the flagship of Admiral Sebastián Cortizia's five-ship fleet that had been trapped in a hurricane in 1649.

Ray and Victor had to be positive of the route that Admiral Cortizia and his fleet had taken 339 years earlier. Accordingly, during the latter part of 1986, Gordel and Jorges had flown to Madrid, Spain, where, with the permission of the Spanish government, they consulted archives in the Admiralty Office. They had also visited Museo de los Dueños del Camino, the Masters of the Path Museum, which contained thousands of old maritime maps and charts and other historical memorabilia.

While working in the museum, Ray and Victor had met Thomas Burstes, another American, who said that he was a tourist. An insurance executive in his early forties, Burstes explained that his hobby was old maps and charts, and that his home was in Miami. Without revealing the true nature of their mission, Gordel and Jorges had told Mr. Burstes that they were also interested in ancient charts, especially from the period when Spain ruled the Caribbean. They also told him that they lived outside of Tampa. Their business? They had not wanted to say they were in the salvage business. Instead, they had told Burstes that they were partners in a bookstore.

They received a big shock when, six weeks after they had returned to the United States, Thomas Burstes, Charles Lombardo, and two of Lombardo's hoods had come to J & G Salvage Company and the smooth-talking Lombardo had offered to buy them all the equipment they might need to find the *Santa Francesca* and bring the vast treasure to the surface. Old records proved that the 680-ton galleon had carried ten tons of Cuban copper, 3,000 gold bars, 2,650 silver bars, and ten large chests filled with religious items made of gold and decorated with precious stones. Two chests had contained a fortune in doubloons and pieces of eight. This money had come from papal indulgences and from a head tax on black slaves sold in Cuba.

Gordel and Jorges had refused Lombardo's offer. Lombardo was a well-known gangster, and they knew their only share of any treasure would be a slug in the head.

"At the time, all we could surmise was that Burstes had gone to Spain to do what Cotton and I did, to check maps, charts, and old records," Gordel explained to McKenna. "We didn't suspect for a moment he might be trying to find out about the *Santa Francesca* or we wouldn't have looked at certain maps and other data while he was with us."

"Burstes must have been working for Lombardo," Jorges said, "and he guessed what we were trying to do. There can be no other answer, Scott."

McKenna had wondered how Gordel and Jorges had deduced the location where the *Santa Francesca* had sunk—and if they had actually found the Spanish warship. He received his answers several hours after he had demolished Charlie Lombardo's men, as he and Gordel and Jorges sat in an all-night McDonald's and ate cheeseburgers.

It was a matter of record that Admiral Sebastián Cortizia and his five vessels had put in at various ports along the east coast of South America. Sailing north, he had entered the Caribbean and had made stops at Trinidad, Santo Domingo, and Baracoa. The last port-of-call had been Havana.

It had been Cortizia's intention to leave Havana, sail west, then turn south through the Gulf of Mexico and stop at Vera Cruz on the southeast coast of Mexico. He would then make the long voyage to Spain. It was a hurricane that wrecked Admiral Cortizia's plans—and his fleet.

Gordel and Jorges, after consulting the old records in Madrid, estimated that Cortizia and his five vessels had only been a day out of Havana when the hurricane struck; they had also calculated the wind speed of the violent sea storm as it had moved north.

Gordel had explained to McKenna that "we judged from the force of the wind—and we guessed the power of the storm from the records we consulted—that the *Santa Francesca* and the four other ships were blown off course. They had to have been pushed north by the wind. Sailing ships are slow at best, and there was little wind when the small armada left Havana. This means that, in all probability, the ships were in a position to be shoved north to a region within a hundred miles west by southwest of the Florida Keys."

Jorges had explained that, as far back as the 1960s, two of Cortizia's galleons had been found, the *Nuestra Señora de la Rosa* and the *Señora de Blanco*. Both had been nine and sixteen miles northwest of the Dry Tortugas, a tiny group of islands that were southwest of Florida and a part of Florida. But the *Santa Francesca,* the main prize, had continued to elude treasure hunters.

"Are you telling me that you haven't actually found the *Santa Francesca*?" Sounding almost angry, McKenna stared at Gordel.

Ray's reply had been instant and curt. "I didn't say that. I didn't mean to imply it either. We're certain we've found the vessel. What we did, we—"

Gordel and Jorges had marked grids on a chart, confident that the *Santa Francesca* was within one hundred nautical miles of Key West, the southernmost city in the United States. For several years they had methodically searched each grid. It was after they had returned from Madrid—now positive that they were on the right track—that they had finished searching the third quadrant of the final grid, making dozens of dives, using both scuba gear and "hard-hat" suits.

Jorges got lucky on the eighteenth dive. He had found a silver bar and seven pieces of eight. Then, as luck would have it, he had to surface because a slow leak developed in his canvas-and-rubber hard-hat suit.

Gordel continued: "It was right after we returned to port that Lombardo and Burstes paid us a visit. We didn't dare go back to the area. We were afraid that Lombardo had people watching us. Besides, we couldn't repair the diving suit. We also knew that if we had found the *Santa Francesca,* we would need other equipment. You were due to arrive and we decided to wait for you."

McKenna did have questions. Why hadn't other treasure hunters over the years found the wreck? McKenna said, "I've read that some treasure hunters have metal detectors that cost as much as fifty thousand dollars. How come they haven't located the wreck?"

"It's not as easy as it sounds," Gordel explained. "No matter how good your detector is, there's a lot of metal down there on the sea floor—cannonballs and other junk from wrecks that didn't contain any treasure. Over the centuries, all kinds of metal has been thrown from ships. To make matters worse, there are iron deposits scattered below the seabed all over the Gulf. Depending where you are searching, you'll get false readings. It all adds up to uncertainty and mostly failure, especially when you get loud pings on your detector, then make a dive and find the wreck of someone's speed-boat or cabin cruiser."

"The ocean itself is deceptive," Jorges said. "In some places the water is shallow and so clear that you could think it wasn't even there. In other places, there are sudden drop-offs and the water is hundreds of fathoms deep—and you never know when sharks or barracudas will put in an appearance. One minute the water is free of danger; then suddenly, there are the sharks."

McKenna had finished drinking his Coke, feeling a new energy flowing through his arteries.

"So you and Cotton are convinced that you've found the *Santa Francesca,*" he offered. "But just on the basis of one silver bar and seven coins?"

"You had better believe it, sport," Gordel said with a hearty laugh. "The silver bar had markings that made it tally with bars listed on the *Santa Francesca*'s manifest. We copied the numbers from old records in the Admiralty Office in Madrid. The bar also carried the number two thousand four hundred in Roman numerals. That is the number used to indicate complete purity in silver." Gordel glanced at Jorges. "Cotton, tell Scotty why you didn't find more bars and coins." He grinned at McKenna. "You were wondering about that, weren't you?"

"Yes, I was," admitted McKenna. "I thought it was because he had to surface when his diving suit started to leak."

Jorges crushed out his Benson & Hedges cigarette. "After I found the bar and the coins, I searched another twenty minutes before I felt the trickle of water coming into the suit. Even if the suit had not begun leaking, I would have had to surface. The longer a diver stays down, the slower he has to surface. Should he come up too fast, he'll get the bends—decompression sickness.

"Anyhow, I found the silver bar and the coins on a large ledge, just as the current shifted some sand. The bar and the coins were almost at my feet. Fifty feet ahead of me the sea floor dropped down into darkness. We think that's where the *Santa Francesca* is. What happened—we think—is that the *Francesca* came down at an angle after her hull ruptured. The chests rolled around in the hold and some were broken open; that's how the coins were released and why I found only a few, plus the silver bar. There has to be more scattered around the ledge, but the majority—ninety-five percent of the entire treasure—is still on board the ship, down in that chasm."

"After Cotton surfaced and was back on board *Little Big Man,* we took numerous soundings," cut in Gordel. "The drop-off is twenty-five fathoms. That's one hundred and fifty feet. There could be a lot of sand down there. Sand is another big annoyance when you're looking for a wreck. You might only be a few feet from what you're looking for, but not spot it because it's covered with sand."

"There's a machine that sucks up sand or blows it away," McKenna said. "I remember seeing one on TV. It was an educational special."

"You're talking about an airlift or an air-blower," Gordel explained. "The airlift sucks up sand and artifacts; an air-blower works underwater by blowing the sand off a wreck. That's why we need you and your money, Scott. We need an airlift and other equipment."

As Gordel looked hopefully at McKenna, Jorges sighed and said, "Scott, you know the risk. Lombardo is bad enough. But we might not even get the treasure. We're positive the gold is down there where we said it is, but until we actually have our hands on it —it's a risk."

"So is living. Make a list of the things you need and the day after tomorrow, we'll start shopping," McKenna said, his reply easing Gordel and Jorges's fears. "And do it right. Get the best equipment available. The first thing tomorrow morning, I'll go to

Tampa and arrange to have a hundred twenty-five thousand dollars transferred from my bank in Boston."

Three weeks later, McKenna, Gordel, and Jorges—and a crew of thirteen—were almost ready to leave port and go to the vicinity where the *Santa Francesca* had sunk. As Ray Gordel had said: "You draw a line seven degrees south of Key West. Then you draw another line that equals seventy-two miles—two point six degrees to the southwest of the first mark. That's where the *Santa Francesca* is waiting for us."

McKenna wrote checks for more than an airlift. He also paid for two hard-hat canvas-and-rubber diving suits, a new automatic air pump, and new air hoses and lines. There were five scuba suits with closed breathing systems, numerous air tanks, and "bang sticks" for protection against sharks. The port diesel received two new cylinders. Small repairs were also made and some items of equipment replaced, such as a brand-new TAS mini-outboard motor for the Sandpiper dinghy, an Aqua 705 radio direction finder, an air compressor to fill the tanks, and a PAR heavy-duty bilge pump that could pump 600 gallons per hour.

Several days before *Little Big Man* was ready to leave port, cases of canned goods, powdered milk, fresh meat, and fresh vegetables were brought aboard, the perishables stored in the large refrigerator in the roomy galley. Then the crew began to arrive— three experienced divers, one of whom, Dominic Zuniga, had previously worked for J & G Salvage; six ordinary deckhands (or seamen first class); Barrett Gulbrandsen, the boatswain, or bosun, who was in charge of the anchor, the forward boom, and the stern winch; and Guadalupe Hernández, a sixty-nine-year-old Mexican-American who always worked as cook whenever Ray and Cotton took *Little Big Man* to sea. The twelfth and thirteenth members of the crew were Alfred Rothweiler and Gene Sisney. Rothweiler was a master mechanic who had put in his twenty years in the U.S. Navy and had retired. Sisney, a Canadian in his thirties, was the radioman and medic. The crew would cost the Ninja Master another twenty-three thousand dollars. One month's work. Professional divers do not come cheap; neither do master mechanics. For that matter, neither do ordinary seamen.

Victor Jorges was the captain. He had to be. He was the only one with his master's papers.

The *Little Big Man* had the sleek lines of a fast patrol boat, which is what she actually was operationally wise. The main feature of her hull design was that it maintained a good reserve of buoyancy forward, deflecting the spray well clear of the forecastle deck where it would interfere with operation of armament. When *Little Big Man* had been a FPB in the Venezuelan navy, she had been armed with an OTO-Melar 76mm (three-inch) gun on the forward deck. The spray was tossed to the sides of the vessel by means of modified round-bilge sections, a spray-deflecting knuckle forward just below the forecastle deck, and a "stake" between this and the waterline.

Little Big Man was strong. The all-welded steel hull was subdivided into seven watertight compartments, while the aluminum alloy superstructure was partly welded and partly riveted. The ship was seaworthy both at high speed and in heavy seas.

The ship was made for battle in that the port and the starboard diesel engines were remotely controlled, either from the soundproof cubicle in the engine compartment or from the enclosed bridge. Another nice feature was that the diesel exhausts were sited at the ship's sides, thus dispensing with the need for a funnel.

Little Big Man was also equipped with a large operations room which housed fire control, radar display with consoles, and a separate radio office located on the after part of the superstructure to starboard. A radar room was at the base of the mast amidships. Finally, the vessel was completely air conditioned.

Raymond Gordel was in charge of weapons. Other than the handguns they had taken from Lombardo's hoods, they were armed with a number of pistols and revolvers, many of them having been brought aboard by members of the crew. Gordel had an autoloader he had used for years, a 9mm Hi-Power Browning. Jorges packed a Walther P-38; he also carried, in a shoulder holster, the .357 Colt Python revolver that had belonged to Jody Karl. But there were other weapons—a veritable arsenal! Ten M16 assault rifles, three Colt CAR-15 submachine guns, and four Ingram M10 SMG's—all obtained by Jorges on the black market. As a Cuban, Cotton had numerous contacts among anti-Castro groups in Miami. He had also used McKenna's money to buy a case of fragmentation grenades and six night-vision devices.

Scott McKenna preferred weapons other than handguns. He had bought a Spanish military combat knife with a "big belly" contoured blade and a dozen ice picks whose plastic handles had been replaced by aluminum pipes filled with plastic putty, the ends sealed with lead. There was also a special weapon he had made— the "Man Hugger," he called it. The Ninja Master had taken thirty-six inches of steel chain and had used the first three inches of dozens of ice picks, welding four of the blades to every fourth link. Each blade, spot-welded at a different spot on a link, pointed in a different direction so that, should the link be forced against the body of a man, one ice-pick blade would be buried in his body while two blades would be parallel to his body. The fourth blade would be pointing away from his body. To each end of the chain he had welded a large steel nut.

McKenna had also made his own version of *shuriken* "stars" —several dozen steel washers two inches in diameter with a half-inch center hole. To the outer rim of each steel washer were four three-inch ice-pick blades, each one pointed to one of the main points of the compass.

The sun was about to pull a cover of clouds over itself for the night when the *Little Big Man,* with Captain Jorges at the wheel, left the long pier in front of the J & G Salvage warehouse, its sharp prow cutting the quiet water as it moved south through Old Tampa Bay. Already the surface of the water was beginning to reflect patterns of color from the dying sun, weaving a mosaic of red, orange, and yellow. Soon, there would be full-blown twilight ushering in the night.

There would be only one stop before *Little Big Man* sailed past MacDill Air Force Base, entered Tampa Bay, passed St. Petersburg's beach, and moved out into the Gulf of Mexico. The ship would stop at Bayview, just north of Clearwater, and take on fuel for the twin diesels.

Scott McKenna, wearing only walking shorts, stood to port on the forward deck and watched three of the deckhands make sure the arms of the cargo boom were secure. The boom mast was bolted to the deck both in front of the superstructure and where the 76mm gun had been mounted.

Forever thinking of security, McKenna studied the three ordinary seamen who had been recommended by Guadalupe Hernández, the cook. Jerry Joe Bilib was only twenty-four. A big man with bulging muscles, he had once tried to be a professional wrestler but had failed. While he knew all the holds, he was a terrible actor and couldn't fake it. Much worse, he couldn't control his temper in the ring. Yet he was a likable individual.

So was Willard Glazier, but in a different kind of way. Quiet, slim, almost forty and with sandy hair, he seemed to be a contemplative individual who had something on his mind. He almost never joked and never talked about himself. "He's an ex-*sacerdote,* Señor Gordel," Guadalupe had told Raymond Gordel. "But he's worked on ships for several years, and he's a good man."

"Okay, so he's an ex-priest," Ray had replied. "As long as he does his job, we don't care if he's the pope in disguise."

Norbert Kling, the third deckhand by the boom, was a beanpole of a man in his thirties. Forever talking—his nickname was "Motor Mouth"—he was either telling jokes or talking about girls. He had a fixation on some actress in one of TV's daytime soap operas, and Scott had once heard him remark that *". . . I'd drag my balls over ten miles of broken glass just to screw her shadow."* He was, however, a good worker—quick and never complaining.

So far so good, McKenna told himself, thinking of the various safety measures he had used to ensure tight security. For one thing, while the crew had been told they were going on a treasure hunt and, in addition to their regular pay, would receive a one-percent share of the "goodies" that were found, they had not been told the true location of the *Santa Francesca.* Nor had they been informed of the phony location.

For the past three weeks, Scott, Ray, and Cotton had indulged in a scenario of deception for the benefit of the "bug" still in place in the office. Since Ray and Cotton had often mentioned the area "southwest of the Keys" before the transmitter had been discovered, it had become necessary to convince Charlie Lombardo that they had made a mistake, that they had made a "new discovery" which indicated that all this time they had been wrong about the location of the *Santa Francesca.* This lie was carried out by Scott, Ray, and Cotton's discussing "new information from the old map" that Scott, with the help of his father, had "discovered" in the Royal Maritime Archives of the Brazilian government. Supposedly, McKenna had gone to Brazil before coming to Florida. Having carefully rehearsed the lie outside the office, the three men then carried on a conversation *inside* the office about the "new map that checks with the other information we obtained in Madrid." Of course! They had been wrong all along. But not anymore. Now they were positive that the *Santa Francesca* had actually sunk southeast of West Palm Beach, in the Northwest Providence Channel, "about forty nautical miles southwest of Freeport." Deliberately, Scott, Ray, and Cotton had refrained from giving the exact longitude and latitude. But would Charles Lombardo take the bait?

A moonless night had fallen over Florida by the time *Little Big Man,* heading southwest, passed tiny Edmont Key and moved into the Gulf of Mexico, her running lights on, her radar arm revolving at the top of the mast on the superstructure.

The arrangement was that McKenna, Gordel, and Jorges were equal partners in the venture. McKenna would receive one third of the proceeds of the treasure, plus his original investment and minus his share of the one percent that paid the crew. Gordel and Jorges were the official leaders of the operation; yet they sensed that McKenna was the real boss, even though he wasn't pushy. It was his organizational ability and his uncanny talent for security that made them defer to his judgment. Thus it was for these reasons that neither Gordel nor Jorges made any comment when the Ninja Master stationed a man at the stern and on the foredeck, each with a Hunter Model-39 infrared night vision viewer with a handle. With an NVD (costing McKenna $950 each), Ellery Thinder and Chester Malbain could see in total darkness. Range of detection was from 300 to 400 feet. Actual recognition at 300 feet; facial ID at 135 feet. In case another vessel seemed to be coming in close, Thinder and Malbain were to signal the bridge with their walkie-talkies.

On the bridge with Gordel, who was at the wheel, McKenna looked toward the oval door when Cotton Jorges came in from the radio room below. Jorges was carrying two Colt CAR-15 submachine guns and a canvas bag filled with twenty spare magazines.

McKenna thought for a moment. "I know this sounds dumb, but I don't suppose we'll have any difficulty in navigation?"

Jorges, putting the SMG's and ammo in a locker, laughed. So did Gordel, who said jovially, "We couldn't get lost or miss our destination if we tried. We're navigating with both RDF and omni."

He explained that RDF—meaning "radio direction finder"—received indicated bearings on a network of Coast Guard–operated radio antennas whose locations were fixed on navigation charts. Gordel pointed out that RDF wasn't all that reliable once a vessel was well outside U.S. territorial waters. That's where omni came into the picture. It picked up signals from radio beacons established for the use of aviators and had a much broader range. Omni meant "visual omnirange radio."

Jorges cut in, "We also have what is called 'loran.' It's the best of all." He then gave the Ninja Master his second lesson in a vessel's "black box" electronic gear.

Meaning "long-range navigation," loran was an electronic system that enabled a skipper to pinpoint his location with a simple radio manipulation and practically no calculations, even when he was out of sight of land. Useful and reliable over extreme ranges, it was free from the vagaries of transmission that afflicted radio-direction-finder bearings taken over the longer spans.

"So you see," Jorges finished, "there isn't any danger of our sailing to the South Pole and not knowing about it." He finished lighting a Benson & Hedges. "And in case you're worried about the dive, either the fake one or the real one, don't! We'll first take soundings. The only real danger is from Lombardo and his scum. There will be a lot of pleasure craft and commercial ships in the channel, and a pleasure yacht could close in pretty fast."

"All we can do is watch for any ship anchored in the distance, that's within sight of us," Gordel said. "Unless you have a better idea?"

The Ninja Master admitted that he hadn't, then said, "I'm going to the radar compartment. I've never seen one. I don't suppose Sisney will mind?"

"It wouldn't do him any good if he did," Gordel said. "I made it clear to the crew that it was your money that was paying for the hunt. Anyhow, Gene won't mind. He's a nice guy."

In a few minutes, McKenna was in the radar compartment and Gene Sisney, who had a long, angular face, a big brush of a mustache, and a slight lisp, pointed out the radar set in front of him. To the left of the radar box was a sonar display unit.

"With radar, the antenna and the feeder wave-guide at the top of the mast toss out the signals and send them down here when they come back," Sisney explained. He then indicated the various features of the unit, beginning with the cathode-ray tube screen and the bearing ring.

"Right here—this is the tuning control," he said, "and this knob is the VRM range-intensity control." He pointed to the various other knobs and switches—the dimmer control, the range selector, interference rejector, rain-snow clutter control, brightness control, horizontal centering, tuning indicator, and so on.

The Ninja Master's finger tapped the unit next to the radar box.

"Is this the sonar unit?"

"Yeah, that's the sonar unit," Sisney said. "Way back when it was called 'asdic.' See for yourself. It has a cathode-ray screen just like radar. The way it operates is that it uses a transducer housed in a sound dome attached to the hull."

"Sonar is used to detect submarines. Correct?" McKenna said.

"That's the general idea. This baby here"—Sisney tapped the control panel beneath the round screen—"could pick up a sub at five miles in open sea. The only reason a high-powered set like this is on board is that this boat used to belong to the Venezuelan navy. Ray told me that the radar and sonar sets were still installed when Captain Jorges bought the vessel."

"What about ordinary pleasure boats and commercial vessels?" McKenna asked. "They also use sonar, don't they?"

Sisney nodded. "Yeah, they use sonar, but have much smaller sets. They don't have to worry about subs. All their captains are interested in is making sure that they don't run into some large underwater obstruction. It's not very likely, but always possible." He blinked at McKenna. "Is there anything else you'd like to know?"

(Yes, but not even Master Nawa knows the answer. There is no reality outside our own perception. In this material continuum, all is a reflection of reality in a mirror of illusion.)

"No, I was just curious," McKenna said. He left the midship housing, went out onto the main deck, and headed toward the stern, pausing for a time where the flat-bottomed aluminum skiff was secured to the swing-out davits. There was a strong, clean breeze that smelled of freshness and open water. The night was as black as the center of the interior of Mount Everest, with a billion beacons of the Milky Way winking and blinking. However, the water was not all black. There were those places where it was faintly luminous, this phosphorescence caused by trillions of microscopic sea creatures floating by the vessel. When excited by *Little Big Man*'s rushing through the water, these lights assumed the form of round masses of greenish hue, at times appearing to be eighteen to twenty-five inches in diameter. At other times, during a strong breeze, when billows would break and foam, the lights would resemble fields of flashing fire.

Enjoying the solitude of the wind blowing in his face, McKenna moved along the port side to the stern, where Ellery Thinder was stationed with a Hunter night-vision viewer. All around him was intense blackness, except for the stars and the luminous masses in the water. Yet the Ninja Master sensed that something else was out there waiting . . . death in the form of Man.

I can feel it! I can smell it!

CHAPTER 4

In spite of all the trouble that had recently fallen on his head and shoulders, and in spite of all the unwelcome publicity, Charles "Chuckie" Lombardo always felt relaxed when sitting on the lawn of his twenty-acre estate northeast of Tampa. Everything on the lawn and in the garden was expensive. The very lawn chair on which he was sitting had been imported from the United Kingdom and was made of the best Empire wood—Burma teak—as were the table and the other two lawn chairs occupied by Jody Karl and Felix Battaglia. This hot Saturday afternoon, both men were reporting to Lombardo, Battaglia having brought him the latest shortwave message from Vincent DiVarco, who was in charge of the men aboard the *Golden Dolphin*. Vinnie Fats had radioed that everything was going according to plan: *Little Big Man* had pulled out on schedule, and Captain Hill, the skipper of the *Golden Dolphin*, had not had the least bit of difficulty in following at a distance of several miles. Gordel, Jorges, and the extremely dangerous McKenna could not possibly be suspicious. There were any number of vessels headed in the same direction, especially small yachts; and when *Little Big Man* turned past the Keys and headed east, there would also be a goodly number of ships in the Straits of Florida, as well as in the Northwest Providence Channel, south of the Grand Bahama Island. At the time that Vinnie Fats had sent the message, the *Golden Dolphin*, following *Little Big Man*, had just swung east and, fifty miles south of Key West, was entering the Straits of Florida.

A crafty look came into Lombardo's black eyes and his hand tightened slightly on the glass in his left hand. "Felix, you're certain that Vinnie's messages can't be picked up by the damned Feds?"

"I keep telling you, Chuckie, there ain't no danger of Uncle Sugar's boys picking up any message between Vinnie and me," said Battaglia, who had a little face that looked as if it had been carved from rock by a crazy sculptor who had made the melon-head too small for the wide shoulders, barrel chest, and massive hairy arms. "The way them radio sets works, they got more than scramblers that chop into bullshit what him and me say to each other. Hell, we're using military radios that can frequency-hop over more than sixty thousand channels on UHF. That means that what goes out over the air sounds like a lot of friggin' static. Shit, the Feds couldn't figure it out with computers."

Jody Karl's bony face clouded with concern as he shifted his weight.

"It's that motherfucker McKenna we gotta worry about. That Jap-thinking son of a bitch ain't human. And him and Gordel and that Cuban spic sure as hell don't think we've forgotten them."

Lombardo couldn't disagree. Three weeks ago, when Jody and his demolished strong-arm boys had returned from the salvage warehouse, Lombardo's reaction had been one of total astonishment. After Jody and the others had given him Scott McKenna's message, he had been filled with even more amazement and naked rage. But he hadn't laughed at McKenna's predictions. Scott McKenna was a ninja, and Lombardo, an educated man, had read some very strange and frightening things about the deadly ninja. Scott McKenna's predictions had come true.

Ellis Joost had died at two-fifteen in the afternoon. One moment he had been alive and well; the next second he was letting out a long sigh, closing his eyes, and falling back. A doctor had not been able to revive him. "Heart attack!" the doctor had said.

Christ on a crutch! Joost had not even been laid out properly at Dormer's House of Eternal Rest when Pete Ratta had bought the big one the very next afternoon! He died the same way that Joost had croaked. Another "heart attack"! Bullshit!

By then, Virgil "Skinny-Boy" Dudenbossle had been so terrified he was almost on the verge of collapse. McKenna had predicted he would die in three days. However, McKenna had not made himself clear. Had he meant three days from the time he had confronted the men in the warehouse, or had he meant that Skinny-Boy would slide into eternity three days after Ratta died?

Dudenbossle was still alive and in good health the day after Ratta died, and still alive, but half out of his mind with fear, the next day. On the third day, Dudenbossle's wife found him stone dead in the bathroom, at one twenty-three in the afternoon—the very day of Ellis Joost's funeral!

"McKenna is only dangerous if he can get close to a man, if he can get his hands on him," Lombardo said firmly, as if making a pronouncement. "Out there on the ocean, he's just another target. I don't mean that he isn't dangerous and a threat, but he will be the first to die. Vinnie Fats will most assuredly act with alacrity and verve at the proper time."

"It sounds too easy," muttered Felix Battaglia, whipping his forehead with a white silk handkerchief. "I read some of them books you had Jody buy. Them ninja killers, they got some pretty weird powers."

"Quit talking and thinking like a superstitious fool," Lombardo snapped acidly. "You're falling into the emotional trap of equating McKenna with some kind of superman. He's flesh and blood and will bleed like any other man. He'll go to hell fast when slugs hit him in the gut."

One of those individuals who could only sunburn and never tan, Lombardo was dressed in sharply creased cream slacks that matched his tailored cream sport shirt, open at the neck. On his left wrist was a wafer-thin gold watch with diamond chip numerals. His black hair and long sideburns were well groomed, and he had a boyish face and youthful appearance that, to the casual observer, shaved ten years from his real age, which was forty-four.

Jody Karl was saying, "That Jap-trained son of a bitch is no superman, but he's one smart cookie. That's why I don't buy that crap about him going to Brazil and digging up new information about the *Santa Francesca*. It don't make no sense. How in the fuck could there be any clues in old records in Brazil where the *Santa Francesca* had sunk? Them spics in Brazil wasn't tailin' her around in no hurricane! I think McKenna and them other two jokers are trying to pull a con on us."

"It does seem convenient," agreed Battaglia. "Hell, how do we know they didn't find the bug, then make up the story about the new location to throw us off track—huh, Chuckie?"

Lombardo laughed without humor. "How do we know what they did? We don't know. And because we don't, Vinnie Fats is following them and their crew. It's that simple."

"Their ship is damned fast," Battaglia commented. He glanced at Karl, who had finished his drink, had gotten up, and was putting his glass on the table. "But I don't suppose it could outrun the *Golden Dolphin* with her souped-up engines."

For the moment, no one spoke. Lombardo was positive that a man like McKenna would not have naively sailed away without expecting trouble of the worst kind and having prepared for it—
Without having prepared some sort of trap!

Lombardo had warned Vincent DiVarco not to assume anything about McKenna and the *Little Big Man.* "Make sure of your moves, Vinnie. Make very sure. One mistake on your part and the whole deal will blow up in our faces. Remember that."

Vinnie Fats had nodded. "Yeah, Chuckie. That McKenna's somethin', all right. But he's in our territory now, and all his ninja know-how won't be worth a fiddler's fuck against machine-gun slugs. You needn't worry. I'll have a few surprises of my own for that ninja son of a bitch."

CHAPTER 5

Scott McKenna enjoyed being on the sea. The morning (after *Little Big Man* had left port) was brilliantly sunny . . . water sparkling, tiny whitecaps, balmy, fleecy cotton-candy clouds. Perfect weather for sailing.

"It's nice now, but bad weather is coming," Forrest Santage, one of the professional divers, remarked to the Ninja Master about ten in the morning. "I was just on the bridge. The barometer is falling fast."

McKenna went to the bridge to see for himself.

"Rain and some wind," said Jorges when he saw McKenna looking at the barometer. "It's nothing to worry about. It's the wrong time of the year for a hurricane or a tropical cyclone. The Coast Guard warning is for a heavy squall. That means a lot of rain, and a wind force of maybe seven on the B scale."

In the distance there were other vessels in the Straits of Florida—large and small yachts, sailing sloops, and now and then a freighter. Toward noon a large cruise liner passed *Little Big Man* to starboard. An hour later, an oil tanker, as long as an aircraft carrier, went by to port. But not once did McKenna and the others see a boat that appeared suspicious.

It was almost four P.M. when they saw the approaching squall-line cloud in the southwest. The sign of a direct wind shift, a squall-line cloud is only the front of the storm, of the wind and rain and of the invading mass of cooler air. It is the only kind of cloud that boils and tears itself apart without sheets of rain interfering with the spectacle, although its blue-black and sulphurous hues can be terrifying. Behind the squall-line cloud was the high-flung thunderhead, the grim-as-death cumulonimbus filled with wind and rain. By the time the ominous thunderhead was closing in, all the hatches and the loose gear on *Little Big Man* had been secured, and every crew member was ready for the onslaught of wind and rain, which came in a sudden cloudburst. Torrents of rain stabbed at the vessel as the angry sea rocked her from stem to stern. Everywhere were white foam crests, the violent waves between ten and fifteen feet high, their speed between twenty and twenty-five knots. Windspeed on the Beaufort scale: seven, or near gale force. Under such conditions, the vessel drifted leeward at about one knot, her leeway over eight degrees. Jorges, at the wheel in the pilothouse, was not worried. Neither was Ray Gordel nor any of the other men, all of whom were familiar with the moods of the sea.

By eight P.M. the storm was over. There was only slight rain, and the surface of the sea was moderate, the more pronounced crests—some only two to three feet high—breaking into white horses. Wind speed: Beaufort force four. A moderate breeze. Nonetheless, Scott McKenna was not about to let down his guard. All through the dark night, men watched and waited with M16's and submachine guns. In the radar room, Gene Sisney kept a careful eye on the radar and the sonar sets.

The next morning the sky was hot and bright, with only thin wisps of high cirrus clouds overhead— "mares' tails" moving along at an altitude of thirty-four thousand feet. The barometer continued to rise, and there was favorable weather for the remaining 214 miles of the voyage to the Northwest Providence Channel. On the morning after the ship entered the Channel, the men went to work in earnest.

Ray Gordel used the end of a lead pencil to tap the Mercator sailing chart on the table in the center of the map and navigation room. Like other sailing charts, this one was on a scale of 1:600,000 and showed all the soundings of the Northwest Providence Channel in fathoms.

"Right here is where we'll make the dive," Gordel said. With his pencil, he circled in red a group of black wavy lines marked 50F. "Right here it's only fifty fathoms. As you can see, the area is thirty-one miles south of the Grand Bahama, far enough so that the Bahamian government can't claim a share of what's supposed to be down there."

"We do have to make the phony search seem legitimate," McKenna observed. "We'll have to continue the fake search for at least two days."

"I'd say three days to make it look good," interjected Jorges.

"The area is okay," said Harry Derr, one of the divers, who had been studying the chart. "But if you ask me, I think it's going to be a lot of work for nothing. Dominic and Forrest will have to go down with me and carry bang sticks. These are shark waters, and I do mean sharks—great whites!"

"We'll have to be precise," Gordel said. "We'll have to lower the hose of the airlift and pretend to bring up gold bars and other valuables. But it's not going to be a lot of work for nothing. We have got to neutralize Lombardo's goons before we go after the real treasure."

"They'll attack," McKenna said. "They have to. Either way, we'll find out very soon."

The "very soon" came nine hours later, although *Little Big Man* did not drop her sea anchor even close to the position that Gordel had chosen. The plan had been changed slightly. To confuse the enemy, McKenna suggested the vessel should first stop over an area so shallow that dives could be made with only scuba gear. Of course the divers would soon "discover" that this was not the place where the *Santa Francesca* had died and gone to the bottom.

The plan worked with the precision of a fine watch. Derr, Santage, Gordel, and John W. Hoover dived the 150 feet in scuba suits with closed breathing system, all four armed with bang sticks as protection against sharks. They stayed down for twenty minutes.

Her twin diesels throbbing with power, *Little Big Man* then proceeded forty-one miles northeast to the section of the channel that Gordel and Jorges had originally chosen. Now would come the big production, the big con. Now the crew could pretend to find the fabled *Santa Francesca,* and, supposedly, bring her vast treasure to the deck of the FPB.

The first day was devoted to preparing the equipment, not that there were many things that had to be done. But because of the three-hundred-foot depth, it would take hours to bring the divers to the surface, depending how long they remained on the bottom—and no one wanted to risk bringing them up in the dark. The danger of attack from Lombardo's men was too great.

The boom on the foredeck hoisted up the two large air compressors and the bulky airlift (or "sand-sweep") while, on deck, men prepared the lifelines and the air hoses of the three "closed dress" hard-hat diving suits. Each suit was a large gray garment made of india rubber, one piece and completely waterproof, though bulky and difficult to handle. A diver does not "slip" into such a suit; he climbs into it from above, as though it were a sack. The heavy shoes, each weighing ten pounds, have lead soles. Even before the large metal helmet is screwed on, the man inside the suit is burdened with a lot of weight, not only from the thick rubber, but also from the large metal ring-collar that, around his neck, extends to the shoulders. The forty pounds of lead around his waist, to help the diver sink and to give him balance in the water, do not lessen his discomfort.

Once the diver is in the suit and the air hose couplings on the helmet checked, the built-in telephone inside the helmet is tested and the air compressor, driven by a gasoline engine, started. Should the engine fail, two men can turn the compressor by hand. The vital air hose is attached to the helmet and the couplings rechecked. The helmet is then placed over the diver's head and screwed onto the collar. A deckhand then closes and secures the faceplate. The diver makes his way to the side of the vessel and climbs down a ladder on the side of the hull into the water. He is then lowered by ropes to the bottom of Mother Ocean.

The greatest danger that the divers would face would be caisson disease, or decompression sickness, commonly referred to as the "bends"—but only if they and the other men were very careless.

There isn't anything mysterious about the bends. On land, we live at the bottom of an ocean of air. At sea level the pressure is one atmosphere—14.7 pounds per square inch. Underwater the situation is reversed. In order to calculate the effects of pressure on a diver, one starts with a surface pressure of one atmosphere. For each additional thirty-three feet the diver descends, another atmosphere—14.7 pounds per square inch—is added. At three hundred feet, the pressure is ten times greater than that experienced on the surface.

The danger comes from nitrogen, which constitutes four fifths of every breath we take. On the surface, nitrogen passes harmlessly in and out of the body. Under pressure, however, the gas is forced into solution in the body's tissues. When pressure starts to fall—when the diver starts to rise to the surface—the nitrogen turns into bubbles of gas, the amount depending on the amount of pressure experienced and the length of time underwater. It is the tiny bubbles of nitrogen that cause the bends.

The only way to prevent the bends is to return slowly to the surface, this gradual ascent allowing the gas to escape naturally (although divers can be brought directly to the surface, provided they ascend directly into a decompression chamber).

To ensure the safety of Derr, Santage, and Zuniga, Gordel, and Jorges would use the U.S. Navy Standard Air Decompression Tables. That meant that should the three divers remain for sixty minutes at the three-hundred-foot level, it would take five hours and sixteen minutes to bring them to the surface. On their way to the surface, the divers would stop every eight feet and remain there for four minutes.

Scott McKenna did not like such a lengthy time factor. Five hours was too long. Five hours would leave the men too vulnerable. Should Lombardo's men attack while the divers were still in the water, they would not have much of a chance, if any. . . .

McKenna made the decision. "They can stay down half an hour," he said. "That way it will only require two hours and thirty-eight minutes to haul them back to the deck."

For three days the divers and the rest of the crew worked and carried out the deception. Six different times the divers went down. The bulky hose of the airlift was lowered. Square wooden dredge baskets were lowered, filled with rocks or sand, then hoisted by the winch to the deck and lowered into the hold.

"Millions of dollars in 'treasure'!" laughed Ray Gordel. "And all of it in rocks and sand! What a joke on Lombardo!"

All the while, the crew kept automatic rifles and SMG's handy, especially at night when there was nothing but darkness and the long silence. *Little Big Man* rode easily on her two sea anchors—large, hollow cone-shaped devices used to retard the drift of a boat with dead engines or a ship hove-to in a storm, and to keep the bow headed into the wind and the sea.

The identification lights of the ship were class three, used for all large vessels and legal in all waters—a twelve-point white light on the stern. It could be seen for several miles. There was a twenty-point white light on the bow that could be seen for over three miles; a ten one-mile light on the starboard and on the port side, and finally another twenty-point white light on the radar mast.

The crew slept in five-hour shifts. All the hatches were secured and at all times five men waited with weapons in the darkened operations room on the main deck of the superstructure. But nothing happened. Not one vessel even came halfway close to *Little Big Man*. . . .

On the fourth day the crew busied itself by putting away equipment, every man tense, convinced that a lot of time and a lot of work had been wasted.

It was 1622 hours—four twenty-two P.M.—when Gene Sisney called McKenna on an Aerotron Tracer-1 walkie-talkie and requested that he come to the radar room. "I think I've spotted something," Sisney said nervously.

Leaving Jorges in charge on the main deck, McKenna and Gordel went to the radar room, where Sisney was glued to the sonar set.

"See for yourselves," Sisney said. He turned back to the round screen and used a finger to point out two large blips. The two blips were together, side by side, and moving steadily away, toward the left, which the bearing ring indicated was due west. The bleeps were regular—*ping, ping, ping, ping.*

Sisney reached out and adjusted the range-selector knob and the gain control. "They were closer to us before I called you. It's as if something came close to us to have a look, and now is moving off."

"How close?" asked McKenna, feeling intensely satisfied. "How close would you say the enemy divers were?"

"How deep are they?" Gordel inquired, his eyes on the sonar screen.

"It's not possible to tell how deep they are, not with any accuracy. I'd say maybe three fathoms. As for distance, I'd say between four hundred and five hundred feet. Understand, that's only a rough guess. If those blips are divers—what else can they be?—they're using scuba gear. Anyhow, they had to come from a ship that's miles away."

"At least six to seven miles," Gordel said, a hard look coming into his eyes. "They could move ten feet under the surface and we'd never be the wiser. By God, Scotty. You knew those sons of bitches would come in at us underwater!"

"I was hoping I would be proven wrong." McKenna inhaled deeply.

"They came in on sea sleds. They must have. A six- or seven-mile swim, and only one way—I don't believe it!" Gordel sounded as if he might be having a conversation with himself. "If you've never heard of them, Scotty, the idea came from World War II. The British and the Italian navies developed underwater vehicles that could carry commandoes underwater to place explosives against the hulls of enemy vessels."

"Yeah," Sisney said. "I was thinking along the same lines. A modern sea sled is just like a little sub, only the men sit on the outside, dressed in diving suits. Hell, it's only a tube with a ballast tank, compressed-air tanks, and an electric engine. Let the water in and you go down. Blow it out with the air and you rise. Speed is about three knots."

He looked at McKenna, indicating he considered the Ninja Master the authority on violence. "If those blips were enemy scouts, when do you think the main force will hit us?"

"Tonight," McKenna said succinctly. "They're convinced we're brought up the treasure. Now they think that all they have to do is take it from us. I'd say they'll return for the attack between three-thirty and four-thirty in the morning."

Sisney nodded slowly, a tight tension on his long face. "Well, at night they could turn off all the lights on their ship, including their masthead and range lights, and creep in closer to us. They wouldn't be counting on us using our sonar. Why should we be when we're not moving?"

Gordel shifted from one foot to the other, a calculating look on his tanned face. "They're not going to come roaring in with their ship. We could rake their decks with slugs, and they know it. Scotty, are you thinking what I'm thinking, the way they'll do it?"

"The reputation of a thousand years may be determined by the conduct of only a single hour," McKenna said. "The first fifteen minutes of the enemy's attack will determine whether they win and we die or whether we live and they fail."

"Give me a straight answer," Gordel said dryly. "I think four or five of them will come in by sea sled. They'll come over the side and try to take control of the ship before we can do anything about it. Then they'll signal for their vessel to come in."

"Exactly," McKenna said. "I only hope that Charles Lombardo will be with them. But he won't be. A man like Lombardo always remains in the deep shadows. . . ."

CHAPTER 6

Scott McKenna and Ray Gordel had been one hundred percent right: the mobsters had come in at three forty-five A.M. and they had made the journey on Maskin sea sleds, wearing scuba suits of the "dry" type and using Emerson closed-circuit, recirculating-air breathing systems.

The five hoods and the two sea sleds had stopped 150 feet from the stern of *Little Big Man*; then four of them had prepared for the silent assault. Donald Stirling would remain with the two sea sleds. He wasn't a gunman. He had been brought along because of his expertise with underwater vehicles. He would remain with the sleds and would be picked up by the *Golden Dolphin* when she came in.

Under the leadership of Joe Barbasta, a ruthless killer, the four had swum to the stern of *Little Big Man*. They had used a small grappling hook and line to secure a rope ladder, which they then used to climb to the main deck of the FPB. Once on board, they had opened the tubular containers strapped to their chest. Each plastic cylinder had contained a Repco VHF walkie-talkie, a pistol and silencer, and spare clips. In addition Barbasta and Dominick "Sally the Sheik" Samenta carried Uzi submachine guns and four spare magazines for each SMG. The SMG's and magazines had been in another watertight container strapped to their backs.

The plan had been dangerous, but uncomplicated—get to the superstructure by way of the main deck, creep upward to the pilot-house, and secure the bridge. Then use one of the Repcos and contact Vinnie Fats on the *Golden Dolphin*. In the meanwhile,

Barbasta and Sally the Sheik would sneak below and machine-gun the crew. That would be the end of it. ¡*Terminado!*

Barbasta and the three other goons had closed in on the operations room on the main deck level of the superstructure. It was here that their plan failed utterly. Scott McKenna and company had been waiting for them in the dark. Ellery Thinder killed Sally the Sheik by crushing his skull with a wrench. Al Coppolo died instantly from a blow to the left temple—John W. Hoover had brained him with the butt of a pistol.

The first thing that Chu-Chu Marika knew was that someone had grabbed his right wrist. During the next moment, he felt pain explode in the right side of his neck, then blackness. Barrett Gulbrandsen had grabbed the .357 Coonan autopistol and had smacked Chu-Chu with brass knuckles.

Joe Barbasta lost consciousness before he realized what was happening. The Ninja Master had grabbed his Glock-17 pistol and slammed him in the right temple with a *seiken* forefist, with only enough force to turn off the hood's consciousness.

Coppolo and Sally the Sheik were dead, and when Barbasta and Marika regained consciousness, they found they were in the engine space, the small area between the engine room and the two big diesel engines that powered *Little Big Man.* They were seated on two cases of engine oil that had been upturned.

This was the first time that Barbasta and Marika had seen McKenna. It was his youth that surprised them. Why, he didn't look at all dangerous. However, they knew that the ice picks around his slim waist, in sheaths on a leather belt, were not there merely for show.

A ninja is also an expert in psychology, both applied and abnormal. For psychological effect, McKenna pulled one of the ice picks with the odd-looking handles from its sheath and moved slowly behind Joe and Chu-Chu. Barrett Gulbrandsen and Harry Derr stationed themselves in front of the hoods.

"You and the others had to come from your vessel on sea sleds or some other kind of underwater conveyance," McKenna said quietly. "We want to know how many others are out there waiting on the sleds. Answer, or I will kill you."

Stalling, Barbasta said, "L-let me get my breath first."

Chu-Chu Marika had a reputation for toughness and for having iron nerve. No one had ever remarked about his intelligence, which wasn't exactly that of an Einstein. If he had had any com-

mon sense, he would have answered promptly. Instead, his own
anger and pride, greater than his fear of death, forced him to say,
"Go fuck yourself, ninja man! We're not going to tell you a god-
damned thing!"

"Why, you son of a bitch!" snarled Gulbrandsen. "McKenna
—" The bosun stopped speaking and his mouth fell open in surprise when he saw McKenna raise the ice pick in his left hand and
as quick as a blink of an eye shove the four and the half inches of
thin blade straight into Chu-Chu's left ear.

A very short, agonized scream jumped from Chu-Chu's throat
and he half rose from the crate of oil. His arms moved upward,
then stopped as if they had struck an invisible barrier. They
dropped at the same time his body sagged and a trickle of blood
began to dribble out of his ear. The expression of surprise and pain
on his face remained, frozen in a time that for him had ended
forever. His eyes opened wide and remained open. His mouth fell
slack. Slowly, he slid from the chair to the floor.

"I'll be damned! You killed him!" exclaimed Harry Derr in a
hollow voice. "I'll be damned!"

McKenna pulled another ice pick from his belt. "Perhaps now
he knows why our days are numbered instead of lettered," he said,
a lilt to his voice. "Now let's get back to our other guest."

He placed his left hand on Joe Barbasta's shoulder and
touched the lobe of the mobster's right ear gently with the point of
the ice pick. "I asked a question. You have to the count of 'one' to
answer it."

Trembling, knowing he was practically sitting on the lap of
death, Barbasta was only too happy to answer.

He talked his head off. "The *Golden Dolphin* is six miles west
of you guys. Me and the others, we was to . . ." Barbasta hesitated, not wanting to anger the Ninja Master by telling him the
terrible truth. But he knew he had to. "We was going to kill the
crew. And the *Dolphin,* by now she's moved to within four miles of
you guys, and she wouldn't have no difficulty in picking up a message on the walkie-talkies we brung along. The plan is for the
Dolphin to pull alongside so we could transfer what you guys found
below in the wreck. Honest, that's the truth."

McKenna drew the point of the ice pick along the right side of
Barbasta's neck, making him squirm and pull away. "And all of
you work for Charles Lombardo." It was not a question. It was a
declarative statement.

"Y-yes. Charlie Lombardo," confirmed Barbasta.

"Who's the head mobster on the boat?"

"Vinnie—Vincent DiVarco." Barbasta's voice shook more than ever. He was doing what he'd sworn he would never do—*singing!*

"Does he have a nickname?"

"V-Vinnie Fats! That's his moniker. I—I call him Vinnie."

"We're going back to the operations room," McKenna said, "and you are going to call 'Vinnie' and tell him the plan worked, that all of us are dead. When you're talking to him on the walkie-talkie, you can try to be a hero and warn him. Let me tell you what will happen to you if you do. First, I'll thumb out your eyeballs. I will then use a hammer to pound your elbows and your kneecaps to pulp. I can assure you, there isn't a doctor in the world who will be able to prevent your being badly crippled—and stone blind—for the rest of your life. Think about it. Now get up and start moving."

Desperation is always the stepfather of hope. Hoping that somehow he would be able to walk away alive when it was all over with, Joe Barbasta did not try to be a hero. He did exactly what McKenna ordered him to do. Using the walkie-talkie, he made contact with Vinnie Fats and reported that he and the other three gunmen had climbed aboard *Little Big Man* and had snuffed every man on board, including McKenna. "Sally cut him in two with a chopper. Anyhow, the ship belongs to us, Vinnie. Over."

Vinnie Fats's heavy and happy voice came back through the Repco transceiver. "Good! Good! Okay. Here's what I want you guys to do. Turn on the deck lights. I'll have Captain Hill bring this tub right over. We'll come in on the port side. See ya in a little way, kid. Out."

"This guy should have been an actor," mocked Ray Gordel, who had come down from the bridge and was glaring at a frightened Barbasta.

"Let's proceed," McKenna said coldly. "It will not take long for the *Golden Dolphin* to get here."

Derr and Rothweiler wired Barbasta's hands behind his back and took him to a cabin on the second deck. With them went Guadalupe Hernández, a shiny meat cleaver in his hands.

"You sit on bunk and you no move," the dark-faced, white-haired old cook snarled at Barbasta. "You move"—he raised the cleaver threateningly—"and the crew will have fried brains for breakfast."

The Ninja Master quickly implemented his plan. Jerry Joseph Bilib, John Hoover, and Chester Malbain (armed with M16 assault rifles, each with four extra magazines) went to the stern carpenter's locker and got down on its starboard side. McKenna, Derr, Thinder, Rothweiler, and Gulbrandsen took positions in the operations room while Santage and Kling waited on the port side of the radio room. Gordel and Jorges waited on the bridge, each man more than ready with his Colt CAR-15 submachine gun. And they were wearing dry-suits, the suits that had been worn by the dead Coppolo and Sally the Sheik.

There was a flaw in McKenna's plan, one that he could not help: the fact that none of the four mobsters who had come aboard *Little Big Man* would be on deck when the enemy ship closed in. Jorges had suggested that they force Barbasta to stand on deck, on the port side of the superstructure—"If he tries to warn the *cagada* with the sea sleds, we can blow him up before he succeeds."

"Yes, we could kill him, and by so doing, we would warn the man with the sea sleds. He would promptly use his walkie-talkie to tip off Vinnie Fats," McKenna had pointed out. "If Barbasta had a single decent thought, it would die of loneliness. He's pure trash, but he's also scared stiff. If we stick him out on deck, he might just try to go over the side into the water, even with guns at his back. We can't risk it. However, I do have another plan."

McKenna's scheme was to have Gordel and Jorges put on wet suits and stand on the port side of the now lighted bridge, where they could be clearly seen. By the time the *Golden Dolphin* was close enough for Vinnie Fats and the other gunmen to see that the two men on the bridge were strangers, it would be too late. McKenna and his men would be sweeping the decks of the *Golden Dolphin* with slugs.

The minutes raced by, with everyone in position and waiting, fingers resting on triggers. The first thing that McKenna and his people saw of the *Golden Dolphin* was the light on her bow—to the southwest. It was the dim light, growing brighter and brighter, that ushered in the sound of the engines a few moments later. The light grew very bright and the sound of the engines increased until all the running lights were visible, as well as the lights in the long deckhouse and on the large command bridge.

One had to have a lot of bucks to own a Trojan yacht like the

Golden Dophin, which ideally fulfilled the requirements of a vessel that could provide long range and rough-water cruising capability at good speed. With an overall length of 139 feet 6 inches, she had a waterline length of 131 feet, a beam of 25 feet 5 inches, and a displacement of 163,000 pounds. Her powerhouse consisted of twin 750-horsepower GM 8V-72TI diesels with superchargers that, driven by exhaust gases, forced the fuel mixture into cylinders under pressure.

The yacht was strong, built of double diagonal mahogany planking with all joints and seams epoxy-glued. From keel to hard-top, she was completely fiberglassed; and she was roomy below-deck, with five staterooms for guests and two staterooms for the captain and the crew of two. There was a large salon, a roomy dinette, and plenty of stern-deck space. Forward was a small lounge, and above, on the foredeck, was a large area for sunbathing. All of it in teak.

The command bridge—up a teak ladder from the cockpit—was modern, spacious and unusual in design. The helm was at a center console with most of the navigational equipment built in. Decca dual tracking loran, SGC single sideband radio, Simpson VHF radio, Ross and Sandpiper depth sounders. Other goodies included Decca radar, hailer, searchlights, and ADF. Steering was hydraulic, with a Robertson autopilot that had remote cockpit control. But only in speed was she a match for a fast patrol boat.

Captain Bernard Hill (he would have killed his own mother if the price had been right) brought the *Golden Dolphin* in fast, the sharp bow cutting the water 150 feet southwest to port of *Little Big Man.* If any of McKenna's people could have gotten a really *good* look at the attack yacht, they would have seen that two men were on the command bridge and several on the stern deck on the starboard side. On the roomy sun deck of the fore section were two more men. These were Vinnie Fats's boys, and each man was armed with a Heckler and Koch 33A2 assault rifle. Behind the stern, at the end of a twenty-one-foot cable, was *Pluto,* the Capri I/O speedboat.

It was now a certainty that Charles Lombardo's sleek vessel was going to close in on the port side. When the yacht was 125 feet from *Little Big Man,* Captain Hill cut speed. Vinnie DiVarco switched on the floodlight mounted on the bridge roof and began to move its wide beam over the port side of the FPB. The shaft of bright light stopped when it came to the port side of the bridge and found Ray Gordel and Victor Jorges. Reflexively, they put up their hands to shield their eyes against the bright white beams, a normal enough action that didn't arouse suspicion. Besides, hadn't one of the men waved?

At less than three knots, the *Golden Dolphin* began to glide in, her starboard drawing closer and closer to the port side of the FPB. There was a difference in size between the two vessels. *Little Big Man,* 116 feet in length, was shorter than the *Golden Dolphin,* but her beam was thirty-six feet four inches. Still, it was the length of the *Golden Dolphin* that mattered, that difference of twenty-three feet between her and the fast patrol boat. McKenna and his men would have to fire at the bridge as she went by, before she came to a stop. Should Captain Hill try to even the sterns, his bridge would be twenty-three feet ahead of the bridge and center superstructure of *Little Big Man.* Neither Gordel nor Jorges nor any member of the crew would be able to fire directly into the bridge once the sterns of the two ships were even. They would have to direct their streams of slugs at her bridge as she glided to a stop, as her bridge went by the superstructure of *Little Big Man.* On the other hand, if the enemy vessel stopped when both bows were even, McKenna and company would be able to demolish the front of her bridge with projectiles.

Worse, but only for Ray Gordel and Victor Jorges, was the fact that their bridge was half a deck higher than the command bridge of the *Golden Dolphin.* This meant they could not fire directly into the starboard windows of the bridge as the sleek yacht passed. They would have to settle for second best—stabbing slugs through the roof.

All this time, Bilib, Hoover, and Malbain had not even seen the enemy vessel. Afraid that they might be detected and give the show away, they remained down by the carpenter's locker. Their signal to open fire would be when the men in the superstructure cut loose.

It soon became apparent that Captain Hill intended to even his stern with the stern of *Little Big Man.* By this time, Ray and Cotton had picked up their CAR-15 submachine guns and had pushed the selective fire levers to full automatic.

In the operations room, Scott McKenna had already told the four men there to begin firing when the front of the enemy's bridge was a mere thirty feet astern of the superstructure of *Little Big Man.*

"That close she couldn't stop even if she wanted to," Mc-
Kenna had said. "Even if she could—and did—it would only put
her bridge opposite us. So much the better."

The final grain of sand fell through the hourglass of waiting.
Little Big Man exploded with gunfire as eight assault rifles roared
from the port side of the superstructure, followed by three more
streams of fire from each end of the carpenter's locker.

Captain Bernard Hill had always said that when his time
came to go, he wanted to die fast and not linger in agony in some
hospital. Hill got his wish. In only three seconds, almost 150
5.56mm slugs stabbed into the command bridge. Gordel and
Jorges fired downward into the hardtop of the bridge. Their twin
streams of projectiles slaughtered the floodlight, blew up the three
running lights, and put sixty-four holes in the roof.

Norbert Kling and Forrest Santage were able to fire through
the starboard windows of the enemy's bridge. Only Kling and
Santage, in the radio room, were on the same level as the command
bridge of the *Golden Dolphin,* Kling firing an M16, Santage one of
the CAR-15 submachine guns. It was their hurricane of slugs that,
in conjunction with the projectiles from Gordel and Jorges, butch-
ered Hill and destroyed the command bridge. Four 5.56mm slugs
hit Hill in the head. The effect was the same as a small stick of
dynamite expoding in the center of Hill's brain. Blobs and bits and
pieces of brain and skull bones and patches of bloody flesh were
plastered all over the inside of the pilothouse. More 5.56mm slugs
stabbed into Hill's right arm and right side, the impact of the
projectiles knocking him all the way to the port side of the bridge.

More slugs—many of these from Ray and Cotton—stabbed
into the center control console, blowing up the DT loran and turning the single sideband and the VHF radios into junk.

Vinnie Fats DiVarco had been lucky. He had left the pilot-
house only a third of a second before the men on *Little Big Man*
had closed the trap and opened fire. On his way to join Frank
Rufferi and Anthony "Joe Beck" Evola, the two hoodlums standing on the sun deck, Vinnie was on the port side of the superstructure and about the step out onto the foredeck when *Little Big Man*
erupted with a thunder-blast of gunfire and and a hail of slugs from
all three decks raked the proud *Golden Dolphin.*

Horrified, ducking shards of flying glass from the port side
windows that were being shot out, Vinnie Fats was just in time to
see Evola and Rufferi dance a short jig of death and then, shot

apart and in a swirling spray of blood, crumble to the deck. The two corpses resembled several piles of bloody rags with twisted arms, legs, and heads resting at odd angles. Very suddenly, "McKenna the Terrible" was no longer a joke.

The men in the operations room of *Little Big Man* had not fired a single shot at the control compartment of the *Golden Dolphin*. The angle of elevation was too high, so they did not waste ammunition. It was they who had offed Evola and Rufferi, and it was they who sent over two hundred slugs through the windows on the starboard side, a wave of 5.56mm metal that washed into the Ultimate Elsewhere everything it touched.

Marlene Sancor, Vinnie Fats's girlfriend, left this life as quickly as Hill, Evola, and Rufferi had departed. Marlene had drunk too many daiquiris during the afternoon and, after having a verbal screaming match with Vinnie, had gone to their cabin to sleep it off. A short time before the Ninja Master sprung the trap that doomed the *Golden Dolphin,* she had awakened, put on her robe, and gone to the main salon to get some coffee, take several Bromos, and put a wet towel over her left eye, which Vinnie had blackened.

Carmine Ne Ne Tortorello and Benny Zinna were also in the salon, playing poker with Rulon Stiffler and Howard Smith, two of the divers. As far as the two gangsters and the divers were concerned, the operation was over, except for transferring the treasure from *Little Big Man* to *Golden Dolphin*. The last thing the four men and Marlene expected was a rain of slugs.

The blast of metal came in so fast that Marlene and the four men never heard the windows shatter. Marlene was killed instantly. A spitzer-shaped projectile stabbed through the left side of her slim neck and sped out the right side. A second bullet came in at a steep angle and practically amputated her right breast before it tore through her heart and made its way out her back. Turned instantly into a bloody corpse, she crumpled to the floor.

Ne Ne Tortorello and Benny Zinna, both sitting at the folddown table, were riddled in twice the length of time it takes a bolt of lightning to strike, the 5.56mm projectiles stabbing into their sides, backs, and heads. They might as well have been dumped into a gigantic meat grinder. Simultaneously, spitzer-shaped slugs speared Smith and Stiffler, both of whom were sitting across the table from Ne Ne and Benny. They fell face downward, their blood mingling with the blood of Benny and Ne Ne.

The wipeout took only fifteen seconds, including the killing of the two crewmen standing on the stern deck. Bilib, Hoover, and Malbain had blown them apart with such precision that the two corpses looked as though they had been hacked to death with several dozen cleavers.

The firing stopped as abruptly as it had started. Although Captain Hill was dead meat, the *Golden Dolphin* continued to move ahead at 3.2 knots.

Other than Vinnie Fats, now making his way toward the bridge, there were eight other men on board, seven triggermen and Junior Orth. The hoodlums had been below, three sleeping in staterooms, two getting ready to go to bed, and two, unable to sleep, helping Orth (who was a chronic insomniac) check and store scuba gear. The roaring of assault rifles had put an end to their complacency and feelings of victory.

Grabbing handguns—Nelson "Spider" Webb picking up a Belgian FNC-M11 assault rifle—the men rushed to the main deck. In an instant, they saw the two bodies of the deckhands and realized what had happened. They also saw the dim shape of *Little Big Man* receding in the distance.

"Son of a bitch!" snarled Spider Webb. "We've been shot to pieces!"

"I wonder if they got Vinnie!" mumbled Nick Cufari, who had a face like an old bulldog's.

"We have to get to the bridge." Junior Orth's voice shook. "They sure as hell would try to shoot the shit out of the bridge."

Orth, Spider Webb, and Angelo "Wimpy" Biello—the rest of the men had gone to the main salon—were soon on the command bridge with Vinnie Fats, who looked like a man who had just seen his house and all his possessions blown away by a twister. Worse, he had only himself to blame. Charlie had warned him: *McKenna will try to trap you. Think before you make any moves. Be very careful.* Vinnie had thought out his moves. He *had* been very careful.

And he had taken the Golden Dolphin *straight into an ambush!*

All of them had to step over the headless corpse of Captain Hill in the port side doorway, and no matter where they stepped, there were either pools of blood or pieces of metal and fabric shot from Hill and from the control console.

Orth quickly pulled down the port and the starboard throttles, and the *Golden Dolphin* began to glide to a stop.

Enraged, Vinnie Fats grabbed a fistful of Orth's dirty T-shirt.

"Are you nuts?" he snarled. "We have to get the fuck out of here!"

"We have to first assess the damage," Orth said angrily, pulling Vinnie's hand away. "We can't go moving ahead in the dark without knowing what's out there, not until daylight anyhow. See for yourself. The radio screen is busted. Everything is wrecked. Hell, they're almost a thousand feet behind us, there ain't no reason they'll come after us. They know we can't make a second attempt."

"Vinnie, he's right," Webb said worriedly. "We'd better listen to him. We don't know a fuckin' thing about boats. He does."

Glaring first at Webb and Biello, then at Orth, Vinnie nodded.

"Okay, but make it fast," he said. "I want us out of here. All the instruments are wrecked and we're sitting in the middle of this friggin' ocean—in the middle of nowhere!"

Within the next fifteen minutes, Junior Orth discovered that the situation had gone from terrible to double-terrible. Not only had the control unit of the automatic pilot been wrecked by slugs but the hand-steering system was also inoperable. The chain on the sprocket, from the shaft of the helm to the drive unit, was broken, a bullet having severed a steel link. The cruise control had also been smashed.

"So what the hell are you saying?" demanded Vinnie Fats, glaring at Orth. "Out with it."

"I just told you. The steering is out," a shaken Orth explained. "We can't turn to port or starboard, either to the left or the right, not until I put on a new chain, if we even have a spare!"

Thinking of Marlene and wondering if she was all right, Vinnie began to breathe heavier from tension. "How long before you can get us out of here?"

"Well, like I said. I have to put on—"

"Listen!" Spider Webb cocked his FNC-M11 to one side.

In only a few seconds, the sound was very clear, the sound of diesels in the distance, growing louder with every moment.

"Son of a bitch!" stammered Angelo Biello. "The bastards are coming after us!"

CHAPTER 7

To Scott McKenna—as a ninja—there was no such thing as partial success. Either one succeeded or one failed. *The* Golden Dolphin *has to be sent to the bottom!* he told himself as he watched the yacht glide by.

As soon as the firing stopped, McKenna told the men in the operations room to remain on full alert. He then hurried to the bridge, where a satisfied Ray Gordel and Cotton Jorges had turned on a small overhead light, opened all the windows to clear the air of powder fumes, and were picking up empty cartridge cases.

Gordel grinned at McKenna and dumped a handful of empty casings into a paper bag. "Well, Scotty, we did it," he said happily. "I don't know how many we killed, but you can bet your last ice pick that they won't be back, and I don't think they'll show up when we go after the real *Santa Francesca.*"

Jorges was not so enthusiastic. "We can't be sure, amigo. A wounded animal often attacks in sheer desperation."

"We have half failed or only half succeeded," McKenna said coldly. "The *Dolphin* is still out there. But they won't return. Not now, not out here."

"Then why do you say we only 'half succeeded'?" Gordel frowned. "Sisney was just in, and he said she's stopped and is about thirteen hundred feet ahead of us. But I'll be double damned if we're going to try to ram her. This bucket isn't built for such rough action."

"Ray, have you forgotten about the diver and the two sea sleds just a short distance from us?"

"What the hell does that have to do with our wrecking the *Golden Dolphin*?" Jorges asked, his eyes narrowing.

The Ninja Master told them what he intended to do—"if the diver and the sleds are still out there."

Jorges shook his head in disbelief while Gordel made "Tch-tch-tch" sounds, then said, "Scotty, those Japs must have taught you to fall in love with death. You're just going to kill yourself the hard way."

Donald Stirling had gotten the biggest surprise of his life when *Little Big Man* had suddenly turned into a battleship. Sitting astraddle one of the sea sleds that he had submerged to three feet, with only his head above water, he had seen the *Golden Dolphin* raked with slugs. Then, much to his horror, he saw the lights of the *Dolphin* grow dim in the distance as she moved off.

Feeling more alone than he had ever felt in his life, Stirling tried to be calm so he could decide what course of action to take. Use one of the sea sleds and go after the yacht? Suppose *Little Big Man* went after her and he got caught in the middle? Another worry was that Vinnie Fats—that sadistic bastard—might order the corpses tossed overboard. Sharks could detect blood for miles. Once great whites smelled blood, they became blood-possessed and frantic to kill, and no power on earth could stop them.

Suddenly the engines of *Little Big Man* throbbed with life and the FPB began to move forward. Stirling was almost grateful when the vessel executed a wide turn and began to cut water in his direction. A searchlight on the bridge was switched on and quickly its shaft of light captured Stirling in its glare. In a short time, the vessel had pulled alongside and men on the foredeck were tossing him a rope.

It did not take long for Stirling to realize that the tall young man meant exactly what he said: Cooperate or we'll toss you back into the sea.

Within ten minutes, McKenna—dressed in shorts and with the ice picks still belted around his waist—was seated on one of the sea sleds with Stirling, who had brought the torpedolike vehicle to the surface.

Stirling quickly explained how the sea sled functioned, beginning with the internal machinery—the forward trim tank, batteries, air bottles, pump, controller, aft trim tank, and buoyancy tank. Far more importantly, he carefully explained the motor control and the diving and steering controls.

Thirty minutes later, McKenna was on his way, wearing two air tanks strapped to his back and a round scuba mask over his face. Only his eyes were above water. In one of the plastic containers strapped to his chest he carried a quart bottle filled with lighter fluid and number two diesel fuel. Next to the bottle, which was wrapped in a towel, was a flare gun. It was not loaded, however. He carried the two 25mm Parac flares in a watertight pouch on the left side of the belt that contained the ice picks.

Ahead the Ninja Master could see the lights of the salon and on the bridge of the enemy vessel, and he hoped that the *Golden Dolphin* would not get under way before he could reach her. He couldn't figure out why she had stopped, unless some of the slugs had damaged her steering mechanism. There wasn't anyone on the stern deck, but he could see figures moving in the long housing and on the bridge. More importantly, now that the yacht was dead in the water, the tow cable of the motorboat was slack and hanging straight down from the rectangular transom.

The short, dark journey did not take long. The Ninja Master stopped the sea sled only 150 feet to the rear of the stern. He removed his scuba mask, unstrapped the air tanks, and belted them and the mask to the center O-ring on top of the rounded hull of the underseas vehicle. It was the air tanks that would keep the vehicle from sinking more than five feet.

McKenna began the swim to the stern of the *Golden Dolphin,* soon reaching the transom. Continuing to kick out his legs, he took several deep breaths and looked at the luminous dial of the diver's watch on his left wrist. In twelve more minutes, Vic Jorges would start to bring the *Little Big Man* toward the target yacht.

Two feet from McKenna was the towline cable, one end attached to a heavy-duty snap-shackle fastened to the stern gunwale, the other end attached to a ring on the foredeck of the Capri I/O speedboat.

In only a short while, he had pulled himself up on the cable and was on the stern deck, his immediate goal the cockpit. He crept across the deck, reached the cockpit, moved down the six steps to its deck, and came to the small doorway of the steps that led to the second deck. Taking two ice picks from his belt and holding them by their weighted handles, he crept down the seven steps to the second deck. He found himself in a long but narrow corridor with the stateroom doors on each side. The doors were of solid teak, plush deep blue carpet beneath his feet. Four lights, recessed into the walls, gave out a soft blue glow. Ahead were the stairs that angled downward to the engine room, the engine space, and the two GM 8V-72TI diesels. Also ahead, to the left of the top of the stairs and surrounded by a stainless-steel guard rail, was the bulkhead to the area underneath the foredeck. Here were frozen-food lockers, freshwater storage, a general storage area, and the forepeak with its anchor section.

The Ninja Master's luck went sour when the bulkhead door swung outward and a man stepped out, a Heckler and Koch 33A2 in his hands. Right behind him another goon stepped through the opening into the corridor. He was armed with a Mini-Uzi sub-machine gun. Both men had come below to get high-powered weapons, just in case *Little Big Man* should attack.

Albert Frasconi and Vito Scimone would have had the advantage if Scott McKenna had been an average man. Neither gunman would have had the least bit of trouble in raising his weapon and stitching the Ninja Master. The reality was that both goons were doomed the instant McKenna saw them.

Frasconi and Scimone recovered quickly from their shock at seeing McKenna and instantly began to raise their weapons. They were too slow, too late, and too dumb to live. By then, the two ice picks had left Scott's hands.

"UH!" The short cry leapt from Scimone's mouth as the rounded blade of the ice pick buried itself high in his throat, so high that the top part of the steel was only a few millimeters under his chin. His body jerked. The H & K fell from his hands, and a river of red started to pour from his mouth and nose.

Vito Scimone's massive legs turned to soggy spaghetti at the same time that Frasconi started to go down. McKenna's ice pick had gone through Scimone's left eye and into his brain, the needle-point stopping when it came to the inside of the rear skull bone. However, as he started to go down (his eye dribbling down his cheek like dark-brown egg yolk), the beginning of cadaveric spasm forced the index finger of his right hand to pull against the trigger of the Uzi. The weapon chattered out a stream of 9mm projectiles that stabbed into the carpet several feet ahead of the falling down dead man.

McKenna raced ahead toward the two corpses.

There was one reason why Vinnie Fats had not ordered the corpses on board tossed into the black water of the channel. He couldn't bear the thought of seeing Marlene Sancor's body disappear beneath the waters. While Junior Orth worked to replace the broken chain on the manual steering system on the command bridge, Vinnie pondered what to do with the bodies of Marlene and the men who had been gunned down. With him in the salon were Nelson Webb and Nick Cufari, and all three of them had to fight to keep from gagging at both the sight and the stench of blood and excrement. Defecation is automatic with a corpse and occurs as soon as the sphincter relaxes.

Vinnie glanced toward the stern doorway as Cosmo "the Bear" Castucci entered the salon. Weighing 271 pounds, Castucci resembled a 100,000 B.C. Neanderthal dressed in twentieth century slacks and shirt. Behind him came Phil Macalusa and Angelo "Wimpy" Biello, both carrying U.S. AR-18 assault rifles.

"Vinnie, Orth said to tell you he'll have that damned chain on in another twenty minutes," Castucci growled. "But what we gonna do with—"

It was then that the six men in the salon heard the Mini-Uzi chatter belowdeck, to starboard.

"What the fuck is going on?" Spider Webb was incredulous. "Al or Vito must have fired accidentally."

"Vito and Al are pros," Vinnie Fats said in quiet alarm. "That burst was no accident. Spider, Nick. You two go forward." He pulled his favorite weapon from his belt, a Mauser M712 *Reihenfeuerpistole*. In spite of its age, the broom-handled Mauser was in excellent condition. "Use the hatch in front of the dinette and head back this way on the second deck. Phil, Wimpy, Cosmo —take the steps in the—what the fuck do they call that square hole in the back deck?"

"The cockpit," supplied Cosmo the Bear. In spite of his brutish appearance, he was not a stupid man.

"Okay. You three use them steps in the cockpit," Vinnie said, pushing off the safety of the long-barreled Mauser. "If Al and Vito ain't wasted whoever is down there, you three will trap the motherfucker between Nick and Spider. Now move it."

Glancing in repugnance at the four bloody corpses at the letdown table, Macalusa stared hard at Vinnie. "Look! Something ain't right! If Al and Vito had blasted whoever it was, they'd been up here by now tellin' us about it. We only heard one burst. So what I want to know is, what the hell has happened to Al and Vito? Maybe it was them who got knocked off!"

"Knocked off by who?" demanded Spider Webb. "You're all nuts! How in hell could anyone be aboard this baby? You think that ninja fucker can *fly*?"

"Get going!" Vinnie Fats snapped angrily. "We'll find out damn soon what's going on. I'm going to the bridge and speed up Orth."

Just as no man can ever step in the same water twice, the Ninja Master also knew that the mobsters—now alerted by the burst of submachine-gun fire—would come at him from both directions. He certainly couldn't let himself be trapped in the engine space. There was only one way into the machinery area, and only one way out.

In spite of the seventeen-inch-long hollow cylinder strapped across his chest, he jumped lightly over the bodies of Vito Scimone and Albert Frasconi and moved into the area beyond the bulkhead, swinging the door shut, but not locking it with the spin-wheel. Again, there were blue lights, their glow revealing that he was in the refrigerated food-storage locker. On top of one vertical locker were several cases of whiskey and a case of gin. McKenna smiled to himself. Why men should put thieves into their mouths to steal their brains was one of the great mysteries of life.

McKenna moved into the section to his left and saw that it was a general storage area. There were crates of canned goods and powdered milk, as well as several boxes of medical supplies. There was a flight of steps at the stern of the compartment. McKenna looked up the stairs, then stepped behind them and took a position behind three large wooden crates, piled one on top of the other and all three metal-strapped to the back of the steps. On each crate was stenciled MKVI BOTTLE/CANISTER ASSEMBLY—air bottles for scuba gear. McKenna removed the hollow container from his chest. It was too bulky and would hinder his movements. He reasoned that whoever would come looking for him would have to come down the steps or through the bulkhead from the corridor that began at the end of the stairs from the cockpit.

The Ninja Master did not have long to wait. The oval door at the top of the stairs opened and two men started to come down, the man in front holding a three-cell flashlight in his left hand and a big blue .357 Colt King Cobra revolver in his right hand. The man behind him with the screwed-up face held an odd-looking Goncz .45 pistol with a long twenty-round magazine.

Spider Webb and Nick Cufari came down the steps, stepped onto the floor, and looked cautiously from left to right, Webb moving the beam of the flashlight ahead of him. At any time, either Webb or Cufari might swing around and decide to look behind the crates. Neither man got the opportunity. As quietly as a shadow, McKenna moved from behind the crates, came in behind Webb and Cufari, and simultaneously executed two blows that only a Master Ninja could carry out successfully. McKenna's arms and hands came down between the left side of Webb and the right side of Cufari, and the hands, moving in opposite directions, connected solidly with the side of each man's neck.

The two gunsels dropped faster than anchors made of lead, their pistols falling to the floor along with the flashlight. The result of the Ninja Master's double *shuto* sword-ridge hand chops was pure catastrophe: contusions of the jugular vein and the carotid artery, as well as contusions of the vagus, phrenic, and hypoglossal nerves. Both hoods were dying from rapid thrombosis, a blood clotting that would rapidly lead to cerebral thrombosis.

McKenna didn't bother to check the bodies—he knew exactly what he could do with his bare hands. He moved through the doorway to his right, reentered the food-storage locker, and took a position by the left side of the bulkhead door. He was in position none too soon. In only eighteen seconds, the rounded bulkhead door began to open very slowly. McKenna waited. After the door had opened several feet, McKenna saw the flash suppressor of a U.S. Armalite-18 assault rifle. The remainder of the barrel and the end of the main part of the weapon followed, a man's hand folded around the foregrip; and McKenna heard the whispered words of the creep behind the clown who was holding the AR-18: "Whoever it is, I think he went to the engine room. Why else would anyone come aboard if he didn't want to wreck us?"

"It's got to be that McKenna son of a bitch," said a third voice, this one gravelly. "Who else would use ice picks? Shit, he don't fight fair!"

"Okay, I'm going in," said the man holding the AR-18.

You are going to die! The Ninja Master attacked, a high, chilling "KIIIIII-EEEEEEEeeeeeeee!" yell exploding from his throat. His arms shot out. Both hands went around the top of the AR-18, and he jerked with such incredible strength that the weapon was pulled from Angelo Biello's grasp, the sudden forward motion of the weapon pulling the trigger against his finger. The AR-18 roared and vomited out a stream of 5.56 X 45mm projectiles that wrecked the horizontal food locker. As the weapon left Wimpy's hand, its motion caused him to lose his balance and pulled him forward so that he half fell through the doorway—straight to his own destruction.

During that split second, the Ninja Master had reversed the assault rifle, and now he slammed the end of the stock full force into Wimpy Biello's face, holding the weapon on its side and hitting the mobster just above the bridge of the nose.

Wimpy might as well have been executed with a fifty-pound sledge! The concussion to his brain was fatal.

McKenna's chain-lightning attack and ninja yell startled Phil Macalusa and Cosmo "the Bear" Castucci, giving the Ninja Master a four-second edge which he used to good advantage. In an instant, he had moved through the bulkhead and was confronting a very startled Phil Macalusa, who had not had time to regear his thoughts and turn the barrel of his AR-18 toward McKenna.

Three feet behind Macalusa and several feet to his right was the Bear and his .357 mag revolver. An enraged expression on his beefy face, he stepped back a few feet and began to move the weapon from left to right in an attempt to get off a round at McKenna. At the moment, he couldn't. Macalusa was between him and the Ninja Master.

Before Macalusa could even begin to defend himself, McKenna executed a quick front snap kick, with an *ashi kubi* instep slam. Macalusa screamed. Not only had the blow shattered his pubic bone, it had also flattened his testicles. In shock, he dropped and sank into unconsciousness.

The moment came when "the Bear" Castucci was positive he couldn't miss. But only for a moment was the barrel of the .357 magnum level with the Ninja Master. McKenna charged straight at the Bear, who squeezed the trigger. The Llama Comanche revolver roared almost at the same time that McKenna moved to one side, the .357 flat-nosed bullet missing the Ninja Master's left side by a fourth of an inch.

The Bear had never been physically afraid of any man—until now. It was impossible for any human being to move with such unbelievable speed. But McKenna had! And now it was too late for another shot. The Ninja Master had him!

Sudden, sharp pain burst in the gunsel's right wrist and right forearm. Startled, Castucci found his right hand reflexively opening, the butt of the Llama Comanche leaving it, and his arm flying upward from McKenna's very fast *mae geri kekomi* front snap kick. The Bear didn't have a chance in a billion. McKenna spun around and let him have an even faster *ushiro kekomi geri* rear thrust kick, his left foot almost burying itself in Castucci's solar plexus.

It was all over for the Bear. In one second, not only had the blow created a fissure in his liver, ruptured his stomach, and torn loose his gall bladder, it had also compressed his pancreas against the lumbar region of his spine.

A howling cry of pain, fear, and defeat poured out of the Bear's mouth. In shock, his strength gone, he staggered back and tripped over the corpse of Vito Scimone. He fell heavily on his back, his lower legs resting across the bloody chest of the corpse.

McKenna glanced down the corridor, then turned and went through the open bulkhead. He knew that *Little Big Man* was not far from the stern of the *Golden Dolphin* because he could hear her engines throbbing. He was leaving the food-locker room and moving into the general storage area when he detected a change in the sound of *Little Big Man*'s engines. Cotton Jorges was bringing her to starboard of the *Golden Dolphin*.

McKenna had come aboard to start a fire in the engine space, hoping that the flames would spread through the luxury yacht. There wasn't, however, any danger that the vessel would explode. "Scotty, diesel fuel doesn't explode like gasoline. It will burn and burn, but no boom."

It didn't matter. McKenna had found another way.

He went behind the crates, opened the watertight container, and took out the flare gun and the bottle of lighter fluid and number two diesel fuel. He opened the quart bottle and poured the contents over the top of the first of the three wooden crates marked MKVI BOTTLE/CANISTER ASSEMBLY, the crate that was the highest of the three. The liquid spread out over the top of the crate and began to flow down its sides and the four sides of the crates beneath it. He saved enough of the liquid to trail a stream of it to the front of the stairs. He tossed down the empty bottle, loaded the flare gun, then went back to the front of the steps and picked up the Colt King Cobra revolver that had belonged to Spider Webb (whose corpse was now decorating the floor). Ready to leave, McKenna looked at the top of the stairs, ran up to the top step, looked around, then pointed the flare gun downward and pulled the trigger. BOOOOP! The flare hit the floor and diesel fuel ignited and the four sides of the three crates started to burn, the fire eating quickly into the dry wood.

McKenna knew he had maybe three or four minutes. He was in a vertical gangway in front of what appeared to be a dinette. At each end of the corridor was a door to the six-foot-wide deck on either side of the long housing containing the salon, dinette, and galley. McKenna turned, moved forward, and entered the galley. *Yes, sir. The bridge has to be overhead.* Judging from the height of the command bridge from the deck, he knew there had to be another compartment between the bridge and the level in which he was standing. But the powerful magnum slugs might reach the bridge.

He raised the Colt King Cobra and squeezed the trigger. The big revolver roared and the .357 bullet tore through the ceiling. Five times he fired and each time, just before he squeezed the trigger, he moved to a different position. With each shot, the bullet stabbed through the pink-and-cream ceiling several feet from where the preceding slug had entered.

On the command bridge, a furiously sweating Vincent DiVarco realized that the intruder aboard must be Scott McKenna. He had heard the AR-18 roaring from below, and knew that if his men had whacked out the son of a bitch, they would have come to the bridge by now and reported it. But how? *How* had McKenna gotten on board? Worse, the goddamn enemy ship was only three hundred feet to starboard. It was just sitting there, waiting. Why? To pick up the crazy McKenna when he jumped into the water—obviously! McKenna had to be insane. No man in his right mind would attack a ship singlehandedly. But McKenna had! And—damn him—he had succeeded!

The Mauser broom-handled pistol in his right hand, Vinnie Fats looked fearfully from port to starboard. Almost as if he expected McKenna to materialize behind him, he swung around and stared toward the stern.

He swung back to Junior Orth, who was on his knees in front of the control console, the two front panels of which had been removed. Spread out on the floor were tools. Orth had taken off his shirt and sweat was dripping from his chest and back.

"Damn it, how much longer?" Vinnie Fats growled.

"I'm finished." Orth turned, looking up at Vinnie, half smiled, and pulled a handkerchief from his right rear pocket. "We'll start her up and see if the chain holds and—"

BLAM! Orth and Vinnie heard the revolver roar from below. They looked down at the floor, glanced at each other, and waited. The .357 bullet had not penetrated the floor. It had gone through the floor of the observation deck below (the ceiling of the galley) and had shot up through the next ceiling, which was also the floor of the bridge—but had been deflected by the head of a small bolt.

BLAM! The second .357 slug came up through the floor and —*wanggg!*— hit the handle of an adjustable wrench and made it jump a foot before ricocheting across the bridge and hitting the port wall.

His mouth open, Orth got to his feet and pushed himself as far as possible against the control console. Vinnie Fats, a silent snarl on his face, hastily backed toward the port door, staring down at the floor as if he expected it to explode in his face.

BLAM! The third bullet came through the middle of the floor and struck the ceiling. But the power of the slug was now almost spent, and it did not penetrate the hardtop.

A fourth BLAM from below. The bore tore up through the floor only a foot in front of Vinnie Fats, who by now was more enraged than afraid.

BLAM! The final .357 projectile zipped through the floor toward the stern of the bridge.

Vinnie Fats waited almost a full minute. When there were no more shots from below, he said in a half-choked voice to Orth, who was still staring down at the bloody floor, "Start the engines and get us out of here. That crazy bastard won't dare come up here. He'll go overboard."

After McKenna fired the last shot, he threw away the revolver and stuck the second big cartridge into the flare gun; he then hurried to to the starboard door of the gangway. Once outside on the deck, he kept close to the wall, raised the flare gun, and fired. He didn't bother to watch the flare shoot upward and burst into a brilliant plume of white-red-yellow-and-orange. Instead, he rushed outward, vaulted over the railing, and dived into the water. He went under, came up, took in a lungful of air, went down again, and began swimming with powerful strokes toward the port side of *Little Big Man,* which had moved a hundred feet closer to the gangster yacht with its cargo of dead. And still no explosion!

There were thirty-two tanks of compressed air in the three
crates in the general storage of the yacht—more accurately, of
compressed *oxygen* and *nitrogen.* A diver does not breathe pure
oxygen. He breathes a mixture of oxygen and nitrogen. Standard
diving mixtures are 60/40, 40/60, and 62.5/37.5.

Slightly heavier than "air," oxygen is not flammable in itself;
however, it strongly supports and rapidly accelerates the combustion of all flammable materials. Nitrogen also is slightly heavier
than air but will not support combustion.

The thirty-two air tanks in the three crates were 60/40. The
mix didn't make any real difference. Compressed oxygen will support combustion, and when compressed oxygen and nitrogen are
heated in diving tanks, both gases expand. But with nowhere to
go . . .

McKenna had swum 125 feet from the vessel when the thirty-
two tanks in the now blazing general storage exploded with a loud
BERRRRUUUUUUMMMMM!, the blast cracking the double mahogany planking and the fiberglass to both port and starboard. The
explosion also caved in the deck of the storage area, ripped off the
control cables to the rudder, and created cracks in the forefoot of
the keel. Equally bad for the *Golden Dolphin,* two vertical braces of
the superstructure were torn from their foundations, the damage so
severe that the command bridge tilted twenty-six inches to stern
and port, throwing Vinnie Fats and Junior Orth backward. The
proud *Golden Dolphin* was doomed. Water began to pour rapidly
through the cracks in the hull, sizzling and creating steam when it
made contact with the fire, which could now be seen by the men
standing at the port railing of *Little Big Man.*

As McKenna closed in on the FPB, swimming for the sea
ladder on the side of the hull, he could see the crew standing at the
port railing, the fire behind him tossing a reddish, flickering glow
over their faces. Unexpectedly, the men raised M16's and began
firing, their concentrated streams of 5.56mm projectiles stabbing
into the black water a hundred feet behind him.

"Sharks! Swim, damn it! Swim!" shouted Ray Gordel.

McKenna swam with all his strength, calling up extra reserves
of power from the subconscious, expecting at any moment to feel
his body in the grip of powerful jaws and sharp teeth. Death is but
walking through a door to a different reality. It is only the true
state for the spirit. This was a part of the ninja Doctrine of Accep-
tance. Maybe so, but McKenna still felt a twinge of bitterness, not

because he might die, but because he would die without being able to defend himself. Not even a Master Ninja can fight a man-eating shark, especially a great white.

Death did not want him this morning. He reached the sea ladder and was very quickly jerked to the deck by willing hands—and none too soon. His feet had not been out of the water for more than a few seconds and he was still being pulled onto the deck when one of the ominous dorsal fins cut the water so close to the vessel that one side of the twenty-five-foot great white raked the hull. Five more fins were moving back and forth only sixty feet away.

"Great whites!" muttered Barrett Gulbrandsen in awe.

"Damned killers!" snarled Chester Malbain. Leaning over the railing, he triggered off a full clip at the shark that had just raked the hull.

"Cease firing," Ray Gordel ordered in a sharp voice. "It's a waste of ammo. Scott is safe and the great whites are only doing what they've been programmed to do—eat!"

"Man, just look at her! She has to sink!" Jerry Bilib said happily. He stared at the blazing *Golden Dolphin* as he shoved a full magazine into his M16 assault rifle.

Burning amidships, the *Golden Dolphin* was beginning to settle in the water. In another three minutes her foredeck and stern would be awash with the hungry waters of Northwest Providence Channel. Dawn had broken out in the east, and everyone could see the yacht very clearly. As they watched the doomed vessel, they saw two men suddenly emerge from the port side of the long above-deck housing and move toward the gunwale.

"Hey! Look! Two of the bastards are still alive!" exclaimed John W. Hoover. "Let's grease those mothers!" He turned and grinned at McKenna. "You must be slipping. How come you didn't kill 'em?"

"We are not going to shoot them," McKenna said firmly. He watched the two men at the stern of the sinking yacht pull in the line attached to the motorboat. "They can't do us any harm."

"Hell no, not now," Hoover said roughly, giving McKenna a dirty look. "They were only going to kill all of us. They're nothing more than a couple of dinks, the very same breed as the Charlies in Nam. With cruds like that, you have to be the meanest motherfucker in the valley. The thing to do is rock-'n'-roll em. The only good dink is a dead dink."

Ignoring Hoover, McKenna turned to Gordel, who was standing next to him at the railing. "Ray, have some of the men bring Barbasta and Stirling up here. We can swing the boat around and they can jump over the side and swim to the motorboat."

"The hell with them!" Gordel's voice was heavy with rancor. "Those two scum-heads can jump from here."

McKenna turned and regarded his old friend with steady eyes. "Ray, you know they can't jump from here and swim. The sharks will get them."

Gordel's expression changed to puzzlement. "Why all this concern for two pieces of trash, and since when did life become so precious to you? After all, you shoved an ice pick into the brain of one creep we captured! And now you're worried that great whites might nibble on Barbasta and Stirling. Man, you are weird!"

"What I did was necessary," McKenna said casually, but still with an icy quality in his voice. "Tossing those two to the sharks isn't."

"It doesn't matter," Gordel said, sounding cheerful. "We don't have time. See for yourself."

The two men on the sinking *Golden Dolphin* had crawled into the Capri I/O speedboat and freed it from its towline. They started the engine and soon were speeding from the yacht, which was beginning to tilt forward. Already her foredeck was underwater, and hundreds of gallons of water were pouring into her main salon, the four corpses awash.

"I don't think that even you, Scotty, can expect us to chase a motorboat!" said Gordel with a slight snicker. "A craft like that can get up to forty knots. Ah . . . there goes the yacht."

The *Golden Dolphin* sank. Her stern reared up six feet so that the men watching on the deck of *Little Big Man* could see the rudder and the propeller. She then slid forward and quickly went under the water. That's all there was to it. For a time the surface bubbled and items that could float began bobbing to the surface. There were no bodies.

There was a long, solemn silence after the *Golden Dolphin* went to the bottom. McKenna, Gordel, and the other men on deck —and Cotton Jorges on the bridge—stared at the debris floating where the yacht had been . . . wooden deck and canvas furniture, plastic dishes, et cetera. Men who spend a good deal of time on the sea never take pleasure in seeing a vessel sink, even the ship of an enemy, except perhaps during times of war. Even the victors have a strong sense of uneasiness. For always foremost in their minds is the thought *It could be us. The next time it might be.* . . .

Ray Gordel put the sling strap of the CAR-15 over his right shoulder. "Now we can go after the real treasure. Ditto to Lombardo!"

Alfred Rothweiler shook his head and stared out where the *Golden Dolphin* had sunk.

"It's like I've always said," he muttered. "Life is all rain and shit, and then you die. . . ."

CHAPTER 8

Sabiendo que vamos a triunfar . . . Sitting in the captain's nook, Captain Ennio Penzula thought of the second line of the Cuban "Hymn of the 26 July"—". . . knowing we are going to win." Penzula, the commander of the *Ernesto Guevara*, was a confident man as he conferred with Major Esteban Cruz de Oviedo, the DSE officer aboard the submarine.

Penzula also felt good because he had sent a long radio report to Colonel Calixto Hevia, using the Soviet-made Angara-PA HF transmitter/receiver, the set scrambling the message and bursting it out as static into the airwaves.

The report could not have been better. Penzula and his crew had shadowed both the *Little Big Man* and the *Golden Dolphin,* all the while staying far enough to stern, and finally to starboard, to outwit any sonar the vessels might be using. Only a highly experienced submarine commander such as Penzula could have accomplished the task, which had not been a simple matter of "trailing behind." Not only did the *Ernesto Guevara* have to remain outside sonar range, but Penzula had been forced to make a lot of guesses as to the possibility of the two target ships changing course abruptly. Much of the time he had concentrated on keeping track of the *Golden Dolphin,* knowing that where *Dolphin* was, *Little Big Man* could not be far ahead.

Penzula had kept track of the two vessels with long-range radar and by having his technicians monitor the two target ships with heat-sensing equipment. Only after the one-sided battle between *Little Big Man* and the *Golden Dolphin* had started had Penzula made a close approach to within six kilometers of the two ships, gambling that no one would be at the sonar sets aboa. two vessels.

After the *Golden Dolphin* had gone to the bottom of Norui-west Providence Channel and *Little Big Man* had started to head due west, Penzula had submerged and had pulled back eleven kilometers. He had also sent a radio message to Captain Armengol Borrero of the *Laughing Lady*. Borrero had been slowly cruising thirty-two kilometers south of the American vessels. By taking a northwest course, Borrero would be able to cut across the bow of *Little Big Man*, if the American ship continued to move due west, presumably on her way back to Florida and to where the real treasure was located.

Captain Penzula had not miscalculated. The *Laughing Lady* had cut across the bow of the American ship, only half a kilometer ahead of her. The rest had only been a matter of patience and caution. Precautions had been taken to prevent the Americans from recognizing the *Laughing Lady* on her various routes past and close to *Little Big Man*. Her flag, on a short mast at the stern, could be changed from the U.S. national ensign (the American stars and stripes) to either a USPS ensign (United States Power Squadron) or to a CGAUX ensign (U.S. Coast Guard Auxiliary). Or Captain Armengol Borrero could use an ordinary yacht ensign. Or the green/white/red flag of Mexico, or the blue/gold/blue (with black triangle) of the Bahamas.

Her real name was actually *Laughing Lady*, and she had been bought at an auction by two DSE agents who had solidly established themselves as American citizens. The name on each side of her bow could be changed by simply taking off the plates and replacing them with names such as *Sea Foam, Swordfish, Jolly Green Giant*, and so on.

Penzula had analyzed all the known factors very carefully. At the present time the American vessel was still moving west and was three fourths of the way through the Straits of Florida. The submarine, submerged at 180 meters, was eleven kilometers to her stern. All that remained, in Penzula's opinion, was for the Americans to sail to the actual location of the *Santa Francesca* and bring up the treasure. The Cuban force would then take the vast treasure from them, even if the pessimistic Major Cruz de Oviedo was convinced that the *americanos* had some kind of scheme in mind to protect themselves.

Esteban Cruz de Oviedo, sitting across the tiny let-down table from Captain Penzula, was saying, "I realize that the Americans don't suspect we are following them, but I am still not satisfied. They were very clever in luring Señor Lombardo's yacht into an ambush."

Major Cruz de Oviedo paused long enough to light a cigarette and inhale deeply. A deep-chested individual who liked to think of himself as *simpático,* he had a face that looked as if it had been squeezed dry and browned by the hot Cuban sun. At times, he reminded the aristocratic-looking Penzula of a cracked, expensive Havana cigar that had been stolen and carried too long by a dirty panhandler. Yet, in spite of Cruz de Oviedo's seedy appearance, he was a first-rate intelligence officer whose disposition toward alarmism never got the better of him.

Penzula, glancing at the small clock on the opposite wall, uncrossed his legs. "Major, it's not McKenna and his people we have to fear. It's the United States Navy."

A look of alarm flashed over Cruz de Oviedo's flat face. "I presume you mean the American navy could detect us with electronic sensors?"

"*Sí.* The Americans keep a very close watch not only on the Caribbean but also on the Straits of Florida and the Gulf of Mexico. The main concern of the Americans is Soviet submarines."

"How good are their detectors? And what kind do they have?"

"There's MAD—short for Magnetic Anomaly Detector," Penzula said. "This has to do with an electromagnetic field that a submarine creates. The Americans also have FLIR—forward-looking infrared. And SOSUS—sound surveillance. In a sense, you might say we're as 'undetectable' as a balloon all alone in the sky."

Cruz de Oviedo tapped ash from his cigarette into an ashtray on the tiny table. "The very possibility that the damned Americans can detect us while we're underwater is cause for concern. I don't know anything about submarines and methods of detection, but I do know that if another sub got close enough, she could detect us with her sonar—*correcto*?"

"*Sí.* With sonar, both hull-mounted and towed," Penzula told him, secretly enjoying the DSE agent's discomfort and trepidation. Penzula did not like Cruz de Oviedo and considered him dirt common, and for good reason: Ennio Vasconcelos Penzula was a product of the upper classes. His father had carved a *colonia* for himself and had been the proud owner of a hacienda, just as Fidel Castro's father, Angel, had owned a ten-thousand-acre *colonia* that had employed five hundred men.

Major Cruz de Oviedo didn't comment. He only inhaled deeply on his cigarette.

Captain Penzula again glanced at the clock on the wall, then got to his feet. "It's time to check with the radio room. Calleja and Borrero should be calling any minute—and don't forget to put out your cigarette."

With a sigh, Cruz de Oviedo crushed out his Moscow Night, got up, and followed Penzula through the narrow door into the hall. He hated the ocean. On top of it was bad enough. Underneath the surface was ten times worse. Piss on Penzula and his assurance about "well-built" Soviet submarines. The damned Russians didn't have the technology of the *americanos*.

The *Ernesto Guevara* was a Soviet type that NATO called "Whiskey-V." The Whiskey variants, six in all, were an old design that the Soviet Union had used from 1951 through 1964. The *Ernesto Guevara* was a diesel-electric boat 76 meters in length, with a beam of 6.5 meters and a draught of 4.9 meters. Torpedo tubes: four 533mm tubes in the bow, and two 406mm tubes in the stern. Power: two 4,000 h.p. diesels and two 2,700 h.p. electric engines. Two propeller shafts. Speed: 18 knots submerged, and 33 km/hr on the surface. Captain, officers, and crew: fifty-four men.

The boat was divided into four pressurized compartments. The stern section contained most of the machinery, the electrical equipment, the air compressors, and the two torpedo tubes. In the aft section were also the diesels and the electric motors, the latter two of which operated on large storage batteries.

Between the diesel compartment—and this included the electric motors—and the midships section were the crew's quarters and the galley; below the deck plates were most of the storage batteries. In the center compartment was the control section—a maze of meters, valves, levers, switches, the gyro compass, the magnetic compass, and the search periscope. The most important equipment was the machinery console and the automatic trim- and depth-keeping instruments, plus the electric gear that controlled the rudder and the hydroplanes.

The forward section of the boat consisted of the radio, sonar, and radar rooms, the map and chart room, the captain and officers' quarters and their mess, the sick bay, a general wardroom, and the bow compartment with its four torpedo tubes.

The conning tower contained the attack periscope, the helm, and the automatic torpedo computer. Buoyancy tanks, trim cells, fuel oil, and freshwater tanks were scattered throughout the boat. As a killer submarine, the *Ernesto Guevara* was a formidable opponent, or rather it had been in its day. However, it was no match for a modern U.S. nuclear sub and its vast array of ECM black boxes and ASW-SOW antisub missiles.

By the time Captain Penzula and Major Cruz de Oviedo reached the radio room, Armando Robles, the radio operator, had almost completed taking down the message that had just come in from *Laughing Lady*. He finished printing the message, tapped out *Received* on the key, turned, and handed the gray sheet of paper to Captain Penzula.

Penzula read the message, which had been scrambled and then automatically decoded; hence there were no cover names. The message read:

Little Big Man *proceeding northwest. 79 degrees west, 22 minutes. We passed her 15 minutes ago and now are 12 kilometers to her stern. Captain Sanchez of the* Independencia *is waiting 64 kilometers west of Marquesas Key. I will give our position in another four hours. Viva Fidel Castro. Viva la Revolución.*

The message was signed: *Calleja.*

Smiling with satisfaction, Penzula handed the message to Cruz de Oviedo, who quickly read it.

"I'm sure of it, the *americanos* are headed for the Florida Keys," Cruz de Oviedo said smugly. He handed the message back to Captain Penzula. "We will have them trapped within a few days. . . ."

CHAPTER 9

Charles Lombardo enjoyed contrast in his surroundings. For that reason, the living room in his mansion had a white ceiling while the walls were of black, red, gold, and cream. In the office he maintained in the Spurds Building in downtown Tampa, he had an executive desk with a plate-glass top, the underside of the glass painted a matte black. Every item on top of the desk—letter opener, penholder, telephone index, and various bric-a-brac—were of brass, which he kept highly polished, delighting in the contraposition of the gleaming brass with the intense black.

This afternoon, however, Charlie was not interested in colors. The disaster was too great; and the insurance he carried on the *Golden Dolphin* could not possibly cover the loss, even if he could somehow explain the yacht's sinking to the insurance company.

Sitting upright in the sumptuous black executive swivel chair, Lombardo glared at a dejected Vincent DiVarco who, in an armchair in front of the desk, faced him squarely.

"Do you mean to tell me that you—you of all people—let that damned McKenna pull you into an ambush?" raged Lombardo, his tone twice as cold as an iceberg. "Damn it to hell, Vinnie! How could you be so stupid?"

Vinnie Fats cleared his throat. What could he say? Total failure always speaks for itself, and in a very loud voice; yet he was not a man either to minimize a situation or to give excuses.

"It happened," he said flatly. "And the plan I had was a good one—to sneak men aboard *Little Big Man* and take over the ship. Them guys I sent aboard and—"

"They sure did!" interposed Lombardo, daggers of vituperation jumping from his eyes. "They must have been grabbed the instant they were on board. That Jap-loving McKenna was waiting for them. There isn't any other answer."

"Yeah, that's the way it happened," Vinnie admitted. "But how in the hell was I to know that? They called on a walkie-talkie and said everything had gone down as planned. I'm not a fuckin' mind reader! How in hell was I to know them dummies had got themselves captured by that fuckin' American Jap? We got the okay from Joe and went in. They shot the piss out of us. That's how it went down."

"Jesus Christ! It was as dumb as using the same hit-gun twice and not going for a head shot!" raged Lombardo. "And I'm talking about your letting McKenna get aboard, kill everyone he bumped into, and blow up the yacht." His voice rose in uncontrolled anger. "How in hell could he even have gotten aboard? Didn't you post guards on the deck?"

"Listen, Charlie—you weren't there!" snapped Vinnie Fats. "We was over a thousand feet away from *Little Big Man.* Who'd think that any man could swim that distance?"

"Hell, he used one of the sea sleds. But I suppose you didn't consider that possibility?"

"Neither would you if you had been there. It was as black as the six hubs of hell. Besides, we was too busy tryin' to fix that goddamn broken chain up on the bridge." Vinnie glared back at Lombardo, reached into the coat pocket of his houndstooth-pattern Piace jacket, and took out his cigarettes and lighter.

"You had enough made-men with you!" Lombardo snarled. "You should have had guys on deck."

"Four of the boys had already been knocked off, and the others was getting ready to battle *Little Big Man* in case she came after us. We couldn't steer. Like I said, who would have thought that McKenna would use a sea sled? Shit, whoever heard of one man attacking a whole goddamn ship!"

"I warned you about that ninja son of a bitch," Lombardo said accusingly. He breathed in noisily and deeply. "I told you over and over that he was not an ordinary man."

"Bullshit! He's still only one man!" objected Vinnie Fats, who again wished he could stop feeling stupid over the way Scott McKenna had outsmarted him. "What it was—McKenna was lucky. That prick's no superman. He just had a lot of luck."

Lombardo ground his teeth. "Yeah? But he and his two pals and their crew are still out there, and you're here! I can't even go to the marine insurance company and put in a claim for the *Golden Dolphin*. You've seen to that."

"What the hell did you expect me and Orth to do?" Vinnie lashed back. "The ship blew up! McKenna must have brought explosives on board. It was all Orth and me could do to get to the motorboat. Or have you forgotten that when she went down, McKenna's ship was only several hundred feet away? It was a wonder that they didn't machine-gun us out of the water!"

Lombardo puffed out his cheeks in exasperation. "I'm talking about what you told the authorities in the Bahamas—that there were only three of you in a small fishing boat and it sank with the loss of one man! How can I go to the insurance company and tell them I've lost the yacht when there's no record of its sinking?"

Vinnie Fats's glare was pure poison. "I suppose you'll say next I should have told them the truth! Shit! We know what them fools in the Bahamas would have done! They would have contacted the FBI, and we would have ended up in a mess, with our names splashed all over the papers—and you know it!"

Lombardo settled back in his chair, looked away, and remained silent for the moment. He couldn't protest against the truth, and he knew that, under the circumstances, Vinnie had done the only thing possible. He had told a story that the authorities in the Bahamas would believe. Small-boating accidents happen every day.

Vinnie Fats deliberately dropped cigarette ashes into a highly polished brass bowl that was there only for show. He enjoyed the pained expression on Lombardo's face as the ashes fell into the rounded depression. But Lombardo only straightened up, put his hands on the desk, and said in a dangerous voice, "By God, McKenna and his friends are not going to get away with it. No, by God, they're not. It's only been several days. We still have time to get out there. This time, I'll be in charge all the way."

"Get out there on the water?" About to sit back down, Vinnie Fats appeared surprised. "You mean to the Keys. In what?"

"My wife's brother has a cabin cruiser we can borrow. The son of a bitch owes me too much money to refuse. His boat is only a fifty footer. Actually, we'll need two boats." Lombardo smiled and his eyes became crafty. "Have you ever heard of a fishing boat named the *Slick Sister*?"

Vinnie cast a dubious eye at Lombardo. "No."

"The *Slick Sister* takes tourists out to fish for marlin and other big ones." Lombardo gave a low, sinister laugh. "And guess who the captain is—Alfredo Jorges, Victor Jorges's brother, his younger brother. Get my drift, Vinnie?"

Now it was Vinnie Fats's turn to smile. "How do you want to do it?"

CHAPTER 10

There was light wind, and moderate seas. Beaufort force five, wind speed of the waves from seventeen to twenty-one knots. This was followed by a light drizzle of six hours. By the time *Little Big Man* was ten miles due west of Marquesas Keys, the rain had stopped. The sea was calm and there were only cirrocumulus clouds drifting across the Dutch-boy blue sky.

It was on the sixth day after the *Golden Dolphin* had exploded and nosed herself to the bottom of the Northwest Providence Channel that Ray Gordel and Victor Jorges began to assemble their maps and charts and plot a course to where they believed the *Santa Francesca* had sunk.

McKenna, who knew very little about navigation (except on land), was curious. "How can you pinpoint the location of the wreck from the evidence you gathered at the Admiralty Office in Madrid?" he asked Gordel and Jorges as the two began plotting a new course in the chart room.

Gordel rubbed the stub of the little finger on his right hand, then, cocking his head to one side, scratched his thick straw-colored mustache. "Well, Scotty. There are some fundamentals. To begin with, all major parallels and meridians are coded by degrees, counting upward from zero. The zero parallel, or base line of latitude, is the equator. From there, the parallels march north and south in progression until they reach ninety degrees at the poles. The longitude base line, or prime meridian, passes through Greenwich, England. From zero degrees along the prime meridian, longitude is reckoned east and west halfway around the world to a maximum of a hundred eighty degrees, where the meridian cuts through the Pacific Ocean.

"Each degree is subdivided into sixty miles called minutes," explained Gordel, "with each minute representing one nautical mile or about two thousand yards."

Leaning over the table, McKenna pondered for a long moment. At length, he said, "If I'm not mistaken, one degree of longitude equals at this latitude approximately fifty miles. I'm basing my calculation on the earth's circumference of about twenty-five thousand miles and the three hundred sixty degrees in a circle. They yield a figure of 69.444 miles per degree, which means an arc-minute equal to 1.1574 miles. The earth's being flatter at the poles would have to make some difference. But I don't know what that difference is."

"If you know what an arc-minute is, you know more about navigation than you think," Jorges complimented McKenna.

"You might say the degrees widen toward the poles," Gordel told McKenna. "The length of a degree of longitude is approximately 24,892 miles divided by 360 and multiplied by the cosine of the latitude. A cosine is—"

"It's the size of the complement of a given arc or angle," the Ninja Master said quickly.

"Well, amigo! Those Japanese did teach you something about trigonometry!" Jorges said good-naturedly.

"Quite a bit and then some," McKenna said, "but they didn't teach me how to navigate on water."

Ray Gordel continued, "At a latitude of, say, 45 degrees, a longitudinal degree is 49 miles, and it increases to 58 miles at 30 degrees north latitude. This range includes most of Europe and the United States."

"So far it's about as clear as ink—black ink," McKenna said.

"If it will help, keep in mind all we have said, then project it to a flat Mercator map of the earth. It's fairly easy from there," Jorges said. "This means we will charge our present course to the spot where we think the *Santa Francesca* went down."

"Right here, Scotty," Gordel said, and, bending down, put his finger on the map. "Roughly, halfway between Key West and the Dry Tortugas. We still have to work out the exact degrees and minutes." All at once he gave a carefree laugh. "You're not afraid that we won't be able to get there, are you, Scotty? I mean that we won't be able to find the spot. And we don't have to worry about Lombardo. We've put an end to his interference."

"It's nothing like that," replied McKenna. "I was only curious about the navigation process. I'm also certain we've seen the last of the Lombardo goons. Just the same, we're going to remain on full alert, especially at night. This vessel is fast. It would be an ideal ship for drug runners. Then there's what Sisney might have heard on the sonar."

For several long moments there was silence, Gordel and Jorges thinking about the early morning when the *Golden Dolphin* had attacked. Gene Sisney, not wanting to miss anything, had left the radar and sonar room as soon as the enemy vessel had begun to close in. He had not returned to the cubicle until after the yacht had sunk and *Little Big Man* had turned around and was headed west. It was then that he had heard the steady *ping-ping-ping-ping* on the sonar, but only for eleven seconds, too short a time for him to get a definite fix. Sisney had immediately alerted McKenna and the others and explained what he had heard.

"So you picked up another vessel out there," Ray Gordel had suggested. "Why get excited? These waters are full of ships."

"I don't think it was a ship." Sisney had been adamant. "In the first place, there weren't any vessels close to us before the *Golden Dolphin* closed in. If another ship had moved in while all the firing was going on, wouldn't we have seen her lights?"

"And in theory, she would have come to investigate the explosion aboard the *Golden Dolphin*," McKenna said in a quiet voice. "She would have wanted to give assistance to another vessel in trouble. Then again, maybe not. These are dangerous waters."

Sucking in his lower lip, Sisney had looked from face to face, as if trying to make up his mind. "I can't be sure, but I don't think what I heard was a surface vessel. I think it was a submarine, a sub just getting out of range of our sonar."

"*¡Qué coño!* That's not possible!" ground out Jorges. "Lombardo couldn't have had a submarine! But"—he stopped and for a few moments appeared to be frozen in time—"but who's to say that an American, Russian, or Cuban sub wasn't out there?"

"What's the difference?" Gordel had pointed out. "Whoever it was—if it was a sub—didn't interfere."

Now, days later, Gordel looked speculatively at McKenna. At length he said, "Scotty, I think you're making too much out of the incident. At the time, Gene said he couldn't be sure about it."

"Scott is right, Ray," Jorges said emphatically. "Personally, I think we would all do well to keep our guns within arm's reach. . . ."

* * *

Under the direction of Harry Derr and Barrett Gulbrandsen,
the crew prepared the diving and other equipment as *Little Big
Man* drew closer to the location of the fabled galleon and its millions in gold and silver bars and other precious items. Hard-hat
diving suits and their long air hoses were inspected. Air compressors and scuba gear were carefully checked. Particular attention
was given to the air tanks, regulators, and hookah gear. The airlift
and its huge hose and bottom "sweep-sucker" were given a minute
going over.

Since this dive and search would be for real, the explosives
chest was opened. The metal chest contained 260 pounds of com-
position C-3 in five-pound demo blocks. A plastic material resem-
bling putty, the C-3 was composed of seventy-seven percent RDX,
three percent tetryl, four percent TNT, and sixteen percent plasti-
cizer containing nitrocotton. The C-3 could be detonated either by
underwater electric timer-detonators or by ten-minute delay fuses.
Or if one preferred, he could drop the wires from the vessel to the
explosive below and use a hand blaster from the deck.

It was doubtful if the C-3 would be needed, or else only very
little. Yet it was always possible that chemicals in the water could
have hardened the sand over the wreck, or, over the span of years,
small earthquakes could have tumbled rocks over the vessel.

It was also possible that Ray Gordel and Victor Jorges had
made a mistake in their detective work and that the *Santa Francesca* was not even there.

By the time *Little Big Man* reached the area directly over
where the galleon was supposed to be, all the equipment was ready,
and so was Victor Jorges. This time, Cotton would be in charge of
the divers and all operations below water. The other three professional divers were not worried about any decision Cotton might
make. He was, after all, an experienced diver and salvager.

With enthusiasm high, the men went to work. Soundings were
taken. The depth was shallow, only 25 fathoms, or 150 feet. In
reply to Scott McKenna's question as to why there was only 150
feet of water when they were so far away from shore, Gordel
laughed and said, "It depends on where you're located. The entire
ocean bed below is the Continental Shelf. The average depth is two
thousand feet. Farther to the west in the Gulf is a large region
named the 'Mississippi Fan.' Sections of it are over three thousand
feet deep."

"But there is only a hundred fifty feet below us," McKenna insisted.

"Because we're above the top of an underwater mountain. Half a mile all around us and the depth drops to almost twelve hundred feet. If the *Santa Francesca* had dropped into one of those deeps, we wouldn't be here. Even hard-hat conventional suits couldn't withstand that kind of pressure. Don't worry, we'll know for sure shortly."

Six hours later, they knew they had found the *Santa Francesca*. They knew when Jorges, Derr, Santage, and Zuniga went down in scuba gear with powerful hand-held halogen powerhouse searchlights and began to search the area.

It was Dominic Zuniga who first found evidence that a very old vessel lay buried in the drifting sand. Zuniga found part of an ancient pistol decorated with brass side-plates. Then Derr found a cast-iron hand grenade four inches in diameter. It was because these first grenades resembled fruit that they were given the name *granadas,* the Spanish word for pomegranates.

Cotton Jorges and Forrest Santage discovered part of the deck and, a little while later, what could have been part of the mizzen-mast, the wood covered and encrusted with white and black coral. Jorges and the other divers knew they had found an old wreck, but was it the *Santa Francesca*? The four divers surfaced and Cotton reported what he and the other divers had found as some of the men examined the grenade.

"Ahead of the stern is nothing but mounds of sand," Jorges said, enjoying a Benson & Hedges and a can of beer. "That much sand—tons of it—it has to be packed and hard toward the bottom," directing his words at Ray Gordel and Scott McKenna. "What I will do is plant about ten pounds of explosive to clear away most of the sand. With some luck, we might blow away enough sand to get to the nameplate. There's no point in getting excited until we're sure she's the *Francesca*."

"Look at this goddamn thing!" said Ellery Thinder, tossing the iron grenade from hand to hand. "Christ, it must weigh more'n five pounds. I don't see how a thing like this could do much damage."

"It didn't," Gordel said. "The hollow ball was filled with gunpowder and—see that large hole? That is where a handle was fitted. In another part there should be a tiny hole for the fuse. Those old grenades made a lot of noise, and that's about all they did."

Jorges and the other divers, now armed with ten pounds of C-3, each block cut into seven pieces, again dived to the wreck, each man also carrying a bang stick. Carefully, they placed the fourteen tiny blocks, each with a timer-detonator, in what they considered strategic positions, then turned each time to its full setting—sixty minutes. Kicking their feet, on which were large rigid fins, they swam slowly to the fifty-foot level, pausing there and at successive ten-foot intervals for decompression.

The C-3 exploded on schedule. There were a rapid series of low, muffled *BERRRUUUMMMMM*s from underneath *Little Big Man,* concussions making the vessel rock back and forth slightly.

In the meanwhile, more soundings had been taken. Only a short distance from where Jorges and Santage had found the stern deck planking, the depth was 435 feet. That is where the mountain-top ended—and the deeper section was the drop-off that Jorges had mentioned even before the voyage had begun.

"Suppose the ship, or at least part of her—the part with the treasure—dropped into that chasm?" McKenna asked Gordel. "Can we still get to it with the hard-hat suits?"

"Oh, sure," Gordel said easily. "Of course, bringing the whole works up will take longer. Think of all the time involved in decompression!"

Once more Cotton and the three other divers went over the side. Two hours and forty-two minutes later they were back on deck, all four so excited they could hardly speak.

"It's her!" Jorges said happily, wiping his great mane of white hair with a towel. "It's the *Santa Francesca!*"

"We knew we were close when we found a sheet of hammered copper," inserted Harry Derr as he unstrapped the air tanks from his back.

"The explosions blew enough of the sand away so that we were able to get to her nameplate," Jorges said. "We had to move a lot of sand, but we found the plate on the starboard side, and it read *Santa Maria Francesca.* Apparently what happened in 1649 was that the *Santa Maria Francesca* finally gave in to the insistent fury of the hurricane and sank some distance to the north of her course, where she now rests. She had narrowly missed sliding into the ravine. She came close, though. Her prow was actually sticking out several feet over the edge."

"She didn't break up when she went down," Gordel added excitedly. "The C-3 did move enough sand so that we could see part of her starboard hull, forward, maybe fifty feet from the fore-castle. She's a four-decker and big for a galleon. Part of her starboard hull is stove in."

"With a little more work, maybe some blasting, we can get inside the ship through the hull," interjected Dominic Zuniga. "I don't think we'll even have to use the airlift, and we won't have to go far to the basket with whatever we find. She's almost directly under us."

"We hit it right," Gordel said with a large victory smile. "Course two-eight-zero, bearing two-point-seven was it."

The dives for that day were finished, because the day was almost finished. Already the sun was going down.

Right after breakfast the next morning, Cotton Jorges, Dominic Zuniga, and Harry Derr went down into the depths. This time they made the descent in conventional hard-hat diving suits—only three of them because the air compressor could not supply air to four divers simultaneously. On this dive Cotton and the other two men would make a complete survey and decide the best and the safest way to get inside the hull.

After Gordel made sure that everything was shipshape on deck, he placed Gulbrandsen in charge, walked over to McKenna at the port rail, and said, "Scotty, you've never been down below. Let's you and I slip into some scuba gear and see what Cotton and the others are doing . . . say fifteen minutes or so."

McKenna did some thinking. All this time, no one had spotted any suspicious vessels in the distance. The closest ship had been a Uniflite motor yacht that had passed four hundred feet to starboard. Her name was *Star Brite,* and she was flying the Mexican flag from her stern. Whoever had been aboard would never know it, but when the ship had gone by a dozen weapons had been pointed at her—M16 assault rifles, Ingrams, and CAR-15 SMG's.

McKenna knew that nothing was going to happen during the next hour. For that matter, not during the entire day. Just the same, he hesitated. The plain truth was that, while he was not afraid of going down into the depths of the water, he was nervous about it. Ever since he had been a child, he had abhorred water closing over his head.

He remembered the words of Yaku Chiyashi, one of the Ninja Masters: "There is no disgrace in admitting fear to oneself. The only disgrace is not facing that fear and conquering it."

"Seems like a good idea," McKenna said to Gordel, vaguely

thinking that he would rather fight an elderly and sick shark than go 150 feet down into the Gulf of Mexico.

"Okay," Ray said. "Come on. I'll show you how to use the scuba breathing system and tell you about the UTEL."

Twenty minutes later, McKenna and Gordel, each with a long bang stick and a halogen search-lantern, were swimming downward toward the wreck of the Spanish galleon. The pressure of the water increased as they moved deeper, a soft blue-green surrounding them. Now and then a blizzard of tiny fish would swim by, or a larger fish pause and stare briefly at the two invaders.

"How do you like it?" Gordel's voice came through the headphones.

"Not too bad," McKenna half lied, thinking that at least this was a new experience with new sensations. He thought, too, that the contrast between a diver in a hard-hat suit and a free-swimming diver was as great as that of a barebacked rider and a knight, weighed down with his armor on his horse.

The UTEL, or AN/PQC-1 radio, permitted one diver to communicate with another, or with a submarine or a surface craft. The transceiver and transponder were worn on the chest. Headphones and a "lung microphone" completed the equipment. Anyone in scuba gear and wearing a UTEL could also communicate with the hard-hat divers. They also wore UTELs, plus having their conventional suit-to-deck telephone line attached to the air hoses.

The sea floor was flat sand; here and there were small reefs covered with brain coral, ginger coral, and gorgonias. Trained as he was in oceanography, Ray Gordel was in his element and swimming in his favorite subject—the Ocean. Yet there was intense danger here. Besides harmless kinds of fish and coelenterates, there were other forms of marine life, lurking on the bottom and in the watery jungle, that were very dangerous to man. There were the scorpion fish, with spines that injected venom, and the lionfish, which, although only three inches long, was very poisonous. Even more dangerous were the moray eel and the barracuda. However, the moray eels and the barracudas seldom attacked, unless they felt their right to their territory was being challenged.

Jorges and the other divers had already been confronted by a barracuda the previous day.

"He was a four-footer," Cotton explained at dinner. "I guess he's been around the wreck so long he thought it was his. When we found the stove-in hull, he came right in and stopped in front of us, just hanging there with those glassy eyes and big jaws, daring us to move one more inch. We killed him with a bang stick. I hated to do it because he was only protecting what he considered his. We didn't have a choice."

The greatest danger, however, was from sharks, even though of the 250 known species of sharks in the world, less than half a dozen different kinds pose a threat to man. Even the ferocious great whites have suffered far more at the hands of man—for sport and food—than the other way around. Norway alone ships over three million pounds of shark meat to Europe each year.

During a general bull session one night, Ray Gordel, an authority on sharks, gave the crew some facts about the marine predators, which play a vital part in the ecology of two thirds of the world's surface.

"A shark is nothing but a set of jaws attached to a stomach," Ray said. "It's not swimming around thinking, *Hot damn, I want to eat a human being.* When a shark does attack, he's only doing what his pea-size brain has programmed him to do—getting a meal. He has a right to. Swimmers are in his territory. He's not vicious in the sense that we apply the word to human beings."

"Yeah, maybe so, but I'd just as soon not meet any of them," Chester Malbain said. "When a great white smells blood, he goes nuts."

"That's true," admitted Gordel, "but you have to put shark attacks in the proper perspective. People simply don't have the facts. Why, fewer than a hundred people a year are killed by sharks —worldwide. More people are killed in the United States by lightning!"

Carrying their bang sticks and powerful lanterns, McKenna and Gordel began to swim to the starboard side of the wreck, where Jorges and Derr were working while Zuniga stood by with two bang sticks. As they swam, several three-hundred-pound groupers accompanied them, the big fish curious about the two strange-looking creatures in black rubber suits. The groupers, however, were more than pests; they were also an alarm system. Should they suddenly vanish, their departure would be a warning that something mean and dangerous was approaching, usually a shark of the harmless variety, or perhaps a sting ray. Then again, it might be a reef shark or a great white.

Gordel and McKenna began the swim to where Jorges and the other two divers were working on the starboard side, all three of whom had air hoses, telephone cables, and lifelines trailing above them. On the way, an octopus, its bulbous eyes narrowed to slits, retreated before the bright beam of McKenna's light. It suddenly spewed out a protective black cloud of "ink," then, using its water-jet-propelled system, shot off into the twilight.

Reaching the three hard-hat divers, Ray and the Ninja Master found Cotton and Harry Derr trying to pull curved planking from the sides of the two-foot-wide gash in the starboard side of the galleon. The wood was encrusted with barnacles and in places dotted with holes, the result of tube worms.

Dominic Zuniga was standing by, a bang stick in each hand.

"I think we're going to have to blast." Cotton spoke into the mike of his UTEL when he saw Ray and Scott. "I didn't want to. I didn't want to risk dislodging the wreck. It could slide into the gully ahead."

"There is an opening toward the stern," offered Derr. "But we sure as hell can't blast there."

Gordel said, "You almost have to blast right here at this perpendicular opening. Any explosion by the stern could cause the wreck to move forward. If she slid a bit to port, it wouldn't be so bad; there's plenty of room."

"Sí," agreed Cotton. "It will have to be here. It will be only a small charge. Six ounces should be enough to enlarge this opening." His voice rose in excitement. "We're so close! The magnetometer indicated the presence of metal. The cooper would account for a lot of it. The rest has to be gold and silver."

Cotton used ten ounces of C-3. The underwater explosion tore a seven-foot-wide opening in the rotted hull and made the interior of the *Santa Maria Francesca* accessible to the treasure hunters.

It was almost four o'clock in the afternoon, after Cotton, Harry Derr, and Forrest Santage went down and Cotton had gone inside the wreck, that his excited voice came through the telephone on the deck of the fast patrol boat converted into a salvage vessel.

"I've found the chests!" he said, almost panting. "There's nine of them. Three of them have broken open—and guess what? They're full of either gold or silver bars. I can't tell. They're too encrusted with growths."

If the men on the deck of *Little Big Man* had given a louder whoop of victory, their shout would have been heard all the way to Key West. Maybe even to Havana!

* * *

The work progressed very slowly during the next four days. Jorges and the two other hard-hat divers were limited in how fast they could move. The wooden chest—bound with brass bands, crusted over with barnacles, and weakened by boring tube worms —were two rotten to be moved. They would fall apart. Even so, they would have been too heavy to move.

Cotton and the other hard-hats carried the gold and the silver bars by hand to metal baskets that had been lowered and were outside the hull. As each container was filled—one hundred bars to a basket, each bar eight inches long by one inch wide on all four sides—it was hoisted to the surface. However, the bars were not scraped and cleaned on the deck of *Little Big Man.* Not taking chances, the Ninja Master had ordered that the treasure be transferred instantly to the forward hold. The major cleaning could be carried out once the FPB was safely back in port.

On the fifth day, Gordel, McKenna, and John Hoover put on scuba gear and went down to have a look inside the galleon. On the way down they passed a fast-moving squid, a school of spadefish swimming in wedge formation, and sweepers massed in a caskage of gold.

The temperature of the water was comfortable. But temperature of water is very deceptive. Most of the sea is too cold for human comfort, and the deeper one goes, the colder it gets. Thousands of feet down, ocean temperatures would be near freezing. On the other hand, one need not dive deeply to experience the problems caused by loss of body heat. Comparatively warm water—86 degrees Fahrenheit (30 degrees Centigrade)—can be fatal if exposure is prolonged, although one is comfortable and perfectly safe in equivalent air temperatures. The reason is that water is an extraordinarily efficient conductor of heat. In water colder than body temperature, an unprotected individual loses warmth two to five times faster than he does in air of the same temperature. How fast one loses heat depends on the age and the health of the person, basically how fast his blood is circulating near the surface of the body. Once deep-body temperature falls below 95 degrees F. (35 degrees C.), temporary amnesis occurs. From 86 degrees F. to 89.6 degrees F., an inactive diver may lose consciousness after hours of exposure and/or suffer a heart attack. As temperature in the body falls below 86 degrees, death comes very quickly.

The inside of the forward hold of the *Santa Francesca* was

eerie, the same kind of uncanny feeling one has when opening a newly discovered tomb of some ancient king. For 339 years the treasure ship had lain in legend, alone with her secrets. She was alone no longer. She had been found and was being robbed of her secrets. Soon the whole world would know that the fabled ship had been found. She would then be permitted to sleep forever.

There wasn't much to see in the light coming from the six halogen spotlights that Jorges and his divers had secured inside the wreck. On each side, to port and to starboard, were the massive wooden braces—"ribs"—that supported the second deck. Overhead were the wide planks of the second deck, all of it, including the floor, covered with barnacles and other marine life that had formed a steel-like crust. The chests—almost empty now—appeared to be a stark warning, and the three skeletons, lying close to the chests, seemed to be silently screaming—"GET OUT!" The only explanation was that the three Spaniards had been trapped belowdecks and had drowned. The uniforms had long since rotted into nothingness, but there were brass and pearl buttons lying between the bones, which gleamed dull white and were surprisingly free of marine growths. Around the bones—around the waist and over the chest—were the disintegrating remains of the leather that had held the weapons of the men. There was an *espada ropera,* or "dress sword"—rapier—by one pile of bones. Two falchions—swords with a heavy single blade—were near the the other two scarecrows in bone. The rapier crumbled into a shower of rust and hardened sea creatures when Hoover tried to pick it up. But the two falchions were solid and seemed to be in good condition underneath their covering of compact crust.

"We're only in the way. Let's get out of here," Gordel said. Cotton Jorges, in conventional diving suit, was lifting gold bars from a chest. Coming in behind Cotton, walking slowly and awkwardly because of the weight of the suit, was Harry Derr, who had just carried some bars to the basket outside the hull.

It took eight days to bring the treasure to the surface. When the tally was made, there were 2,610 gold bars and 1,491 silver bars, the count prompting McKenna to say, "We're lacking 390 gold bars and 1,158 silver bars. I refer to the original number on the manifest."

"Well, they're not down there," Gordel said with a sigh. "Either the records were wrong or maybe some of the chests were transferred to another galleon after the manifest was made. When the *Nuestra Señora de la Rosa* and the *Señora de Blanco* were found, they had a lot of gold bars on board."

"There aren't any more chests in the holds," Jorges said. "I'm positive."

"It doesn't really matter," Gordel said. "Just look at what we already have. I would say it was considerable."

It was an understatement. Besides the gold and silver—worth how many millions?—there were 2,831 doubloons, all of them struck at Spain's royal mint, and a small chest full of pearls (471 to be exact).

There was far more, mainly in religious items—fourteen solid-gold candlesticks; a large gold medallion bearing a portrait of the Virgin Mary; a two-foot-high bronze crucifix, with the nailed Christ of solid gold. The bottom of the cross bore the skull-and-bones emblem of the Holy Order of the Inquisition. The two most valuable items were a seven-inch gold medallion bearing the cross of the Order of Santiago framed by thirty-one diamonds (the cross was made of twelve emeralds) and a brooch shaped like a heart, the heart made of seventy-six diamonds.

Staring at the medallion and the brooch, every man was in awe. Never again would they be close to so much incredible wealth.

"My God!" Gordel said hoarsely. "The brooch and the medal alone must be worth a couple of million!"

There were many other items whose only value was their age, everyday items from the past—glass plates and cups; a silver whistle, complete with ear spoon and a manicure set; six bronze dividers and a bronze astrolabe. More interesting was the pocket calculator which combined a moondial, a vertical sundial, and a compass. There was a rare silver ewer and plenty of weaponry. There were thirty-one matchlock muskets and harquebuses with the lead shot they used, twenty-seven swords, thirty-seven daggers, a dozen stone cannonballs, and ninety-four cast-iron shot.

The ninth day—overcast with a hint of rain in the air—was spent in cleaning and putting away diving and other equipment. The works was finished. The treasure of the *Santa Francesca* had been found and was safely in the hold of the FPB. *Little Big Man* could now make the return voyage to the J & G Salvage dock miles southwest of Sweetwater.

All this time each ordinary seaman had taken his turn as lookout in front of the radar mast on the hardtop of the bridge deck. The lookouts had but one function: to scan all points of the compass through powerful binoculars. At night they used infrared scopes. All this time they had not spotted any vessel that appeared to be the least bit suspicious, any more than Gene Sisney had detected anything out of the ordinary on the sonar, although after *Little Big Man* had dropped anchor over the "X-Marks-the-Spot," he had checked the sonar only sporadically. He and Scott felt that a constant sonar check would be a waste of time since there were too many vessels within sonar range. Trying to pick the one that could be an enemy was impossible.

It was an hour after supper and the sun was setting when Sisney—for want of something better to do—went to the listening room and turned on the sonar. Five minutes later, he used a walkie-talkie to call McKenna, who was by the bow ventilator cowl talking to John W. Hoover about firearms. An ex-Marine, Hoover had been a weapons specialist.

There was an urgency to Sisney's voice as it came through the W-T.

"Scott, you had better get up here. I've spotted a sub. I'm positive!"

McKenna hurried to the listening room, the well-muscled, burr-headed Hoover right behind him. They found Sisney staring at the sonar scope and listening to the fearful *pinggggg . . . pinggggggg . . . pinggggg . . . pinggggg.*

"It's a sub," Sisney said in a low, intense voice. "See the blip on the screen!" He pointed to a tiny patch of white that was slowly moving toward the red circle in the center of the scope. "That's her. I'd say she's not more than two thousand feet off our port and coming straight at us, at maybe ten to twelve knots."

"But how in hell can Lombardo have a submarine?" protested Hoover in honest puzzlement. "Hell, it can't be him or his cruds!"

Sisney tossed a dirty look at Hoover. "I was trained in the Navy. You weren't. I said there's a sub north of us and there is— period!"

Sisney and Hoover glanced at McKenna, who was watching the blip crawl closer to the center of the scope. "We do know that whoever is in the submarine is coming right at us," McKenna said.

"And that's enough for me. Gene, remain here. J.W., come with me. We're going to full red alert."

McKenna headed for the door. No sooner were he and Hoover on the bridge deck than Norbert Kling, who was the lookout, began turning the crank of the siren mounted in front of the radar mast.

The Ninja Master and Hoover, on the port side of the bridge, were close enough to Kling so that, by moving to the railing, they could look up and see him on the hardtop. McKenna turned and cupped his hands to his mouth.

"Norbert, what did you see?" McKenna thought that Kling had seen the business end of a periscope butting through the water.

Kling stopped turning the handle of the siren, stood up, and looked down at McKenna and Hoover.

"Two powerboats to the northwest," he yelled down in reply. "They're headed toward us at full speed!"

CHAPTER 11

Captain Ennio Penzula, standing in the conning tower of the *Ernesto Guevara*, peered through the attack periscope. Knowing that the work of this world does not wait to be done by perfect people, Penzula reflected on the decision he had been forced to make after Havana had sent a message by radio. The Department of State Security had received a report from its special D-unit in Florida, to the effect that DSE agents, shadowing Charles Lombardo, had seen him and three of his top hoods—Vincent DiVarco, Jody Karl, and Felix Battaglia—board a boat named the *Slick Sister*. All four had carried fishing gear. An hour later, the boat had left the harbor in Tampa. The captain of the fishing boat was Alfredo Jorges, Victor Jorges's younger brother.

Colonel Calixto Hevia's message had concluded with: *It is apparent that the American Lombardo is going to exact revenge against Victor Jorges, Raymond Gordel, and Scott McKenna through Alfredo Jorges. It is my conviction that once the craft is at sea, the gangsters will take over the vessel and use it to attack* Little Big Man. *Since the* Slick Sister *is a small vessel, I also feel that before the attack the American hoodlums will make contact with another ship. Should the vessels approach before the* Independencia *arrives, destroy them.*

The Slick Sister *is a Chris-Craft. She is painted white with blue trim. She is seventeen meters in length and five meters at the beam.*

This message is also being sent to Major Calleja aboard Laughing Lady *and to Captain José Sanchez of the* Independencia. *Since you are the closest to the American treasure ship, I have instructed Major Calleja and Captain Sanchez to move in on your orders. Do not fail.* Viva Fidel Castro. Viva la Revolución. *Hevia. End of Message.*

Penzula had received the message two days earlier. Disliking the method he had to employ, he had moved the submarine to within three kilometers of *Little Big Man.* Yet he reasoned that even if the *americanos* were using their sonar and detected him, what could they do? Pull up anchor and go home? This was highly unlikely. They wouldn't leave without the treasure. They would know that whoever was watching would have deduced that this was the genuine location.

A worried Penzula had immediately contacted Major Calleja. He had given Calleja and Captain Borrero the position of the *Ernesto Guevara,* and had asked them for theirs. They had replied that the *Laughing Lady* was only seventeen kilometers west of the American ship. "We are pretending to fish," Calleja had said. "We could remain in this position for days if we had to."

¡Bueno! Calleja could be at the scene in a matter of hours. Not so with the *Independencia.* For three days she had been only seventy-three kilometers northwest of the American ship. She had dropped anchor. Some of her crew had then lowered a boat, rowed to the stern, and pretended to work on the rudder, men going down in scuba suits. After four days, Captain José Sanchez had pulled up anchor and moved on. He had been afraid that he might attract the attention of the American navy. He was now 724 kilometers southwest of *Little Big Man.* It would take him several days to cover that distance.

Penzula had replied to Captain Sanchez: *Proceed to this area with all possible speed. Coordinates follow.* . . .

Penzula had then set up an intensified watch on *Little Big Man* and the activities of the *americanos* aboard her. The bow and the stern torpedo tubes were loaded, and the crew of the Soviet "Whiskey" submarine placed on alert two. Penzula and his officers had then watched the last of the treasure hoisted aboard *Little Big Man.*

At 1910 hours of the second day, after Penzula had moved in close to the Americans, the technicians in the sonar room detected the sounds of two vessels, apparently traveling together, moving closer to the area from the northwest. The vessels could not be *Laughing Lady* and the *Independencia.*

After ten minutes, it became apparent that the two ships were headed toward the *Little Big Man.* Penzula ordered the crew to battle stations.

With the awareness that the two surface craft had to be the loco Charles Lombardo and his *gamberros,* Penzula waited and watched while the men waited to fire the Soviet "Talikin" acoustic-homer torpedoes.

Soon Penzula saw the two ships coming fast from the north-west. They were too far away for him to make out their names; yet only an *idiota* would not have been able to deduce their intention. Both vessels were about the same size, although the one that was white with the blue trim on the hull and the housing—it had to be *Slick Sister*—was slightly larger than its companion. Cutting the water at an estimated twenty knots both ships would cross Penzula's bow at a distance of 1,219 meters, or 4,000 feet.

"We'll use the tubes in the bow." Penzula spoke into the throat mike to First Officer Luis Morúa in the control room below. "Prepare to fire."

Panifilo Navarro, the second officer, was to Penzula's right. Behind the two Cuban submariners stood Major Esteban Cruz de Oviedo, so nervous he had forgotten about the no smoking rules and had lighted a Moscow Night.

Penzula watched the *Slick Sister* and the other cabin cruiser draw closer—racing toward their destruction. He could see figures on the flying bridge of each vessel, which had a tuna tower and platform and was equipped with spreaders and outriggers.

He looked at the range computed by the torpedo computer and transferred to the selector on the attack scope. Ahhh—*¡ahora!*

"Fire one," Penzula said, some slight excitement in his voice.

There was a hissing sound and the boat shuddered slightly as the torpedo shot from the tube and began to streak toward the targets.

"Number one fired, sir." Morúa's voice came through the headphones over Penzula's head.

"Fire two."

Another shudder and another hissing sound.

"Number two fired."

"Fire three and four." Then, after a few seconds, Morúa said, "All four are running straight and smooth. No deviation, sir."

Penzula stepped back from the attack periscope, looked at his wristwatch, and began counting the seconds. . . .

CHAPTER 12

The three most miserable men in the Gulf of Mexico were Vinnie Fats DiVarco, Jody Karl, and Felix Battaglia. All three hoods had been opposed to another attack on the two partners of J & G Salvage and their friend Scott McKenna. Their main reason was very logical: an attack was too dangerous. There were other reasons. Not only would Gordel, Jorges, and McKenna and their men be on guard against another attack, but suppose the U.S. Coast Guard or the U.S. Navy appeared on the scene.

There had been no reasoning with Charlie. He was a man possessed with the burning desire not only of obtaining the treasure, but also of killing Ray Gordel and Victor Jorges, and especially Scott McKenna, whom he held responsible for the loss of the *Golden Dolphin*.

There had not been a problem in obtaining *Zephyr II*, the Viking sedan fisherman that belonged to Charlie's brother-in-law. Nor had there been any difficulty in renting *Slick Sister*, the Chris-Craft owned by J & G Salvage and skippered by Alfredo Jorges. The younger brother of Victor Jorges had not been the least bit suspicious when Charlie approached him about renting the boat for a day, telling him that "my friends and I would like to go after a marlin or two."

Charlie himself had shot and killed Alfredo Jorges and Willy Kuntz, the deckhand. *Slick Sister* was forty miles out of Tampa and had been met by *Zephyr II* with the twelve mobsters aboard her when Charlie walked up to Alfredo, pulled a Bauer autopistol from his pocket, and snarled, "Here's where you get off, spic!" He had then put two .25 slugs into Alfredo's stomach, after which he shot Willy Kuntz. Both men were then dumped overboard.

The two vessels had then started toward the large area where *Little Big Man* might be. There was a lot of water out there, and they only knew the general area of where the treasure lay hidden.

For eight days the two ships crossed and recrossed the huge area, using the spare fuel, water, and food that had been brought along on *Zephyr II,* which, with twelve men and extra provisions, was a very crowded ship.

"We're going to have to snuff Charlie," Vinnie Fats whispered one morning to Felix Battaglia. "He's gone off his rocker. We keep up with this shit, we're either gonna get killed or end up in a Federal joint!"

"Goddamn, Vinnie! I dunno. . . ," Battaglia said. "Maybe we could find another way. . . ."

"Yeah! What way? We can't talk no sense to him. He's as nutty as two sacks of walnuts when it comes to that joker McKenna. He ain't thinking with all his marbles. He ain't playing with a full deck."

Another nagging worry for Vinnie Fats, Karl, and Battaglia was that vessels and helicopters of the United States Coast Guard would begin searching for *Slick Sister*—if it wasn't looking already! The vessel had been scheduled to return to port the evening of the first day. The harbor master must have reported her absence.

There was Charlie's plan, so fuckin' full of holes it might have been dreamed up by some creep high on Latin grass! Charlie's "master plan"—as he called it—was to sink *Slick Sister* and return to port in *Zephyr II.* The treasure aboard *Little Big Man*—"They must have found it by now!" Charlie reasoned—would be transferred to *Zephyr II.* When DiVarco, Karl, and Battaglia pointed out to Charlie that there wasn't room for sixteen men aboard *Zephyr II,* much less a couple of tons of gold and silver and whatever, he had only snarled, "Then we'll make room."

It was during the late afternoon of the tenth day, and supplies were running low, when the lookout of *Zephyr II* spotted *Little Big Man* in the distance.

Charlie's attack plan was simple and stupid, just like his other scheme to sink one vessel and load everything onto the other ship —rack along the sides of *Little Big Man* and rake her deck with the Heckler and Koch assault rifles aboard *Zephyr II.*

Vinnie DiVarco, Jody Karl, and Felix Battaglia now did what they had to do, the three realizing that they no longer had any choice in the matter. The *Slick Sister* and *Zephyr II* were less than three thousand feet from *Little Big Man* when Vinnie Fats used his .45 Grizzly Win Mag pistol and pumped four big .45 HP slugs into Charlie's back. Charles Lombardo couldn't begin to be shocked or surprised. Stone dead, he dropped to the deck. He would only be astonished in eternity. . . .

It was also too late for the other mobsters. Every man on board the two vessels had eaten of bread baked in blackness and in bitterness. DiVarco, Karl, and Battaglia died within the space of a microsecond, the blasts of twelve hundred pounds of explosive charge in the two torpedoes turning them into nothing more than drifting atoms.

The other hoodlums on board *Zephyr II* might as well have been trapped by a star that had turned into a nova. A tenth of a second later, the red-and-white *Zephyr II* and the men on board were turned into scattered molecules of metal, wood, and fiberglass, flesh, bone, and blood. . . .

CHAPTER 13

The Ninja Masters in Japan had said that leadership is action. It is never rank or position. They also had a philosophy in regard to practical living—by assuming the future, man makes his present endurable and his past meaningful.

Now, standing on the stern and watching the two cabin cruisers approach, McKenna wondered if any of them had a future. It was all within the will of the Tao. He and the others had done all they could do. In less than five minutes after Norbert Kling had sounded the alarm, the crew had been ready for violent kill-action, the hands of the men filled with either M16's or submachine guns, ammo bags slung over their shoulders. They waited in the superstructure, most of them in the operations room on the first deck, the others scattered out. Two men were even in the carpenter's locker at the stern.

On the port side toward the stern, Victor Jorges watched the two approaching ships through 8X Fujinon binoculars. Jorges suddenly lowered the glasses and stepped back, his mouth open, a look of fear on his strong face.

"One of those ships," he choked out. "One of them is our vessel—*Slick Sister!*"

Looking startled, Gordel reached over and took the binoculars from Jorges's hand, made an adjustment in the focus, and looked out at the two vessels in the distance. He saw at once that the cabin cruiser that was a hundred feet ahead of its companion was indeed the *Slick Sister*, the fishing boat that he and Cotton owned. Before he could say anything there was a thunderous explosion and the *Slick Sister* vanished in a giant ball of red fire, tendrils of flame, some a hundred feet long, leaping out in all directions. Before any of the men cold catch his breath, there were two more thunderous explosions—so close together they might as well have been one—and the other cabin cruiser was replaced by a solid wall of fire and smoke. Then there was nothing left accept for thousands of parts and pieces of wreckage floating on the surface and falling from the overcast sky, the light from the setting sun glinting red, orange, and yellow against the million pieces of debris.

"What the hell!" started Al Rothweiler, who was standing six feet to the right of Jorges.

"The submarine," McKenna said brusquely. "The sub sank them with torpedoes. Everyone on board—" Remembering that Alfredo Jorges might have been on board the Chris-Craft, he didn't finish.

"I'm a big boy, Scott," Cotton said in a cold but even voice. "If my brother was on board, he's dead. Superman couldn't have lived through those explosions."

Ray Gordel offered, "That son of a bitch Lombardo no doubt had his men grab Alfredo so that he could use him as a bargaining chip—Alfredo's life for the gold and silver. And it would have worked!"

"I don't believe it!" Rothweiler turned and looked doubtfully at Gordel. "Who the hell would come looking for us in a submarine?"

"Look!" shouted Willard Glazier.

Everyone saw that something was coming to the surface thirteen hundred yards to port. First the blunt prow of the submarine burst from the water, then came back down hard as the foredeck, the conning tower, and the rest of the U-boat broke the surface.

"I don't—I don't believe it!" whispered Ellery Thinder, who had crept out of the carpenter's locker with Jerry Bilib and was now standing next to McKenna. "Maybe it's a U.S. submarine," he said hopefully. "But how would her captain know that the two ships were coming to attack us? Come to think of it, we don't know for sure they were Lombardo's men, do we?"

"We know that the sub is headed toward us," Scott McKenna intoned, his eyes appraising the underseas craft that now was fully on the surface and moving at a fast rate of speed toward *Little Big Man.*

"That damned sub is fast," Gordel said angrily, "and we don't have time to start the engines and run for it. Even if we tried, her skipper could put a torpedo into our side."

"He wouldn't want to sink us," observed Jorges, "not with all the treasure we have on board. But he would if he had to. Ships and divers could come back to this spot and bring up the treasure. And he knows we know it—the son of a bitch!"

Harry Derr called down from an open window on the bridge. "Who do you think it is, Scotty?"

The Ninja Master turned and looked up at Derr. "We'll know shortly. He knows he has us and that we can't run."

The U-boat came straight toward the sleek gray fast patrol boat. As the Russian sub drew closer, McKenna and the other men could see who they presumed to be the captain and three of his officers on the bridge on top of the conning tower, one of the men attaching a large bullhorn to the rounded front rim of the bridge. Presently the submarine stopped one hundred feet to port of *Little Big Man,* and the man in the center—neither he nor any of the other men wore a uniform—picked up a microphone.

Captain Ennio Penzula's voice, amplified by the electric bullhorn, floated clearly across the quiet water to McKenna and the other men, a strong accent to his English.

"AMERICANS, YOU AND YOUR VESSEL ARE MY PRISONERS. SHOULD YOU ATTEMPT TO MOVE THE SHIP, I WILL SINK YOU WITH A TORPEDO. WE KNOW YOU HAVE THE TREASURE FROM THE *SANTA FRAN-CESCA.* WE WATCHED YOU BRING IT UP FROM THE BOTTOM OF THE SEA. YOUR VESSEL WILL REMAIN STATIONARY. IN A SHORT WHILE A SURFACE VESSEL WILL ARRIVE AND SOME OF HER PEOPLE WILL BOARD YOUR SHIP. SIGNAL THAT YOU UNDERSTAND AND WILL COMPLY BY REMOVING THE STANDARD FROM YOUR STERN. COMPLY AT ONCE OR I WILL SINK YOUR SHIP."

"He's got us cold," murmured Jerry Bilib. "How can we fight a submarine?"

"I think about now we could do with one of Motor Mouth's bad jokes," sighed Gordel, wondering if any of them would be alive to see the sunrise.

Jorges glared at the Ninja Master, pure hellish rage on his face.

"The *minga* who just spoke over the bullhorn—that *tió de*

mala leche!—is a Cuban—and don't try to tell me I don't know a Cuban accent! I would rather be dead than surrender to an asshole stooge of Castro! And don't give me any *cagada* about 'while there's life there's hope'!"

"Crap it might be and trite it certainly is, but it's the truth," McKenna said soberly. "By dying now, you would only prove that you have more hatred than common sense."

"We can't fight a torpedo," Gordel said angrily. "Committing suicide! That's all we would be doing. Better to stay alive and see what develops. I'm going to remove the flag from the stern."

"They'll kill us anyhow, as soon as their other ship arrives," Cotton said furiously. "They only want the treasure. We aren't of any use to them."

"Yeah. . . .Well, maybe we'll be able to take some of the commie bastards with us," Gordel called back over his shoulder. "At least it's a chance."

Scott McKenna began to inhale slowly and deeply, breathing from the stomach and all the while concentrating on a spot in the center of his forehead. It was only the beginning of the exercise to Stroke the Death Bird. He had to increase his Kime, or Ki, which was the gathering of all the body's physical and mental forces.

Ki is the vital energy that exists in every human being. It is original energy and permeates the universe; it is physical and mental force and power. Above all, it is being and is beyond all physical, chemical, and natural phenomena.

Ki could only be increased by the Way of Understanding the Breath; and when one is trained in Understanding the Breath, *one can pull the tremendous energy from the pineal gland.*

His hands on the railing, the Ninja Master inhaled, then exhaled, one part of his mind recalling the wise words of Master Yoshiaki Nawa: "I will tell you of a Master from Hishomata who one day wanted to show the true power of Kime. He gave the following demonstration to his class: He suspended a bamboo stick on two paper discs held up by two razor blades. One had only to touch the construction to make it tumble down. The Master took a *bokken,* or wooden training sword, and, after concentrating, he struck a sharp blow in the direction of the bamboo, but stopped within a hair's breath of it. The bamboo split. . . ."

"We've seen that ship before now," Ray Gordel muttered in a sad voice when he and the other men saw *Laughing Lady* approaching from the west. None of the men could see her name on the bow since it was middle twilight, but they could see the general construction of the ninety-five-foot-long aluminum Uniflite yacht.

They couldn't see the *Ernesto Guevara,* either. The submarine had submerged, the men on board *Little Big Man* realizing that her skipper didn't want his boat seen by any ships that might innocently enter the area. But they realized that whether he was submerged or on the surface, the bow torpedo tubes were pointed in their direction. They also knew that they were being watched through the periscope because the sub's radio antenna was bobbing on the surface of the water.

"That damned yacht has passed us a dozen times or more," Jorges said in a tight voice that was on the brink of rage. "Each time she was flying a different flag and wearing a different name. Clever. Now we know how the Castro shitheads monitored our position."

"It was not our fault," McKenna said. "We didn't even suspect that Castro was after the treasure."

"Well, we know it now, for all the good it does us," Jorges said, frowning with helplessness. "Castro wanted the treasure, and now he has it."

The *Laughing Lady* turned to port and began the approach to *Little Big Man,* finally stopping three hundred yards to the stern of the FPB. Cuban seamen lowered a large inflatable rubber boat, to the stern bracket of which was attached an outboard motor. Four men then climbed into the boat from the starboard side. One of them started the outboard motor and began to guide the rubber boat toward the port side of *Little Big Man.*

"They're certainly cautious," muttered Ellery Thinder. "They're not about to put that big baby between us and the sub."

The rubber boat reached the port side of *Little Big Man* a short time later. McKenna, Jorges, Gordel, and some of the men moved to the sea ladder and, in a kind of loose semicircle, watched with stone-faced expressions as the four Cubans, one by one, climbed from the boat to the deck. Three of the men carried AKR "Shinkov" assault rifles—SMG versions of the Soviet AKR—and wore pistols in leather flap-over holsters around their waists. While they took up defensive positions, the fourth man climbed to the deck. He also had a pistol belted around his waist, and from his manner it was apparent he was the leader of the group.

With a slight smile, he stepped forward. A tall, muscular man with a flat waist and a sure, confident manner, he had wavy coal-black hair and a full, tanned face decorated with a long mustache whose ends met the bottom portions of long sideburns. Like the three other Cubans, he wore dark-brown pants and a dark-brown short-sleeve shirt with shoulder tabs. But while the other three had dark-brown utility caps, he was bareheaded. He stepped confidently forward.

"Gentlemen, I am Major Emilio Calleja," he announced in a friendly voice, in a tone that one might use in greeting a next door neighbor. There was no trace of an accent in his English. Unexpectedly, he gave a hearty laugh. "Come now, boys! Why the sad looks? Life is like that. Some win, some lose. This time you lose and we win."

"Sure," Ray Gordel said dryly. "Life is all rain and shit, and then you die."

Calleja's eyes went to Gordel. "What is your name?"

"Raymond Gordel. I'm half owner of this boat."

Calleja nodded, and his eyes moved to Victor Jorges, who faced him with arms folded defiantly over his broad chest.

"You must be Victor Jorges?" Calleja said. "No one else has your kind of hair. It's like a trademark."

"I've thought about dyeing it," Cotton mocked, "but if I did, people could tell when I had dandruff. This way they never know."

If Calleja knew that Jorges was being sarcastic, he didn't show it. He took another step forward and for a long moment stared at Scott McKenna, who looked directly into the Cuban officer's eyes. What Calleja saw was a young man who was six feet two inches tall and weighed 201 pounds. His muscles were lean, the tendons showing against moderately large bones. Calleja, having seen men like this before, sensed that standing in front of him was a very unusual man, a steel-hard individual—especially so since McKenna was a Ninja Master.

He judged that McKenna was twenty-six or twenty-seven years old. Oddly, though, his face didn't have any of the usual rounded youthfulness. But it was a serious face, a strong face that revealed character and a steadfastness of purpose. The intelligent copper-colored eyes were spotted with gold, the hair combed straight back, the way many *japonés* males, especially businessmen, wore their hair.

A deep feeling of satisfaction flowed through Major Calleja. McKenna was no longer a threat. Calleja didn't care what Colonel

Hevia and General Dorticos might do with McKenna and the other two fools who owned *Little Big Man.* The crew would not be a problem either. Once the treasure was off the ship, they'd be locked belowdecks and would drown when the ship was sunk. The vessel would eventually be found, and in waters this shallow divers could easily go down and find the bodies. It would not do to have the corpses filled with bullet holes.

"I'm Scott McKenna," the Ninja Master said in reply to Calleja's questioning eyes. He noticed that the three Cubans with AKR submachine guns were also wearing walkie-talkies in leather cases on the left side of their belts.

"Yes . . ." There was a subtle sneer in Calleja's voice. "I figured you were the so-called 'Ninja Master.' But you won't be 'walking on water' from now on."

"All right, Major. What happens now?" Ray Gordel was blunt. "We assume you'll transfer the gold and silver we brought up to your ship, whatever her name might be."

Calleja smiled broadly. "If you wanted to know the name of our ship, you should have come right out and asked. It's the *Laughing Lady.* That's a helluva name—right? No, the treasure will not be placed aboard her. It will be transferred to a freighter named *Independencia.* She's on her way right now and should be here between midnight and one A.M."

"What about the crew?" demanded Jorges.

"After we have the treasure, we'll go our way and you will go yours," Calleja said easily—and too quickly. "None of you have any need to be concerned, as long as you do what you're told. But for now"—he poked a finger at McKenna, Jorges, and Gordel— "the three of you will be guests aboard our submarine. We don't intend to have you inciting the crew to try something foolish."

Ray Gordel gave McKenna a quick glance, as much as to say, *You know he's lying. Fidel Castro can't afford to have us tell the press about Cuban piracy on the high seas.* Nonetheless, he remained silent.

"Do you have a gun locker on board?" asked Calleja.

"No," Gordel said flatly.

"I want all your weapons collected. We'll find a place to put them." Calleja's voice now had a take-no-prisoners quality to it. "Two of my men—Osmelo and Miguel here—will remain on board and every fifteen minutes report the behavior of the crew. Should there be any nonsense, the submarine will put a torpedo into your hull. These are international waters. We can always come back and get the treasure from this vessel. Now let's get on with it."

It took less than ten minutes for the silent crew to turn in their assault rifles, SMG's, pistols, and revolvers. The arsenal was placed in the carpenter's locker on the stern; the door was secured and two of the Cubans positioned themselves in front of it.

Major Emilio Calleja surveyed the locker. Barrett Gulbrandsen had locked the door and given him the key. It didn't mean anything. The door was wood and could be kicked in. Calleja turned to the assembled crew of *Little Big Man.* When the weapons were being handed in, he had shamelessly appropriated Ray Gordel's 9mm Hi-Power Browning and the .357 Colt Python revolver that had belonged to Jody Karl.

He said to the crew, in a loud threatening voice, "All of you listen to me. Any man who gets within ten feet of the carpenter's locker will be shot instantly. Remember that."

None of the men said anything. They only watched in silence as one of the AKR-carrying Cubans pulled a walkie-talkie from the case on his belt and handed it to Calleja, who turned it on and made contact with the *Ernesto Guevara.*

"Everything has gone according to plan." Calleja spoke in Spanish, his mouth close to the small receiver. "Come to the surface. We'll be ready to come on board in ten minutes. Acknowledge. Over."

"We understand. We'll surface at once," came the reply. "Over."

"End of message—out." Calleja turned off the walkie-talkie, handed it back to Carlos Bazea, and said curtly to McKenna, Gordel, and Jorges, "Let's go."

It required only a little time for the rubber boat and its five passengers to reach the U-boat that had risen to the surface. A large spotlight from the bridge on the conning tower illuminated the foredeck. The light was necessary. Twilight was gone and while there was a full moon, it was playing hide-and-seek most of the time with a heavy cloud cover and losing the game.

Sailors on the foredeck tossed a wide rope ladder, on which were mounted large wooden floats, down over the rounded port side. Bazea remained in the rubber boat; he would return Major Calleja to the *Laughing Lady.* McKenna, Jorges, Gordel, and Calleja crawled up the rope ladder to the walkway in the center top of

the hull and moved to the open hatch, through which light shone
upward, twenty feet in front of the tall conning tower. Soon they
had crawled down the ladder to the first deck. They found three
Cubans waiting for them in the narrow corridor, two with Soviet
Stechkin machine pistols in their hands, the third man, an officer
judging from the insignia on his light blue shirt, with a holstered
Soviet Vitmorkin machine pistol.

"This way," Aguero Robledo said in strongly accented English. The chief warrant officer, he was the short, roundheaded
Cuban with the Vitmorkin M-P. He turned and started sternward
down the hall. A few minutes later, McKenna, Jorges, and Gordel
found themselves in a wardroom being shoved into chairs at a table
in the center of the room.

A fourth Cuban had been waiting in the wardroom. About
forty, he was barrel chested, had an ugly bunched-together face,
and in general looked as if he had spent too much time living in the
middle of the Great Empty Quarter in Saudi Arabia.

While Major Calleja and the three submariners watched in
amusement, Major Esteban Cruz de Oviedo produced lengths of
thin but strong rope and carefully proceeded to tie the wrists of the
three Americans to the metal arms of the chairs.

"That one is Scott McKenna." Major Calleja indicated.
"Keep an eye on him. He could be tricky."

"He could also be dead if he gets cute," Major Cruz de Oviedo
said without humor, glaring at McKenna, who was on one side of
the table, his chair turned slightly to Cruz de Oviedo. "How about
the crew? Do you anticipate any trouble from them before Captain
Sanchez arrives?"

Calleja shook his head. "As long as they know this sub is
pointed at them and as long as they think there's a chance for life,
they'll behave. I even intend to use them to transfer the treasure
from *Little Big Man* to the *Independencia.*"

"How do you intend to sink the *americano* ship?"

Calleja appeared surprised. "Didn't Captain Penzula tell you?

"No, he didn't. He's a stickler for rules when anything is on a
need-to-know basis."

"We'll place a Zorntov mine against her bow and another one
against her hull amidships," Calleja said. "She'll go to the bottom
in five minutes, and her crew, locked belowdecks, will drown."

"A good plan," commented Cruz de Oviedo.

"You goddamn son of a bitch!" Cotton Jorges spit out at Calleja. "That's cold-blooded murder. I hope all of you rot in hell!"

"Watch your mouth, stupid," warned Cruz de Oviedo, "or you'll go to Cuba without your teeth."

In contrast, Major Calleja didn't take offense at Jorges's words.

"Sorry about your crew," he said matter-of-factly. "We all have our jobs to do in this world. I am only doing mine. But enough of this small talk. I have to get back to my ship."

Aguero Robledo stepped forward. "Sir, the Russian mines are in Captain Penzula's cabin, should you want to take them with you now."

"Gracias, but I'll pick up the mines after the *Independencia* arrives," replied Calleja. "Right now, I want to return to *Laughing Lady* and make a report to Havana. *Hasta luego,* Major Oviedo."

"Adios, Major." Esteban Cruz de Oviedo smiled, then glared again at McKenna and his two friends, pulled a 9mm Makarov pistol from his right pants pocket, and sat down on a chair by the stern wall. He glanced to his right as Major Calleja and the other men left the wardroom and one of them closed the door.

Ray Gordel cleared his throat. To his left sat Cotton, his wrists also bound firmly to the aluminum arms of the chair. Across the oval table was the Ninja Master, half facing Major Cruz de Oviedo, thirteen feet away. The only sounds were the low, steady throbbing of the spillover pumps and the almost inaudible hum of the battery rechargers.

McKenna, relaxed in the chair, began to make "Ber-oop" sounds with his mouth— "Ber-oop, ber-oop, ber-oop."

Ray and Cotton looked at him in puzzlement. So did Major Cruz de Oviedo, who said, "What are you doing? Why are you making those sounds?"

"No particular reason," McKenna replied. "I'm bored, that's all."

"Well, stop it. They annoy me," said Cruz de Oviedo.

All this time, ever since the submarine had surfaced an hour ago, the Ninja Master had been increasing his Ki. He could now feel the pure Power waiting to be released, the pure Force flowing from the pineal, surging through every muscle cell, every blood cell; and with that explosive physical energy was a tremendously increased mental capability, an almost preternatural faculty that made his judgment acute and gave him supreme confidence. Just as he knew he was occupying space in a universe of matter, of tangibility, he was also positive that within a few minutes Major Esteban Cruz de Oviedo would be a corpse.

As if sensing what McKenna was about to do, Ray Gordel went about getting Cruz de Oviedo's attention by saying, "Major, why aren't we submerging—if you don't mind my asking?" He noticed that Cruz de Oviedo was holding the Makarov loosely in his right hand, the muzzle pointed downward.

"Why should we submerge?" sneered Cruz de Oviedo. "It's dark. Should any ships approach the area, the men in the sonar room will hear them. Then we can submerge."

"I see. I only asked becau—"

Scott McKenna exploded across the room, the chair and its legs pointing outward behind him. He moved with such astonishing speed that it would have taken a high-speed camera to capture his movements.

Gordel and Jorges's mouths were falling open, and Major Cruz de Oviedo was frantically trying to raise the Makarov when McKenna's left leg streaked up and the tip of his foot connected solidly with the underside of the Cuban's right wrist, the vicious kick fracturing the ulna, making the arm fly upward and the hand open. The Russian pistol hit the wall and fell to the floor.

Cruz de Oviedo let out a hoarse cry of pain and in desperation tried to turn and pick up the pistol. He was not even half turned when the Ninja Master—chair and all—made a high leap and twisted his body into a horizontal position so that his head would not strike the low ceiling and his legs would be in place. Both his legs—at the bend of the knees—went around Cruz de Oviedo's neck. He had him! In a microinstant, he tightened his legs and was pulling the now terrified Cruz de Oviedo to the floor. McKenna landed on his right side, the right arm of the chair breaking his fall, the momentum forcing the flesh of his wrists to cut into the ropes. Steadily he applied the pressure, tightening his legs. Making choking and gasping sounds, Major Cruz de Oviedo clawed at McKenna's legs, while his own legs beat the floor and his body squirmed from side to side. But like a butterfly pinned by a needle, he was trapped. As frantic as he was and as strong as he was, he could not free his neck and throat from the killing vise of the Ninja Master's legs. Very quickly, the top of his trachea, the top of his esophagus, and his thyroid cartilege (or Adam's apple) were crushed and mashed together and his gasping changed to a death rattle, to the once-in-a-lifetime sounds a man makes when he is leaving this world and plunging into eternity. For several seconds, Cruz de Oviedo's left leg twitched as his arms relaxed and his limp hands fell from McKenna's legs. Then his body relaxed completely and became a useless corpse.

"N-never again will I k-kid you about your training as a ninja," Cotton whispered in awe. "Never again."

Not answering, McKenna pulled his legs from around the dead Cuban's neck and stood up. He then sat down with the attached chair, took a deep breath, and exerted pressure on his left wrist. The rope, crossed five times over the top of his wrist and underneath the aluminum arm, began to break. In seconds he was free. He pulled on his right wrists. One-two-three-four-five snaps and he was free. Now free of the chair, he moved to Ray and Cotton and soon had removed the ropes from their arms.

"Be very quiet," McKenna whispered. "We have a lot to do and a long way to go, and little time for both."

"We can get off this sub the same way we came in," suggested Gordel, who had picked up the Makarov pistol. "That hatch is only a short distance forward." He noticed that a subtle change had come over McKenna, or was he imagining that there was now a machinelike quality to his friend, as well as a deadly ruthlessness of purpose?

"First, we render this submarine and its crew useless," McKenna said. "We must, or risk the deaths of our own men."

"But . . . but how—?" began Jorges, stopping when he saw McKenna open the door of the wardroom and look out into the hall, first up the corridor, then down the corridor. McKenna then motioned with his right hand.

Once they were in the corridor with its dim overhead lights, they looked sternward and found themselves confronted with four closed doors to their left and two to their right—narrow doors, the kind that front cabins. And only officers have cabins on submarines. Sternward, at the end of the corridor, was a closed bulkhead with a push-pull handle. Toward the bow, only twenty feet from where they were standing, was the ladder to the now closed hatch in the top of the hull. Six feet bow-ward from the ladder was a half-open bulkhead, this one with a lockwheel in the center of the large oval door.

"This is a Russian submarine," Gordel whispered, so nervous his voice shook. His hobby was collecting die-cast models of tanks, armored cars, ships, planes, and submarines, and he was a voracious reader of military books. He quickly explained why he knew the U-boat was Russian—because of the bulkheads. The one toward the stern end of the corridor had a push-pull lever while the one toward the bow had a lock wheel.

"That's how the Russkies build their subs, with protection against flooding always facing in the direction of the control room. All the lockwheels will be on one side and the regular hands on the other side. Past the control center, in the stern, the arrangement will be just the opposite."

The Ninja Master said, "Then if we lock the bulkhead toward the bow, anyone in the compartments ahead of us will be imprisoned. Correct?"

"That's right," Gordel said. "And once we step through the bulkhead toward the stern and secure it, everyone in this section will be locked in, if anyone's in the cabins."

The Ninja Master whispered orders. "Cotton, close and lock the bow bulkhead. Ray, keep your pistol trained on the stern bulkhead. I'm going to have a look in those cabins on the left-hand side." His eyes followed Jorges, who had run to the bow bulkhead and was swinging it shut. "When Cotton comes back have him investigate the two cabins to the right, and tell him to be very careful."

"Why bother with this section?" Jorges demanded in an intense voice. "We can seal off all this section by locking the stern bulkhead. The control center has to be on the other side of it."

"Think!" McKenna said evenly. "If just one Cuban is in one of those cabins and learns what is going on, after we take over the control center, he could go through the hatch on top of the hull and warn Major Calleja on the *Laughing Lady.* When we take over the control room, any Cuban in this compartment has to be dead. Now, watch that stern bulkhead."

McKenna moved to the first door, very quickly pulled it open, and looked inside the darkened room. A bunk, a small let-down table, a chair, and a wall locker. The cabin was empty.

He closed the door and moved to the next cabin, noticing that Cotton, having locked the bow bulkhead, was moving toward the first door on the other side of the corridor. McKenna put his hand on the handle, turned it, and very fast pulled open the door. He was not surprised to see a man seated at the let-down table and the small light on the wall on.

Panifilo Navarro, writing in his diary, looked up, utter amazement on his chubby face. Before he could blink a second time, the Ninja Master was on him. His right arm slashed downward as the officer was coming up from his chair, his hand chopping against the back of Navarro's neck, the *shuto* chop killing the man instantly. The blow had broken his neck and severed his spinal cord.

Cotton Jorges also scored. The moment he opened the door of the first cabin on the right-hand side, he saw the room was dark, but he also heard the heavy breathing of a man sleeping in the bunk. He crept across the small room to the bunk and slammed his fist into the man's face, just above the bridge of the nose. Justo Díaz, the day engine-room officer, groaned, his eyes barely opening. *"¡Hideputa!"* snarled Jorges, and again smashed his fist into Díaz's face. This time the man lay still. To make sure the man would die, Cotton removed a shoelace from one of Díaz's shoes and tightened it around his neck before tying it. Díaz struggled only briefly, his arms and legs flapping like broken wings. Quickly he relaxed in death.

Cotton was leaving the cabin—with a fully loaded 9mm Vitmorkin machine pistol he had found in a holster hanging on the handle of the locker—by the time Scott McKenna was pulling open the door of the third cabin on his side of the corridor.

Aguero Robledo, who had to go on control-room watch at 2400 hours, had gone to his cabin after reporting to Captain Penzula that the three *americanos* were aboard and that Major Emilio Calleja had left the boat and returned to the *Laughing Lady.* For a time, Robledo had caught up on his reading. He then decided to grab four hours of sleep before had to go on duty. In his stocking feet, he had stepped out of his pants and was hanging them up when McKenna opened the door.

Stark-naked alarm flashed over Robledo's balloonlike face for only a moment; he then made a dive for the Vitmorkin M-P lying on the desk table—and walked right into the Ninja Master's left hand, right into a *yon hon nukite* four-finger spear thrust. The chief warrant officer stopped as if he had hit an invisible steel wall and immediately began to choke to death. The trachea with vocal cords, thyroid cartilage, carotid artery, vagus nerve, et cetera—everything was crushed and bleeding. Blood bubbling between his lips, his eyes bulging and great gasping sounds coming from his wrecked throat, Robledo tried to move his hands upward. He knew he was dying, but he couldn't do anything about it. He sagged to the floor and was three fourths dead and his world beginning to go black by the time McKenna had picked up the Vitmorkin and was leaving the cabin.

The Ninja Master—giving a quick glance at Jorges moving into the next cabin across the corridor—handed the machine pistol to Gordel, walked to the fourth and last cabin, and pulled open the door. The light was off and there was no one on the neatly made bunk. He turned on the light over the desk-table and looked around, his eyes narrowing when he saw the officer's cap with the gold-and-red braid above the bill. The cap was hanging on the wall. He was positive he was in Captain Penzula's cabin when he spotted the small wooden crate against the wall, to one side of the built-in locker. The box was marked with Russian words and had heavy rope handles at each end. Approaching the box, McKenna lifted the lid, looked inside, and saw the six round mines, stacked three in a row, each mine ten inches in diameter and four inches thick. He hurried from the tiny room, a plan forming in his mind. Still, he was concerned—*How many men are in the bow torpedo room?*

He found Gordel and Jorges waiting for him, Cotton now armed with a Vitmorkin and saying, "I strangled the son of a bitch in the first cabin. The second cabin was empty." He looked at the Vitmorkin in Gordel's hand, then turned again to McKenna. "I see you scored. Our luck had better be as good once we're past the stern bulkhead."

"We'll go through fast." McKenna carefully took the Makarov from Gordel's hand. "Keep in mind that the door swings outward, away from us. We have to be on the other side before anyone can close it."

"Look, Scott. We might have to use guns," declared Jorges, sounding as if he expected McKenna to say, *Positively no shooting.* "There will be four or five Castro slime in the control room, and they aren't just going to stand there!"

"Make sure you hit what you aim at and kill what you shoot," McKenna said. "No one outside will hear the shots, not inside a closed submarine."

"But suppose the hatch in the conning tower is open?" offered Gordel, playing the devil's advocate. "The sub has moved back a few hundred feet, but they'd sure hear the shot on *Little Big Man.* Those two goons at the stern would be on their walkie-talkies in nothing flat!"

"There isn't anything we can do about it—but hope that all

the hatches on this boat are closed," McKenna said. "Ray, you push open the door in the bulkhead. I'll go in first. You two follow —and fast."

With the Makarov in his right hand, McKenna moved quickly to the stern bulkhead, Gordel and Jorges, Vitmorkin machine pistols in their hands, beside him.

"Ready?" Gordel put his hand on the metal door and looked at McKenna.

"Do it!"

Gordel pushed against the gray door, which, balanced on large hinges, swung effortlessly outward in the direction of the control room. McKenna stepped through the opening, Ray and Cotton following.

Just beyond the bulkhead were the radio room and the radar and sonar room, the latter to the left of the corridor. Beyond the two cubicles and an ordinary rectangular door was the large control room with its consoles, guidance controls, and other equipment.

Instantly, the Ninja Master and his two companions were eyeball to eyeball with the enemy. The doors of both the radio room and the radar/sonar room were open, but only one of the "listening" operators was on duty.

In the radio room, Armando Robles had just finished sending a coded message from Captain Ennio Penzula to the DGI Center in Havana. He had switched off the Angara-PA HF transmitter and was shoving back his chair when he caught sight of a figure from the corner of his eye. At about the same time, Orlando Paredes, the technician on sonar watch, glanced from the scope-screen, saw a tall bronze-skinned man, and reacted like a man who was looking at a ghost. Only, "ghosts" can't kill. The Ninja Master could and did—and he was as expert with a handgun as he was with his bare hands, feet, knees, and legs. The Makarov cracked and Paredes fell back, a bullet hole an inch above his nose. His eyes were wide open, his mouth slack. There was the much louder crack of a Vitmorkin machine pistol, then another explosion from the same weapon as Cotton Jorges put two 9mm projectiles into the chest of Armando Robles.

Within the confined space, all three shots had been very loud. The magnified echoes were just getting off to a bouncing start by the time McKenna was moving through the rectangular door into the control room in which were Captain Penzula and five of the crew. All six, momentarily paralyzed by the sounds of the three shots, were only beginning to reorganize their thoughts. They only succeeded partially.

Captain Penzula, in his commander's chair by the two periscope heads, had only enough time to get to his feet. By then, McKenna, Gordel, and Jorges were inside the control room at the bow end.

Five feet from Penzula, Luis Morúa, the first officer, was about to sit down in the chair in front of the guidance controls. He was quick-thinking but foolish. He reached for a Beretta 92F pistol in a left side belt holster. Ponce Portocarrero, a technician at the console at the stern end of the control room, was also anxious to die. He, too, tried to pull a Beretta 92F from a belt holster. During that same single second, Jesús Giscisa, a diesel engineer who had been standing in front of the open bulkhead at the stern end, darted through the opening and pulled the door shut behind him.

McKenna fired twice in quick succession. His first 9mm Makarov bullet caught Morúa high in the chest, several inches below the hollow of the throat. The first officer let out a short cry, spun to his left, and fell. McKenna's second slug popped Portocarrero, who had his Beretta half out of its holster, in the pit of the stomach. A hundredth of a second later, Ray Gordel's 9mm Vitmorkin projectile went through Portocarrero's mouth. It tore off his tongue and bored out the back of his neck. With blood dropping on the panel and on the floor, Portocarrero crumpled to the floor.

With two of the crew snuffed in less time than it takes to count to five, Captain Penzula and the two other men in the control room raised their arms high, fear and hatred in their eyes. Rufo Frente, a large man with a boyish face and a blob of a birthmark on his left cheek, was the technician by the console on the starboard side. José Ygleses stood in front of the gyro and the magnetic compasses, both of which were part of the initial guidance system. A control-room officer with the rank of lieutenant, he was also a political officer in the Cuban Directorate of General Intelligence and would report only to El Tiburón—General Rolando Dorticos. His orders from "The Shark" on this voyage had been to watch Captain Penzula and Major Cruz de Oviedo.

"Gentlemen, you are being foolish," Penzula said tersely and in good English. "There isn't anywhere you can go. We have your ship and your crew. I advise you to give me your weapons. You have my word that you will not be harmed."

"Ray, lock that bulkhead," McKenna said, happy that he now had proof that Gordel had been right about all lock-systems being pointed toward the control room. The bulkhead across the control room did have its lock wheel on *this* side, *inside* the control room.

"Right." Gordel moved across the control room, and McKenna and Jorges covered Penzula and the two other Cubans with their pistols, the Ninja Master motioning with his Makarov, indicating to Frente and Ygleses that they should move over to their captain.

A cool, calculating man under fire, Penzula again made a try. "I assure you men, you won't be harmed if you surrender. I am the captain of this submarine and I—"

"Captain, how many of your men are in the bow torpedo compartment?" McKenna asked, stepping closer to the submarine commander. "And don't try to play games with me. We haven't the time. Lie and I'll know it. Refuse to answer and I'll kill you."

"Scott, the overhead latch is closed," said Jorges, who had checked the overhead hatch above the ladder that moved to the conning tower.

An angry look dropped over Captain Penzula's face, and his mouth tightened. Frente and Ygleses stared sullenly at McKenna and Jorges, then at Gordel, who had returned from locking the bulkhead.

"I will not give you information," Penzula said evenly, his tone measured. "And you won't shoot. Why should you? It's impossible for you to kill everyone on board this—"

The unexpected explosion of the 9mm cartridge inside the firing chamber of the Makarov made even Frente and Ygleses give a start. They weren't half as shocked as Penzula, who looked as flabbergasted as a man who has just learned he has won the grand prize in a lottery. His eyes opened as wide as possible. His lower jaw moved up and down. He did manage to look down at the blood oozing from the bullet hole in his chest and staining his blue shirt. His legs melted and he sank to the floor, only moments from the Ultimate Elsewhere, for the 9mm metal had gone through the aortic arch above the heart.

McKenna swung and turned to Rufo Frente, who drew back slightly, now even more afraid of dying. Ygleses, his mouth like dry cotton, was also very worried. He assumed the tall young *americano* was the "McKenna" he had heard Major Cruz de Oviedo talk about. Cruz de Oviedo! He had been forward. *¡Dios!* Had they already killed him? They must have. They must have killed everyone forward.

Frente said quickly, "There aren't any men in the forward torpedo room. Why would they be there?"

"Because a torpedo is pointed at our ship, that's why!" McKenna said. "Or have you forgotten what I said about lying?"

"I'm telling the truth," Frente said even more quickly. *"Sí,* the tubes are loaded, but it isn't necessary to have personnel in either the bow or the stern torpedo rooms in order to fire. The firing is done from here, from the control center."

Ray Gordel interjected, "What about the deck hatches? How many hatches are on the stern deck behind the conning tower?"

Frente, a small-faced man with a neat short beard, seemed surprised. "There aren't any hatches on the stern deck. There are only the forward hatch and the two in the conning tower, the one to the bridge and the one that opens to the port-side."

It was the more intelligent José Ygleses who deduced that the three *americanos* intended to somehow sink the *Ernesto Guevara.* Why else would they want such information about the deck hatches? The enormity of it horrified Ygleses. There were almost eighty crewmen locked in the aft section of the boat, locked in without any means of escape. *¡Puta!* Even with cutting torches, it would take them an hour or more to burn through the tough and thick steel of the bulkhead. And how many men were forward? Ygleses knew there were several in the sick bay. The murderous *americanos* had probably locked them in behind the first bulkhead. And what would the *americanos* do with him and Rufo, lock them up in one of the compartments, or—

"The *Independencia,"* McKenna said to Frente. "What was her position an hour ago?"

Frente, whose arms were beginning to tire, swallowed and though for a moment. "I can't—I don't know the exact position of the *Independencia.* I can only tell you that a few days ago she was seven hundred kilometers to the southwest. That's why it took her so long to get to this area. She's scheduled to arrive in this area between twenty-four hundred and zero one hundred hours."

The Ninja Master smiled. Southwest. *That means she's moving northeast!*

"Could we lower our arms?" began Frente began. "There—"

He had spoken the last six words of his life; yet neither he nor José Ygleses heard the two shots from the Makarov in McKenna's hand. They didn't even feel any pain. They died too quickly for thoughts to form in their brain cells. The both dropped to the floor at the same time, expressions of disbelief on their faces.

The Makarov almost empty, McKenna tossed the weapon to the floor, and glanced at the solemn faces of Ray and Cotton. He realized that since they were both decent men, they felt uneasy about being a party to shooting men down in cold blood. As a Ninja Master, he was more realistic. He regarded it only as common sense to kill a murderous enemy before he could kill you. Moral abstractions did not have a place in the fine art of survival.

"Don't feel guilty about these Cubans," McKenna said, moving rapidly across the control room to pull the Beretta from the holster of the dead Luis Morúa. "They were going to kill every man on board *Little Big Man.* We only turned the tables on them."

"Guilty!" sneered Jorges. "I wish the whole goddamn island of Cuba would sink beneath the waters, but only after I personally strangled Fidel Castro!"

Ray Gordel glanced from the still-open bulkhead forward, then back again at McKenna, who had pulled the Beretta 92F autopistol from the holster of the first officer and was now pulling a Beretta from the stiff hand of the dead Ponce Portocarrero.

"Sooner or later the rest of the crew trapped aft will send a few men through the stern torpedo tubes. We have to get off this damned boat, kill those two Cubans on our own ship, and get under way before Major Calleja on the *Laughing Lady* knows what's going on. All we need is a fifteen-minute start."

Scott McKenna did not like to run from any enemy, nor leave any job uncompleted. He had other plans.

"Ray, what do you know about magnetic mines?"

CHAPTER 14

To make sure that the two Cubans on the stern of *Little Big Man* would not see them—although it was not likely that they could in the dark—McKenna, Jorges, and Gordel left the *Ernesto Guevara* by way of the port side door in the conning tower. Gordel and Jorges were in agreement with the Ninja Master's plan to blow up the submarine with several of the Soviet Zorntov mines he had found in Captain Penzula's cabin; yet they thought he would be playing Russian roulette when he tried to capture the *Laughing Lady*.

"We have six mines," Ray had pointed out. "Why don't you just swim over and place a couple of mines against her hull? That would be the end of her and Major Calleja."

"Because we need the *Laughing Lady* to fool the Cubans on board the *Independencia*," McKenna had explained. "The Cubans on the *Independencia* may or may not know what our ship looks like, but her captain and crew will surely know the *Laughing Lady*."

It was at this point that Gordel and Jorges had been in total disagreement with the Ninja Master.

"Amigo, in the first place, you can't be sure that you will even get to the *Laughing Lady*," Jorges had said fiercely. "There are sharks in these waters, and from this sub to that yacht the distance is slightly more than a thousand feet—and you'll be weighed down with four of the mines!"

McKenna had shrugged. "I'll have to take my chances with the sharks. So will you and Ray when you swim to *Little Big Man*. And the mines—"

"But from here to our ship the distance is only a hundred feet," Gordel had said. "Our chances are far greater than yours!"

"The mines will have a great deal of buoyancy in the water," McKenna had said. "Each mine had a U-ring in the side. I'll carry them by making loops of the ropes Major Cruz de Oviedo used on us. One rope and two mines around each shoulder—after I'm done with this sub."

"Why not let us take the four mines?" Jorges had offered. "We're not going to have any trouble taking out the two guards at the stern. All we have to do is come up over the transom and the railing and creep in behind them."

"Too much could go wrong. I don't want to risk our men with those mines."

Neither Gordel nor Jorges had been easy to convince. "Suppose we do get control of the *Laughing Lady,*" Gordel had said. "How in hell do you think we can attack a freighter? There'll be over a hundred men on the *Independencia.* Or do you intend for us to only get close enough for you to swim over and slap a couple of the mines against her hull? If that's it, we could do that as easily with our own vessel. Another thing—what are you going to do with the mines when you reach the *Laughing Lady*? They sure won't float!"

"I'll explain later," McKenna had said. "First, the two of you have to regain control of our ship, and I have to eliminate the crew on Major Calleja's tub. There shouldn't be more than fifteen or twenty of them."

McKenna's two friends only stared at him.

Solving the operation of the Zorntov magnetic mines had not been difficult for Gordel. Each mine, weighing five pounds and carrying four pounds of the Russian equivalent of TNT, was exploded by a detonator set in the top center of the casing. Protruding from the center of the detonator was the timer and its control knob. The mine could be set to detonate from ten minutes to sixty minutes.

"The way it works," explained Gordel, "you set the timer before you go into the water. And see this red seal on the side of the detonator?" He held up the mine for McKenna and Jorges. "You pull this tab and the seal comes off. Behind it, in the opening, is a little knob at the end of a short, thick wire. You pull the wire out as far as it will go. That begins the timing. The lever is on the other side of the detonator. See, it's on the top casing. Pull it up and it turns on the magnet. That's all there is to it."

They made a final check in the darkness beside the conning tower. The six Zorntov mines, on three short ropes, dangled from McKenna's shoulders. In addition, he and Gordel and Jorges had removed belts from the dead men in the control room and had used them to slip through the trigger guards of the Vitmorkin machine pistols and the two Beretta autoloaders; and although being submerged in water for a short period of time would not prevent the weapons from firing, they had used pencils to stuff lengths of handkerchiefs into the barrels of the four weapons. Ray and Cotton wore two of the belts around their waists—the two Vitmorkins and one Beretta. McKenna carried the other Beretta.

"Remember what I said about the mines," whispered Gordel to McKenna. "Place them against the hull, then turn on the magnet. If you turn on the magnet before you place them, the hull will 'grab' them and they'll clank against the plates. The crew inside will hear the noise. We don't want them coming out the stern tubes ahead of schedule."

In the darkness, Cotton Jorges's face looked grim. "I don't think half an hour is long enough, Scott. You should have set the timers to a full hour."

McKenna sounded amused. "Why? I can place two mines against this boat and swim to the *Laughing Lady* in less than half that time. Anyhow, nothing is certain in this life. All we can be positive of is death. We know what we have to do. Let's do it."

Do it they did. They moved to the rounded port side, sat down, and began pushing themselves forward. Ten seconds later, they had slid down the hull and were going feet first into the water.

Gordel and Jorges came up, took in big gulps of air, went under again, and began swimming toward *Little Big Man*. McKenna swam in the same direction—south—toward the bow. But while his two companions continued on, he stopped when he came to the end of the bow. Kicking his legs in the chilly water to keep afloat, he removed one rope and its two magnetic mines from his left shoulder. He untied the loop, removed one mine, and retied the rope. After slipping the mine and the rope over his shoulder and holding the free mine in one hand, he inhaled, dived fifteen feet, and found the rounded keel of the submarine. He pulled the seal from the mine, reached into the opening with thumb and forefinger, found the knob, and pulled. Knob and wire moved outward 2.8 inches. Carefully, as though the mine were made of eggshells, he placed the mine against the hull and pulled up on the lever. Testing, he then tried to remove the mine. He couldn't. It was as solid as a giant rivet head.

Shooting to the surface of the dark water, the Ninja Master took in air and swam to the stern of the U-boat. Again he took a deep breath, dived, and found the hull twenty feet in front of the rudder and the two four-bladed propellers. Once more, he repeated the process with the mine, this time not bothering to remove the rope. Once the mine was tight against the plates, he went to the surface and swam around the stern of the boat, continuing until he was fifty feet to starboard of the doomed 250-foot sub. Treading water, he looked around. Slightly more than 350 feet in front of him was *Little Big Man*. And $250 million bucks worth of treasures—at minimum! Not only were her running lights on, but also her deck lights, and he could see the two Cubans near the stern. God help them when Ray and Cotton got their hands on them.

By now, Ray and Cotton must be about ready to come up out of the water behind them, but I don't have time to watch.

To the southwest, 1,150 feet from where he was treading water, was the *Laughing Lady,* ablaze with light. He could hear the faint sounds of Spanish music, either from a record player or a radio.

Determination flashed in McKenna's copper eyes. So Major Calleja and his cruds were celebrating! In a short time, they wouldn't even be able to hear and appreciate their own funeral dirge. Concentrating on the spot in the center of his forehead, he began to swim toward the the the *Laughing Lady,* taking long powerful strokes. In spite of his dislike of water, he was an expert swimmer. He had been forced to become an expert in the water. He was a Master Ninja, and now his Ki was demanding to be released, screaming to express itself.

One side of his mind thought of the third principle of the Hsi Men Jitsu, the Way of the Mind Gate. This third principle dealt with Chikairi No Jitsu: the Nine Methods of Prevailing. One of those methods was Minomushi No Jitsu—destroying the enemy from within, attacking him suddenly at his home base. It was only a matter of timing and speed—and the Will of the Will of the Will of the Will of the Will of the Tao. . . .

* * *

Ray Gordel and Cotton Jorges had submerged three times. When they came to the surface the third time, they were only six feet to the stern of *Little Big Man*. Rapidly they unbuckled the belts from around their waists and pulled the wet leather from within the trigger guards of the two Vitmorkin machine pistols. Jorges, who also had the Beretta pistol, left it on the belt, which he rebuckled around his waist. They pulled the pieces of handkerchiefs from the barrels and, holding the weapons out of the water, swam the short distance to the stern. The problem of pulling themselves over the transom was solved by first balancing themselves on the top of the frame brace of the rudder assembly. Once on the frame brace, they could reach for the gunwale. Once they were to the gunwale, they could pull themselves the rest of the way by reaching for the bottom cross-section of the railing.

Ray and Cotton had one thing going for them: desperation. They wanted to live and, most of all, they wanted revenge. They were soon past the gunwale and crawling over the top railing, ready with their Vitmorkins. Should one of the Cubans look around the corner of the carpenter's locker, six feet in front of them, he'd get his head blown off, even though Ray and Cotton preferred to slam out the Cubans without any noise. The sound of a shot would surely carry to the *Laughing Lady*.

Slowly, quietly, Ray crept up one side of the locker while Cotton moved up on the right side. They could hear the two Cubans talking and knew that Harry Derr, Jerry Bilib, and the three other men standing on the stern boat deck could see them creeping in on the two guards. Why else would Derr suddenly point straight up at the sky as if he had spotted a flying saucer, if not to get the attention of Bazan Zaldo and Manuel Uruita, the two Cuban guards. Bilib and the other men, including members of the crew on the main deck, also began to look up and point at the sky. The ruse worked. Zaldo and Uruita stood up and began to search the black sky for something that wasn't there, neither suspecting that they were about to die.

Jorges chopped Zaldo across the back of the neck with the long barrel of the Vitmorkin machine pistol in his right hand, the savage slam breaking the man's neck. Gordel used a different method, but he achieved the same result.

The holder of a black belt, second *dan,* in Shotokan—a Japanese karate system characterized by powerful linear techniques and deep, strong stances—Gordel preferred to kill with his bare hands. At the last moment, when he was only a foot behind Manuel Uruita, he threw his left arm around the man's neck and instantly tightened it, pressing the rear of his forearm into the Cuban's throat. Simultaneously, he slammed the heel of his right hand against the back of Uruita's head, a terrific blow that fractured several of the cervical vertebrae and twisted the cord. Manuel Uruita was dead by the time he had finished blinking.

Now that the Cuban guards were dead, the crew rushed forward to congratulate Ray and Cotton. All of them asked, "Where's McKenna?"

Gordel told them about the submarine and what the Ninja Master intended to do with *Laughing Lady,* then the *Independencia.*

Chester Malbain wasn't happy about the submarine. "Sweet Jesus! She's only a hundred feet away! Won't her going down swamp us?"

"Of course not," Gordel said, continuing to watch Motor Mouth Kling, who was using a short pry-bar to force open the door of the carpenter's locker. "We might rock a bit when she goes down, but that's all. The water is this area is too shallow for any great situation."

Gene Sisney commented, "Well, if you ask me—and no one has—I think McKenna is either the bravest or the craziest man in this part of the world. One man against the whole crew of a yacht! Those spics will blow him apart!" At once he remembered that Jorges was Cuban, and was embarrassed. "I—I didn't mean that remark the way it sounded, Cotton. Sorry."

"Don't be." Jorges hunched a shoulder, and accepted a cigarette from John W. Hoover. "Anyone living on the island of Cuba is a *minga* spic. Me, I got my final papers last year. I'm a Cuban-American. I'm a citizen."

Gordel laughed, happy now that Kling had forced open the door.

"Yeah, well, if something goes wrong, you're going to be a dead Cuban-American. Let's get the guns out of there and dig in. If McKenna fails, we're going to have one hell of a battle on our hands."

It was a few minutes later that Dominic Zuniga, picking up an M16 assault rifle, said to Sisney, "Gene, you don't seem to remember what McKenna did to the *Golden Dolphin.* Personally, I feel sorry for Major Calleja and the other bastards aboard *Laughing Lady.* None of them will see the sunrise. I'd bet a used roll of toilet paper on it."

Zuniga might have been willing to wager toilet paper, but Scott McKenna was gambling his life. Not even tired, he swam the remaining 150 feet underwater and came to the surface beneath the stern of the *Laughing Lady.* At once he saw that instead of a free-floating sea anchor, her skipper had used the regular anchor at the starboard bow. McKenna could see that the slanting anchor cable was as tight as a violin string.

McKenna moved close to the anchor cable, pulled the rope and its two mines from his left shoulder, and untied it. He then tied each end of the rope to the anchor cable, a foot below the water. The rope and its two Zorntov mines soon joined the other rope and its two rounded canisters of high explosive.

Now, to get to the foredeck. Closing in on the yacht, he had seen two men walking back and forth on the forward deck, and they were still there. He looked at the anchor cable. His hands were wet and the cable was wet. Could he do it? He had to. Climbing the cable was the only way he could reach the deck. The port side and the sea ladder? He suspected that if the railing were open and the sea ladder in place, the area would be well guarded.

With the Beretta pistol tight against his left side, McKenna took three slow and very deep breaths, then two quick "snap" breaths. He reached up, put both hands around the cable, and began to pull himself out of the water. It took him only a minute to reach the top of the cable, where it moved though the hull just below the forecastle. A few feet overhead was the two-foot-long hawser slot in the short, solid railing of the forecastle. It was a chance, but he would have to take it. Jackknifing his body and rearing upward, he managed to grab the bottom rim of the hawser slot with both hands. With a tremendous effort, he pulled himself up by his arms, just high enough to look through the twenty-seven-by-six-inch slot. One of the Cubans was only six feet away, and from the position of his feet and legs, he was looking east toward the stern of *Little Big Man.* What to do? *I can't hang here forever!* McKenna got his answer when Gabriel Bartana turned and strode back to the port railing to join Fernando Ameijeiras.

From his position by the hawser slot, McKenna could see both men clearly by the port railing. They were dressed in short-sleeved white shirts, white duck pants, and white canvas shoes. Yes, sir, just like Americans enjoying themselves on their boat— "Americans" because *Laughing Lady* was flying the Stars and Stripes from her stern. Leaning on the railing, the two men were talking in low tones, their backs turned to the Ninja Master.

Wondering who might be looking out the windows of the bridge or the decks below, McKenna pulled himself up and over the railing on the starboard side. Now on the deck, he silently crept toward Bartana and Ameijeiras. He was halfway across the deck when Ameijeiras half turned, spotted him, and yelled "Behind us!" in Spanish to Bartana. By then it was too late for both men. McKenna made a running leap, one that turned his body into a two-hundred-pound horizontal projectile. Both his bare feet smashed into Bartana in a flying dragon kick that shattered the man's teeth, broke his lower jaw, and fractured his breastbone. He dropped with a loud cry of agony while the larger Ameijeiras prepared to deal with the *americano* who had apparently materialized out of nowhere. He might as well have tried to kiss a king cobra on the mouth!

All members of the Cuban armed forces are trained in the basics of Sambo, the Soviet school of karate. Ameijeiras thought he would batter his opponent senseless with a series of ridge-hand chops to the face and neck. He changed his mind when McKenna, coming down from smashing out Bartana, twisted his body in midair so that, when he landed on his feet, not only was his back turned to the Cuban, but he was again in a horizontal position, supporting his torso with his hands flat on the deck, as though he were trying to do push-ups!

Thinking that McKenna was one *americano estúpido,* Ameijeiras rushed in, his intention to jump on the small of McKenna's back with both feet. *Sí, break the cabrón's spine!* It was Ameijeiras's final, fatal mistake.

"¡Que te la mame tu madre!" Ameijeiras yelled, not for a moment realizing how he had been tricked. He had stopped for only a split second and was preparing to jump when McKenna's left leg came up like a reversed battering ram in a short hook-kick, a *ushiro kaka to* backside of the heel slam that trapped Ameijeiras's testicles and flattened them. The explosive agony was instant and unbearable, so excruciating that Ameijeiras was immediately too sick and too weak even to scream. With a wild, petrified look, he started to make blubbering sounds as he sank to his knees.

He did not whimper long. In an instant, the Ninja Master was on his feet, had spun, and was delivering a short right *tsum saki* tip-of-the-toes kick to the left side of Ameijeiras's neck.

McKenna glanced up at the bridge in front of him. A man was staring down at him. . . .

At the time of McKenna's attack, only Cosme Torriente was in the steering compartment on the bridge deck, half asleep in the captain's chair. Major Emilio Calleja and Captain Armengol Borrero were in the radio and chart room, directly behind the steering compartment. They had just completed a long radio report to the Center in Havana, and were congratulating each other with rum mixed with Coca-Cola. And why not? The mission was a success. McKenna and the two other Americans who owned the ship were onboard the submarine, and *Little Big Man* and her crew had been captured. All that remained was for the treasure to be transferred to the *Independencia,* and the crew of *Little Big Man* dispensed with . . . a minor matter. Then home to Havana.

It was the muffled blast a thousand feet to the northeast that made Calleja and Captain Borrero begin to have doubts. The same explosion awakened Cosme Torriente and made the five Cubans in the long lounge and the four on the stern deck pause and wonder. Torriente got up from the high leather chair, went to the window of the steering compartment, and looked out. He could not see the submarine; it was too far away and the night was too dark. However, the deck of the yacht was brilliantly lighted and Torriente could see the tall man, dressed only in walking shorts, looking up at him from the foredeck. Just as quickly the man sprinted to Torriente's right. It was then that Torriente saw the bodies of Gabriel Bartana and Fernando Ameijeiras, Bartana lying on his back, Ameijeiras face down. Horrified and confused, Torriente turned and looked fearfully at Major Calleja and Captain Borrero, both of whom rushed into the steering compartment from the radio and chart room.

"I'm sure it was an explosion," Calleja said soberly, a look of deep concern on his face. "Did you see anything?" He and Borrero stared out the windows, for the moment not seeing the bodies of Bartana and Ameijeiras.

"A man!" Torriente said dumbly. "A man on the forward deck. He's killed Bartana and Ameijeiras. See! There to port."

Calleja and Borrero looked down and saw the bodies of the

two Cubans. They swung back to Torriente, rage in the eyes of both officers. "A man! Where did he—"

BBBERRRROOOOMMMMMMMMM! The Zorntov mine on the stern of the *Ernesto Guevara* exploded, the blast forcing the last fifty feet of the submarine to rear up several feet. The first explosion of the mine attached to the keel of the bow section had blown an eight-foot hole in both the outer hull and the pressure hull and tons of water were pouring into the boat.

The second blast had ripped a ten-foot cavity in the underside of the stern hulls, the concussion alone killing twenty-two of the crew members locked in the aft section. Six tons of water a minute began rushing into the aft section, sweeping everything before it, including screaming men who knew they were about to die. It was a tidal wave that could not be stopped and would only come to a halt when it reached the closed bulkhead door at the stern end of the control room. It took only sixty-seven seconds for the water to completely fill the aft section of the submarine.

By then, Captain Borrero and Major Calleja had picked up night vision scopes and were staring in dread at the death of the *Ernesto Guevara.* They saw the bow end of the sub rear up twenty feet in the air, due to the thousands of tons of water in the second half of the boat. Stunned by this very sudden turn of events, Calleja and Borrero saw the pride of the Cuban Submarine Service slip beneath the waves. The exact depth of this position in the Gulf of Mexico was 171 feet. The stern stopped its downward plunge when the two propellers dug into the sandy bottom, leaving more than seventy-five feet of the upper section of the boat out of the water, pointing at the sky at a forty-degree angle. Very quickly the weight of the tons of water in the bow won out and the section ahead of the conning tower—it was underwater—began to drop toward the water. The sinking took only thirty seconds. Then no trace of the *Ernesto Guevara* remained. The submarine was gone.

"It's not possible!" mumbled Armengol Borrero in a daze. Slowly he lowered the infrared scope. "How? How could she have exploded?"

"Scott McKenna! He's responsible!" Major Calleja said hoarsely. He didn't know how he knew, but he *knew.* Worse, the Ninja Master had done more than the impossible! Somehow the son of a bitch had gotten aboard the *Laughing Lady.*

Captain Borrero's hooded eyes darted to Calleja. "Bartana and Ameijeiras must have been by the port railing," he said, puzzlement on his fat face. "Why didn't the men guarding the sea ladder see McKenna?"

"That McKenna is on this ship is enough," snarled Calleja, who glared at Cosme Torriente. "Which way did he go? Pronto!"

"He ran to starboard." The words jumped from Torriente's mouth. "I think he'll try to get inside the lounge."

"We have to find him!" He almost said, *Before he kills any more of us!* but caught himself in time. He pulled a Star M-28 pistol from his belted holster. "Come on. We'll use the steps in the radio room to get to the lounge."

After seeing the man staring down at him from the bridge, McKenna had darted to his left, to the starboard side of the housing amidships. He assumed there had to be Cubans guarding the sea ladder on the port side. Then again, perhaps not. What would they be guarding against? *Little Big Man* and its crew had been captured.

He paused by the side of the housing, unstrapped the Beretta 92F pistol, pulled the length of handkerchief from the barrel, pushed the safety to fire, then moved past the door that opened to the captain's cabin. Twenty feet later, he came to the starboard door of the main lounge.

The six men in the lounge had been drinking rum and listening to music from Havana on the radio. After the two mines had exploded they had shut off the radio and looked out the port windows, knowing that something was wrong. At the same time, the four Cubans who were supposed to watch the port side and its sea ladder but had gone to the stern to relax in deck chairs, ran from the stern along the port side to the foredeck, where they found Ameijeiras and Bartana.

The men inside the lounge had turned from the windows, and Díaz Balerri, muttering, "That sounded like it came from the submarine!" had started for the radio room to confer with Major Calleja and Captain Borrero.

McKenna opened the door on the starboard side of the lounge and charged forward. He wanted to kill as quickly and as silently as possible. At the same time, he realized that by now the man on the bridge had given the warning that the vessel was being invaded. On that basis, he might as well use the Beretta.

Astonished at seeing the Ninja Master, the Cubans rushed him. The short but powerful Díaz Balerri was the first to come within range. McKenna raised the Beretta and pulled the trigger. The hammer fell. There was a click. But there wasn't any explosion. As fate had decreed, the firing pin had struck a defective cartridge.

Balerri attempted to grab McKenna's right wrist and at the same time slam a hamlike fist into the Ninja Master's face, but all he got for his double effort was double trouble—a lightning fast *yoko geri keage* side snap-kick to the solar plexus, the TNT kick throwing the Cuban commie into instant shock. Besides rupturing his stomach and severely injuring his liver, spleen, and pancreas, the kick had torn the abdominal aorta and he was bleeding internally. He would be dead within a few minutes.

So would Alberto Chaviano and José Guerra, the two members of the crew who took care of the Cummins V-12 diesels. Chaviano, who resembled a barrel with arms and legs, rushed straight in with a snarl on his face. The more clever Guerra darted wide to McKenna's left, almost falling over a chair in an effort to get behind him.

Chaviano tried a short snap-kick and a left chop to the right side of McKenna's neck, his leg and his fist as easy to dodge as molasses flowing in January. McKenna—he had thrown away the useless Beretta—struck so fast that Chaviano didn't even see death coming at him. A right *yubi basami* knuckle-fingertip strike to the center of Chaviano's throat and a left *seiryu toh* palm edge slam to the side of the neck stopped the Cuban as though he had been hit in the head with an ax.

Simultaneously, as McKenna's hands shot forward, he executed a very quick, perfectly timed *ushiro kekomi geri* rear thrust kick, his foot smashing into the groin of José Guerra. A great gasp of agony poured from Guerra—and for good reason. His bladder had been ruptured and blood and urine were leaking into the abdominal cavity. To make matters worse, his pubic bone had been fractured.

Only five of the Cubans had charged McKenna. Lázaro Caridad, the sixth, still clung to his foolish dream of becoming a concert pianist. At all costs he wanted to protect his hands and precious fingers. Instead of rushing in with the other men, he darted to the stern end of the lounge and picked up a Spanish Star Z-70 submachine gun that had been lying on the short bar. By the time McKenna had taken out the first three attackers and the last two were having second thoughts about attacking him, Caridad was ready to fire.

McKenna, forever watchful, had not missed what Caridad was doing. He rushed straight at Luis Romayo and Barrera Castellanos a blink of a second before Caridad's finger squeezed the trigger of the chatterbox. The SMG roared, the barrel spitting out a stream of 9mm *cartucho largo* slugs that skimmed very close to McKenna's left side and, at an angle, shot through one of the open windows to starboard. By then, McKenna had reached Luis Romayo, who tried an "X" block with both arms and attempted a short front snap-kick to the Ninja Master's right knee.

The four Cubans, returning from the foredeck, saw what was going on through the open port side door of the lounge. They began to pour into the lounge, several pulling Beretta pistols from holsters.

It was at this point that Caridad made his mistake. If he had been patient, he might have been able to pop McKenna with 9mm *cartucho* projectiles. Instead, he ran out the stern door of the lounge, intending to rush up the starboard side, outside the lounge, and come in at McKenna from behind.

McKenna sent Romayo to his Maker with an *ippon nukite* one-finger-spear strike to the throat. Then, grabbing the choking man's shirtfront with both hands, he lifted him a few inches off the floor and flung him in the path of Barrera Castellanos and the four Cubans who had just entered the lounge from the port door. Cursing to cover his fear, the heavily bearded Castellanos staggered back, lost his balance, and fell into Lino Carrillo and Basilio Sagua. They and the other two Cubans who had been on the stern were now forced to stop and regain their balance. Taking advantage of the confusion, McKenna turned and darted to the short flight of steps at the forward end of the lounge. These steps led down to the second deck of the yacht and were next to the steps that slanted upward to the sonar and the radar room behind the radio and chart room.

Just as McKenna started down the steps, the door at the top of the other set of steps opened and Major Calleja stepped out, a 9mm Star pistol in his right hand and a dark cloud of fury on his tanned face. For only a blur of a moment he saw McKenna darting down the steps, and just as quickly snapped off a shot. But he missed, the bullet hitting the fourth rug-covered step down with a muffled clang.

There was also the explosion of a Beretta. Antonio Rabi, one of the Cubans who had rushed in from the port side, had also gotten off a round. His bullet came close to McKenna. It zipped half an inch above his head and buried itself in a section of horizontal molding above the doorway. McKenna then reached the door at the bottom of the steps, raced through the opening, and slammed the door shut.

"Get him! *¡Adelante! ¡Adelante!* Get that *hijo de puta!*" shouted Major Calleja, his lips pulled back over his teeth. He hurried down the steps, followed by Captain Borrero and Cosme Torriente, and glanced in disdain at Lázaro Caridad who had just come into the lounge through the starboard door, the Star Z-70 SMG in his hands.

"Get rid of that machine pistol," Calleja ordered. "We can't use it inside. It's too dangerous."

"Yes, sir," Caridad said, placing the submachine gun on a cushioned couch, then covering it was several pink and blue cushions.

On the other side of Calleja, three of the men had moved down the steps, Castellanos in the lead. Coming to the door at the end of the small landing, Castellanos hesitated. Lino Carrillo and Basilio Sagua, behind him, didn't urge him on. They, too, were afraid of the deadly *americano,* even though they knew he wasn't armed.

Calleja turned to Captain Borrero. "Armengol, how many of the men are belowdecks?"

Borrero's fat face screwed up in thought. But it was Pancho Pérez who answered. He was standing at the top of the steps that led to the second deck. "I think Rique and Testifonte are in the engine room, oiling the diesels. I am not sure."

Thinking of what Scott McKenna had done to the *Golden Dolphin*—according to Captain Penzula—Major Calleja assumed he would try to to blow up the *Laughing Lady,* or at least sink her.

Calleja said to Borrero, "Contact Rique Garrigo and Testifonte Baroni on the phone and tell them to stay put in the engine room. That son of a bitch McKenna is not going to blow up this ship."

Calleja was breathing so heavily that little whistling sounds came from his nostrils. He suddenly became aware that three of the men were still standing at the top of the stairs to the second deck.

"What the fuck are you doing—saying your prayers?" he screamed at the startled men, his face turning purple. "I said go after him! Find that *americano* son of a bitch and kill him!"

More afraid of Major Calleja—at least for the moment—than of the Ninja Master, Barrera Castellanos pushed open the door and timidly stepped into the softly lighted corridor while the other men came down the steps. Castellanos looked from port to starboard in the short corridor. Then he crept to the port end and looked up and down the long main hall. The corridor was empty. Scott McKenna had vanished.

There was more bad news in the main lounge. Captain Borrero had picked up a phone from a shelf and had tried to contact the engine room.

"No one answers," he said fearfully to a frustrated Major Calleja.

Calleja cursed.

Determined not to let himself be trapped belowdecks, McKenna did a lot of rapid thinking while rushing down the steps. He reasoned that since the interiors of luxurious yachts were similar, there should be a flight of steps from the second deck to the control centers of the vessel and that those steps should be only a short distance ahead of him. He quickly learned that he was correct. As soon as he left the short hall and stepped into the stern-to-bow corridor, he saw a set of metal stairs only ten feet ahead of him. He rushed forward, sprinted up the steps, and very carefully opened the door and saw that he was in a short hall between two rooms. Once he was in the hall, he looked through the open doors of the two rooms and saw that the room to starboard was the captain's cabin, the room to port the radio and chart room. He decided to go to the port side. He was moving across the radio room when the plaque on the stern wall caught his eye. Evidently, the American who had formerly owned the yacht had been either a collector of knives or a Nazi lover. On a highly varnished piece of wood, shaped like a triangle with the point downward, were five large knives. The knife in the center was a fifteen-inch SS dress dagger. On one side of the SS dagger were two white-handled Luftwaffe dress knives; on the other side were two dress daggers of Wehrmacht generals. McKenna tightened the belt of his walking shorts and the wider belt that had held the Beretta pistol. He then pulled the five knives from their holders on the wooden plaque and thrust each one under the two belts, after which he opened the port door and looked up and down the deck, which, between the side of the housing and the railing, was not quite six feet wide. Not one Cuban was in sight.

He moved sternward past the lower deck and the bridge deck, hunching down so low as he moved past the windows of the lounge that no one inside could see him. Twenty feet later, he had to stop when he came to the open door on the port side. With great caution, he looked around the edge of the doorway into the lounge.

Jackpot!

Only a quarter of a minute after Barrera Castellanos and the five other Cubans were in the main corridor on the second deck, they saw Rique Garrigo and Testifonte Baroni coming in their direction from the engine room toward the stern. The two men quickly explained that they had heard a submachine gun and pistol shots from the top deck and had come from the engine room to investigate. Castellanos explained what had happened, finishing with, "We saw him come down the steps. He has to be on this deck."

"Maybe so, but he can't be in the engine room," the brutal-looking Rique Garrigo reiterated, motioning with his Llama Omni DA pistol toward the engine room sternward. "We locked the door to the machinery compartment. If he's down here, he's in one of the cabins, or in stores or the galley, or maybe up in the forepeak."

"We're not being smart," Basilio Sagua said, his eyes narrowing. "He's not anywhere down here. He would be stupid to let himself be trapped. See those steps ahead of us. He's made a fool of us. Right now he's in one of the compartments up top."

"*¡Adelante!* Let's get out of here," Castellanos said angrily.

Jackpot indeed! McKenna saw that only fifteen feet in front of him were Major Emilio Calleja—the same man who had stared down at him from the bridge—and the captain of *Laughing Lady.* The globe-headed heavyset man wore captain's shoulderboards on his shirt. Calleja had holstered his Star *pistola,* but Captain Borrero and Cosme Torriente were still holding Beretta autoloaders loosely in their hands.

The Death Bird had been stroked! McKenna took a deep breath, held it for three seconds, exhaled, and pulled one of the big Nazi daggers from his waistband. Holding the dagger by its handle in his left hand, he sprang up and charged into the lounge with the speed of a cannonball. He was positive that he would have at least one second on his side. It would take that long for the three men to get over the shock of seeing him.

Torriente let out a frightened cry and started to bring up his Beretta toward McKenna, whose left arm shot forward and upward. With a snap of his wrist, the German air force dagger left his hand and cut through the air, the twelve-inch blade burying itself high in Torriente's stomach. The bridge officer let out a loud gasp. His eyes went wide, his mouth opened, the Baretta fell to the rug, and he staggered back, blood starting to trickle from the corners of his mouth.

A terrified Armengol Borrero managed to get off one round, his Beretta booming. Only five feet from the skipper of *Laughing Lady*, the Ninja Master knew he couldn't reach Borrero before he fired. He jerked his body hard to his left, and the 9mm hollow point projectile cut across his right side, the metal raking his rib cage for three inches, the quick pain like a slash of a razor blade.

Borrero did not have time to pull the trigger of the autoloader a second time. By then, McKenna had closed in on him as well as Major Calleja, the latter of whom was frantically trying to pull his Star autopistol from is flap-over holster. McKenna's right arm shot out and his strong fingers closed tightly around the top of the Beretta in Borrero's right hand while, at the same instant, his left hand closed around Calleja's right wrist. As McKenna pulled the Beretta upward and twisted it out of Borrero's hand, he kneed the man viciously in the groin, let the pistol fall to the rug, and ducked to avoid a snarling Calleja's left-hand *shuto* chop aimed at his neck. As Calleja tried to free his right arm and drew his left arm back for another blow, McKenna finished Borrero off with a right-handed *yon hon nukite* four-finger-spear-stab to the jugular notch, the "soft spot" in the front of the neck.

With Borrero now choking to death, McKenna turned his full attention to Major Calleja. Releasing his hold on Calleja's right wrist, McKenna did not intend for the man to die fast. Calleja deserved to be brutally punished for what he had intended to do to the crew of *Little Big Man.*

No fool, Calleja knew he didn't have time to pull that Star from its holster. He tried to defend himself by feinting with a left *seiken* forefist as he tried to connect a right *hira ken* knuckle-joint punch to the top of McKenna's nose and deliver a left foot stomp to the Ninja Master's right instep. Calleja was very fast, but compared to McKenna he was as slow as an elderly turtle crippled with arthritis.

McKenna slammed the Cuban with a left-handed *nakadaka ippon ken,* the middle finger-knuckle blow landing on Calleja's upper lip and breaking off three of his teeth. With equal speed, McKenna slammed him just below the bottom lip with a hard *hitosashi ippon ken,* his forefinger knuckles slam-breaking off two bottom teeth. A right *ura ken* back fist to the Cuban's nose made him cry out with more pain while he tried to spit out teeth from a mouth filled with blood. A *goju ryu* karate square knuckle *seiken* blow to Calleja's solar plexus made him helpless, yet did not cause him to lose consciousness and go down. McKenna had deliberately pulled the punch, hitting him only hard enough to take all his strength. When the bloody-mouthed and gasping Calleja started to double over, McKenna grabbed him by the hair and prepared to chop him in the back of the neck with a right *hiji* elbow strike. He would then have permitted the battered Calleja to fall, and would have broken the top of his spine with a foot stamp. He didn't because the door at the top of the stairs opened—it was the door to the sonar and radar room—and Lino Carrillo stepped out, a Beretta in one hand. Behind him came three more of Calleja's men.

Carrillo couldn't fire and neither could Barrera Castellanos, the man behind him, both afraid that they would hit the half-unconscious Major Calleja. McKenna had jerked the agonized Calleja upright and was holding him as a shield, keeping the beaten man between him and the Cubans who were now coming down the steps. He knew that several would attempt to get behind him; yet he realized he didn't have time to pick up the Beretta on the floor or pull the Star semiautomatic from Major Calleja's holster.

Carrillo and Pancho Pérez rushed to the left of McKenna. Castellanos and Testifonte Baroni, thinking they were being clever, charged to his right while McKenna, still holding Calleja upright with the right hand, kept his eyes on the four Cubans and, with his left hand, pulled one of the German daggers from his belt. The back of Calleja was to the other Cubans and none of them could see the dagger in the left hand of the Ninja Master. Now it was more than a matter of training. The outcome depended on the Will of the Will of the Will of the Tao.

If Castellanos had been willing to fire and take the chance of hitting his boss, he might have been able to shoot McKenna. His trouble was the weakness of all inexperienced fighters who found themselves confronting a Ninja Master. He wanted to be positive. He wanted to get in close.

No sooner had he and Baroni darted to McKenna's right than Scott pulled his left arm from behind Calleja's body and very quickly threw the long-bladed dagger. It went exactly where he wanted it to go—straight through the throat of Barrera Castellanos. The silver guard rested firmly against his Adam's apple. The handle stuck out like a misplaced penis while four inches of the blade, dripping blood, protruded from the back of his neck. Gurgling blood, which poured from his mouth and from the blade of the dagger through his throat, Castellanos started to fall. Approaching death tightened his muscles, and his finger contracted against the trigger of the Beretta, causing the weapon to discharge.

Simultaneously, the Ninja Master sensed that Carrillo, the other Cuban craphead with a pistol, was almost behind him and getting ready to shoot him either in his left side or in the back. Very fast, McKenna swung himself and Calleja around in a half circle and pulled another dagger from his belt. As Carrillo's Beretta boomed, Pancho Pérez moved toward McKenna from the left and Testifonte Baroni rushed forward to pull the pistol from the dead hand of Castellanos, whose blood was making a soggy mess of the rug.

Castellanos's projectile had sped by McKenna's back as the Ninja Master had spun around to confront Lino Carrillo, the slug coming within an eighth of an inch of his flesh and narrowly missing the right side of Carrillo, whose 9mm H.P. bullet struck Major Calleja in the center of the back, the slug coming to a halt only when it struck the underside of Calleja's breastbone. Horrified at his mistake, Carrillo hesitated, not quite knowing what to do next. But Scott McKenna did!

With tremendous effort of will and muscle, he shoved the corpse of Major Calleja at Carrillo, the dead man's back hitting the startled Carrillo in the chest, his dead weight forcing Carrillo to stumble back and fall heavily to the floor. Then McKenna leapt several feet into the air, came upward and out with his right leg, and tossed the Luftwaffe dress knife at Baroni, who was about to pick up the Beretta pistol. The steel blade buried itself in Baroni's liver and caused him to scream with all the agony of a man being tortured by having needles hammered underneath his fingernails— all of it only a micromoment before Scott's right foot rammed into

Pérez's face. The *mawashi geri* roundhouse kick broke the Cuban's nose and his upper and lower jaws, and knocked him into instant unconsciousness.

Only Lino Carrillo remained a threat. He had dropped his Beretta when he had fallen and was now frantically shoving the dead Calleja from him. McKenna was about to move over and kick him into eternity and would have, if he had not been forced by the Cubans outside to change his tactics.

The four had separated from the group as soon as the eight Cubans had come up from the second deck. These four had taken the same route as McKenna—through the radio room to the port side of the vessel. Now, McKenna had spotted Basilio Sagua and Rique Garrigo moving sternward, past the lounge windows, on the port-side deck. Behind them were Antonio Rabi and Lázaro Caridad. By the count of ten, Sagua and Garrigo would reach the port-side door of the lounge.

By the count of five, the Ninja Master had stepped over to the body of Castellanos, pulled the Beretta from the stiff fingers of the corpse, and was squeezing the trigger. His first 9mm hollow point popped Lino Carrillo in the left side of the head. PLOP! The slug rammed through flesh and bone and made mush of Carrillo's brain. The Cuban had managed to push away the body of Calleja and had been reaching over to pick up his Beretta.

Scott's second projectile—he fired as he jumped up and ran forward—bored into the chest of Basilio Sagua as he was coming through the door and raising his 9mm Hi-Power Browning *pistola*. He uttered a short "OHHHHhhhh!" and staggered back against Rique Garrigo, who ducked around him and snapped off a shot at McKenna, now only seven feet away. McKenna twisted to his left and the bullet burned air underneath his right armpit, the projectile cutting slightly into the flesh, enough to draw blood that would mingle with the dried blood on his right side.

McKenna fired. His 9mm H.P. put an end to all Garrigo's ambitions, the hollow point popping him high in the right side of the chest and the impact shoving him back toward the open door.

Lázaro Caridad was next on the Ninja Master's list. The Cuban was about to fire through one of the open windows on the port side, but McKenna was faster. He snapped off a round with the Beretta as Caridad was shoving his own pistol through one of the windows. PLOP—the bullet stabbed into Caridad's face below his left nostril. The slug skidded across the roof of his mouth and took its exit through the back of his head.

Antonio Rabi, the last Cuban alive on the *Laughing Lady,* was not armed. Even if he had been, he would have panicked, being all alone to face the terrible *americano.* With a wild cry of fear, he turned and started to run toward the bow, not having the least idea where he was going. At the moment, all he wanted to do was get far away from the Ninja Master. McKenna tore out the door, raced up the port side, and caught up with Rabi as he was about to run through the door of the radio room. He didn't bother to shoot the Cuban, who made a desperate attempt to defend himself by throwing a left hook and a straight right punch. A child could have ducked. McKenna grabbed him by the left wrist, jerked on the arm, and executed a high *mae geri keage,* his foot smashing into his left armpit and paralyzing Rabi's left side. McKenna grabbed him by his shirt and by his pants at the crotch, lifted the moaning man over his head, and pitched him over the port railing into the water, fifteen feet below.

All the deck lights were on, their glow making it possible for one to see seventy to eighty feet on all sides of the yacht. That is why Scott was able to see Rabi struggling in the water. In a few moments, he also saw the menacing dorsal fin cutting the water, some fifty feet to the left of the Cuban. McKenna couldn't see the great white. If he could have seen the ocean's most perfect killing machine, he would have seen its upper jaw and teeth come down and the membranes roll over its eyes a split second before it struck. For a shark never sees its victim a micromoment before it strikes. The water churned. Antonio Rabi screamed. Then the great white pulled him under and he was gone.

Death is that after which nothing is of interest. Thinking of the Japanese proverb, McKenna walked into the radio and chart room and headed for the steering compartment. It was not possible for him to contact Ray Gordel and Cotton Jorges on any walkie-talkies or the radio of *Laughing Lady.* Their frequencies were different, and the *Independencia* might pick up the message. A simpler method would be to turn on the spotlight on the hardtop of the bridge and flash it on and off half a dozen times as a signal that the Cuban vessel was now his.

He thought again of the sharks. They had to eat, too, didn't they?

CHAPTER 15

As soon as the yacht and the fast patrol boat were close enough together that their hulls were almost scraping, Ray Gordel, John Hoover, and Victor Jorges leapt from the stern deck of *Little Big Man* to the aft deck of *Laughing Lady,* where Scott McKenna was waiting for them. All three wore belted pistols and carried Ingram M10 submachine guns, and all three stared at the Ninja Master as if trying to reassure themselves that he was still alive, that he was really flesh and bone.

"By God, you actually did it!" Gordel said, with an expression of amazement. "You killed every one of them!"

"Sixteen to be exact—or was it seventeen?" McKenna said matter-of-factly. "They were slow, and I did have a lot of luck."

"Uh-huh," grunted Jorges, looking at the dried blood on McKenna's right side. "But from the looks of you, some of them were pretty damn good."

John Hoover, who had looked up the port and the starboard sides and visually inspected the lounge from the open stern door, appeared and sounded puzzled.

"But, Scott, where are the bodies?" he asked.

"I threw them overboard after I contacted you with the spotlight," McKenna said. "Bodies lying around only clutter up a ship."

Jorges was all business, as usual. "Where did you put the magnetic mines?"

"We'll have company now when we go after the *Independencia,*" Gordel said with a sigh. "All that 'fresh meat' will bring sharks from within a radius of only God knows how many miles."

"So what?" Hoover said. "They can't get to us."

Ray Gordel sat down on a canvas-and-aluminum deck chair and gave Hoover a long are-you-dumb look. "Yeah? How do you think we can sock those mines to the hull, below the waterline, with sharks around?"

"But the sharks are here, not there," Hoover said. He glanced at his wristwatch. "It's nine forty-five right now. By the time we get going and reach the freighter, we should be twenty or thirty miles from this spot."

McKenna thought of the four Zorntov mines he had tied to the anchor cable, a foot below the water. He had thought of going down after them before *Little Big Man* had arrived, then had decided he wouldn't have the time. Again fate had intervened, and he had been saved from certain death.

Gordel looked hard at Hoover. "Let me tell you something about a great white, John. Of the four living fish that are warm blooded, the great white is one of them. Of the 250 different species of sharks, the great white is the most dangerous—precisely because he is warm blooded. A great white has sensory receivers above his snout, you might say something like sonar. That's why he can detect prey for miles. And when blood is in the water—well! Right now every shark within fifty miles is headed toward us. The sharks already here associate this ship with food and will follow us."

"And I repeat: they can't get to us!" Hoover said.

"And what will happen if one of us falls into the water when we do our 'pirate' act and board the *Independencia*?" Gordel stood up and looked straight at McKenna. "Provided Scott ever gets around to telling us how we're going to do it."

The Ninja Master didn't seem concerned as he answered Jorges's previous question. "I tied the four mines to the anchor cable. We'll have to raise the cable slowly and stop it when the mines are close to the hull. Some of you will have to hold my legs while I lean over the side and untie them."

Jorges pulled a pack of Benson & Hedges from his shirt pocket. "It's a good thing you didn't go into the water after those mines. You would have been dinner for a great white."

"Yeah, well, that doesn't tell us how we're going to attack the freighter," Gordel said, looking again at McKenna. "There are only sixteen of us, and there'll be at least a hundred Cubans on the *Independencia*."

* * *

At twenty knots, the *Laughing Lady* headed southwest, Ray Gordel at the wheel in the steering compartment. Next to him was Jerry Joe Bilib. In the main lounge, McKenna, Hoover, and Jorges were busy wiring mop handles to the rounded sides of the four magnetic mines. After they had completed their work with the mines, they would have to prepare the four ropes on the metal chair.

There were five other crew members of *Little Big Man* on board the captured enemy yacht. Gene Sisney was in the radar-sonar room. Will Glazier, Ellery Thinder, and Norbert Kling would work the ropes and, later, serve as gunners. Alfred Rothweiler— "hurting" because he had run out of Bull Durham to smoke in his pipe—was below, watching the diesels. He would take over the wheel when Gordel went aboard the *Independencia* with the Ninja Master, Jorges, and Hoover, the latter of whom had volunteered.

McKenna's plan was simple and direct. The *Independencia* would dwarf the fast patrol boat. The freighter would have a draft of twenty-seven to thirty feet, and her depth would be from thirty to thirty-five feet. This meant that not even the hardtop of the steering compartment of *Laughing Lady* would be level with the main deck of the *Independencia.* Considering the difference in size of the two vessels, it was logical to assume that the Cubans were not planning to go to the trouble of using a derrick boom to hoist the treasure from the hold of *Little Big Man* to one of the holds of the *Independencia.* The transfer could be carried out more expediently by using the cargo opening in the port side of the freighter, the same cargo opening that freighters often used at dockside. Lift trucks could take cargo directly inside a ship from the dock, thereby saving loading time. The side cargo opening would be almost level with the deck of *Little Big Man.* All the Cubans would have to do was secure the much smaller vessel with mooring lines; the crews of the two ships would then be able to transfer the treasure within a matter of hours.

It sounded easy, until one thought of the "supposes" involved. Suppose the Cubans planned to use one of the cargo booms to hoist the treasure aboard the freighter? It really didn't matter. The *Little Big Man* wouldn't be there. She would be five miles behind *Laughing Lady* with the six remaining members of the crew. After the attack on the *Independencia* had been completed, the ten men

aboard *Laughing Lady* would return to the FPB and the lady
would be sunk with blocks of C-3 explosives. *Little Big Man* and its
happy, newly rich crew would go home. That was the plan. But the
plans of mice and men and Ninja Masters often fall apart. . . .

There might not even be an attack against the *Independencia,*
not in the sense that McKenna and his four helpers would board
the freighter. Some oceangoing freighters had cargo doors in their
hulls; others did not. If the *Independencia* did not have side cargo
doors, there wouldn't be any way that McKenna and his tiny raid-
ing party would be able to get aboard.

"But at least we'll be able to sink her by placing mines against
her hull," McKenna said. "I'll set each mine for ten minutes. Even
if the Cubans wise up in a hurry, the mines will explode before they
can get to them."

Jorges chuckled. "As dark as it is, it would be an hour before
they could even find the mines."

"The only thing that bothers me is that we'll have to go at not
more than five knots when you place the mines," Gordel said
thoughtfully. "You and the others would be clear targets to anyone
on deck of the freighter. It's something to think about, Scotty."

"I have," McKenna said. "Unless the Cubans are waiting for
us with men who have lights and weapons ready, we'll have the
advantage of five to ten minutes. We'll have only our running lights
and the lounge lights on and it will be difficult for the Cubans to
see what we're doing on the stern."

"Why not leave the lights in the lounge off?" Jerry Joe Bilib
suggested. "Without them the stern will be pitch dark."

McKenna shook his head. "A darkened lounge would immediately make the *Independencia* suspicious. Why would everyone
on board the *Laughing Lady* be sitting in the dark?"

There were several "supposes." Suppose the Cubans aboard
the freighter tried to contact the submarine, or had already tried to
reach the *Ernesto Guevara* by radio?

There was one certainty. When the captain and the crew of
the *Independencia* saw the *Laughing Lady* coming at them, they
would assume there had been a change in plans and instantly try to
contact the yacht.

"That's not all that much of a problem," Jorges said. "I speak
Spanish without an accent—the Cuban dialect. I can stall them
long enough for us to get in close."

Cotton made a face when McKenna reminded him and the

rest of the men of "internal security." Everyone, even Gordel and Jorges, was silent and attentive when McKenna explained that any real change of plans would have been considered in advance by the Cubans and would be reported with possibly recognition phrases to prove the new plans were genuine and to identify the sender of any such message.

They were not even sure they knew how to operate the Soviet-manufactured transceiver aboard *Laughing Lady*. Instruction plates had been replaced and were in Spanish. However, "I'm not sure, but I think there's a scrambler attached to the receiver," said Gene Sisney, the unofficial "electronics expert." "The whole business is probably automatic. I can't be sure. And see this other deal over here? I think it's part of an arrangement that makes it possible for all transmissions to be 'condensed.' Sort of 'buzzed' out into the air in seconds."

Gordel was impatient. "Damn it, Gene! What can you tell us for sure?"

"Only that if the *Independencia* calls us, and all the circuits aren't automatic, we'll be in serious trouble. All they'll receive from us is nothing—or gobbledegook!"

"It's possible that the *Independencia* won't want to call," McKenna said slowly. "Even if the messages can be 'buzzed' out, it may be that the Cubans aboard the freighter are under orders not to initiate any radio contact. There are a lot of American government listening stations in the area."

"I disagree," said Jorges. "We heard Major Calleja tell one of the men on the submarine that he was in a hurry to get back to *Laughing Lady* and make a report to Havana. He wasn't afraid of American navy or CIA stations."

"That's true," admitted McKenna. "But that doesn't mean that the *Independencia* is permitted to transmit. Either way, it's going to be a crap shoot."

"In more ways than one if the weather doesn't hold," Gene Sisney said. "Haven't you guys heard the thunder in the distance?"

As the yacht drew closer to the freighter, some changes were made in the plan of attack. The Ninja Master had intended to place the mines while tied into an aluminum-and-canvas deck chair that would be lowered by rope five feet over the starboard side, at the stern. From such a position, he would be able to place the mines almost at the waterline of the freighter.

Ray Gordel had talked McKenna out of the "nutty idea."

"I'll have to steer the yacht as close as possible to the side of the freighter. I can take a straight course for a short distance, but we're not on tracks like a train. Should the freighter move even a few feet toward us, you could be crushed, or at least have your legs broken."

Instead, McKenna would place the mines from the deck of *Laughing Lady.* The mines were powerful, and portions of the holes they would blow in the hull would be below the waterline. At least one hole would be. Five pounds of C-3 would be taped to the mine.

However, neither Gordel nor Jorges had been able to talk McKenna out of taking the "Man Hugger" with him, the thirty-six-inch chain to the links of which ice-pick blades had been welded. Hard pieces of cork had been shoved onto the tip of each blade. Even so, carrying the deadly weapon over the shoulder would be cumbersome. Be that as it may—"I'm taking it with me," McKenna insisted. "I want to make sure it's balanced properly."

Gene Sisney detected a large vessel both on radar and sonar at ten thirty-seven. He estimated the distance between ten and fifteen miles.

"Of course there isn't any way we can be sure it's the freighter," he said. "It could be another cruise ship. The Gulf is full of them."

"We won't know until we intercept her," Scott McKenna said. "The darkness is to our advantage. The enemy won't be able to make out our shape until we're within a hundred feet of her. But she could use a spotlight to pick us up before we're in close."

Jorges said, "We'll have to use our own searchlight to get the name of the ship, to make sure she's the *Independencia.* That will put shivers sliding up and down their spines—I hope."

With the freighter moving toward the yacht and vice versa, it did not take long for *Laughing Lady* to close in on the much larger Cuban vessel. By the time the yacht was five miles to the port bow of the *Independencia,* the Ninja Master and the men were in position. In the steering compartment were Gordel, Sisney, and Rothweiler, the ex-Navy man and mechanic having come up from the engine room. McKenna, Hoover, Jorges, and Bilib were on the stern deck. Strapped around their waists were pistols, and spare magazines for the autoloaders in their pockets. McKenna had the four mines, at the end of five-foot-ten-inch mop handles, ready. He had changed from walking shorts and bare feet to khaki shirt and pants and white canvas deck shoes with thick rubber soles. Like the other men, he wore a pistol, the 9mm Llama Omni DA that had belonged to Rique Garrigo, and had a Tracer-1 FM/VHF walkie-talkie in a leather case on his left side.

In the cockpit were Thinder and Glazier. Also in the cockpit were the spare bags of SMG ammo that McKenna and the other attackers would carry if and when they boarded the *Independencia*. In Gordel and Jorges's bags were also ten pounds of C-3 in six packets, each package with a time-detonator attached. If they couldn't sink the big bastard one way, they would do it another—from inside the freighter. Thinder and Glazier were armed with Colt CAR-15 SMG's. A CAR-15 in his hands, Norbert Kling stood in the stern doorway of the lounge.

Very rapidly the five miles narrowed until there were only twelve hundred feet separating *Laughing Lady*, moving at twenty knots to the southwest, and the *Independencia*, cutting water at fifteen knots to the northeast.

The freighter was big—though, built in 1961, she still wasn't as large as some modern freighters built after 1970. Between the perpendiculars, she was 510 feet long with a 60-foot beam. Life on the vessel, for the eighty-four officers and crew, centered in two "islands." Amidships were the bridge, wheelhouse, chart room, radio shack, gyro room, sick bay, and officers' quarters, all of them contained in the three-deck-high superstructure. Beneath the superstructure at second-deck level and to port and starboard of the engine and boiler casings were situated the refrigerated vegetable, dairy, meat and fish rooms, clean and soiled linen rooms, dry storerooms, and the engineers' stores.

Aft was the second superstructure. It contained the galley, the officers' mess, the crew's mess, the engine officers' and crew's quarters, and the engine room. A catwalk above the low well deck joined the two superstructures; crossing it in heavy seas called for a 207-foot dash.

Below the upper deck was the boiler room and the engines. But there weren't any "hairy apes" shoveling dirty coal into raging and hungry fireboxes. Only a fireman–water-tender in unsoiled dungarees had to adjust flaming oil jets and keep an eye on the water level in the three boilers. Aft of the boilers were the three turbo-electric engines and the engineer watch room.

The basic design of the *Independencia* was of a vessel of the full scantling type, with a cruiser stern, a raked stem, a single screw, and a balanced rudder. The second deck was continuous throughout, and seven watertight bulkheads, all extending to the upper deck, divided the vessel into five cargo holds, fore and aft peak tanks, and four deep tanks. The inner bottom tanks, eight on either side, were fitted as fuel-oil tanks, but were also able to carry water ballast. Two forward deep tanks were situated under number one hold, and the third was situated aft of the machinery space. The fuel-oil settling tanks were located at the sides of the ship not far from the boilers. Five cargo booms handled all cargo, three on the foredeck and two aft, two of them heavy-lift derricks, one forward, one to stern.

On a mast behind the wheelhouse were the radio direction finder, radar antenna bar, gearbox and transceiver, pilot flag, and blinking red and orange lights. Behind the mast was the dummy funnel. The smoke pole was at the stern of the midships superstructure. To port were six steel longboats, each twenty-four feet long, hanging on davits. From the flag mast at the stern flew the flag of Argentina.

Finishing a silent Our Father, Ray Gordel took the *Laughing Lady* straight at the freighter.

"Al, Gene. Don't bother with the CAR-15's," he said. "As close as we'll be to her, you won't be able to see her railing."

Alfred Rothweiler cocked the SMG in his hands. "You'll cross her bow and we'll be far enough away to see her bridge deck and steering compartment. If she's not wise to us by then, we won't fire."

"That makes sense," agreed Gordel. "Gene, get on the walkie-talkie and tell them on the stern that I'll make the first one by port to see if she has cargo doors. If she has, I'll cross her stern, cut speed, and go up close to starboard and McKenna can play superman with the first mine. Then I'll cut across her bow and come back to port."

"I still don't know what to think of McKenna," Sisney said, pulling the Tracer-1 W-T from the case on his belt. "I can't decide whether he's crazy or knows exactly what he's doing."

"He thinks like an Oriental," Gordel said, thinking that in many ways he no longer knew his old friend.

By the time Cotton Jorges had taken the message from Sisney on his walkie-talkie and had told the other men, the yacht was so close to the *Independencia* that the freighter loomed up like a small mountain.

Gordel turned the wheel, and very quickly the yacht was moving past the port side of the freighter at a distance of only fifty feet. In the stern all the men waited with Ingram SMG's and M16 assault rifles, all except the Ninja Master, who stood as calm as a tombstone, looking for the cargo doors. He had set the timers on the four Zorntov mines. All he had to do was magnetize each mine and pull the wires.

He and the other men saw the cargo doors: two of them together in the port side, directly below the second boom. Opening outward, the doors were square, each one ten by thirteen feet, their bottom edges ten feet above the waterline, and only two or three feet higher than the main deck of *Laughing Lady*.

"Well, there are the cargo doors—damn it!" Jerry Joe Bilib said resignedly. "It looks like we're going aboard the big bastard."

No one answered him.

Ray Gordel took the yacht a hundred feet to the stern of the freighter. He executed a wide turn to starboard, turned again, and, as he approached the starboard side of the large vessel, cut speed to a slow-drag five knots.

Scott McKenna placed the end of the last two feet of the mop handle on top of the deck railing, pulled up the magnet lever on top of the mine, took off the seal, and jerked the activating wire. Eleven seconds later, he leaned forward over the railing, with the end of the mop handle in his right hand while he held on to the railing with his left hand. He waited as the yacht moved so close to the starboard side of the freighter that it seemed, for an instant, that the hulls of the two vessels would come together. They didn't. They did come so close that they were only six feet apart. NOW! McKenna shoved the mop handle forward and downward, the steel hull of the freighter grabbing the bottom of the magnetized mine four feet above the waterline and thirty feet forward of her propeller and rudder.

All the while, the other men looked upward at the railing of the freighter, watching for any signs of danger. They could see the forms of a dozen men, but because of the darkness they could not be sure whether the Cubans were armed.

Once Gordel saw that he was amidships, he increased speed to twenty knots; the yacht shot forward and very quickly moved ahead. Gordel then turned to port a hundred yards ahead of the freighter, which by now had begun to slow down. Once again Ray took *Laughing Lady* up the port side of *Independencia*. Only, this time he moved in very close and cut speed when the prow of the yacht was pointing west.

Soon McKenna was placing the second mine against the outside of the first cargo door, toward the lower corner where the bottom hinge, inside the ship, would be. It was right after he'd placed the third mine against the lower outer edge of the second door that six Cubans from the top port-side deck opened fire, three with pistols, the other three triggering Soviet AKS 74 assault rifles. The AKS 5.45 X 39mm projectiles were popping into the yacht when seven automatic weapons—Ingrams and M16's—roared from the stern of the *Laughing Lady* and a tidal wave of slugs washed over the Cubans, butchering them to the extent that bits and blobs of flesh and blood were dropping into the water by the time the corpses were sinking to the bloody deck. For good measure, Motor Mouth Kling riddled the bottoms of the lifeboats as the yacht moved by and the Ninja Master prepared to place the fouth and final mine, the one with the five-pound block of C-3. He placed this last mine five feet above the waterline and forty feet forward of the rudder and the propeller.

The yacht continued west, Gordel taking the vessel six hundred feet to the port stern of the big freighter, which had shut off her engines and was coming to a full stop in the water. Ray swung the vessel around so that her bow was pointed in the same direction as the freighter, cut her diesels to a full stop, and turned to Alfred Rothweiler.

"Al, do you have everything straight?"

"I'd have to be an idiot if I didn't," Rothweiler said, sounding peeved. "After the four blasts, I take her forward a hundred feet past the bow of the target, turn, and come back along her port side. You'll give the distance to Gene from the stern, over the walkie-talkie, and he'll relay instructions to me and tell me when to shove off. I wait five hundred feet to starboard and come back to the cargo doors when we get the 'Come and pick us up' from you birds on the walkie-talkie. If you don't get your balls shot off!"

"You got it!" Gordel gave a lopsided grin. "I'll see you both later. Keep the coffee hot."

"One more thing," said Rothweiler, becoming very serious. "If you come across a can of pipe tobacco over there, grab it for me. I can't stand smoking cigarettes. Every time I light up, I think of lung cancer."

"I'll ask the captain when I see him," joked Gordel. He turned, headed for the radio-chart room door, and soon had joined McKenna, Jorges, and the others on the stern, all waiting for the four blasts.

All things do not always come to those who wait. But sometimes a few things do. The first explosion by the starboard stern shattered the quiet night at the same time a light drizzle started to drop from the silent sky. There was a BERRRRUUUUUM, a bright flash of fire, some smoke, and a miracle was performed— and without a big, bright star in the east. A jagged eighteen-foot hole was created in the side of the *Independencia,* the freighter rocking from starboard to port and back again. A six-by-eight-inch section of the hole was below the waterline and immediately the Gulf of Mexico began to pour in.

Minutes later, the second blast blew apart the first cargo door and tore off many of the hull plates. Seventy-one seconds later the third mine exploded and sent most of the other cargo door crashing into the water. Again the big vessel rocked from side to side.

The fourth explosion was the loudest, a big blast that blew a twenty-three-foot hole on the port side of the freighter. The tremendous concussion also ripped apart part of the shaft tunnel, the tunnel recess space, and the lower part of the shaft tunnel escape trunk. Worse, the blast had twisted the propeller shaft and wrecked much of the tail shaft casing and four of the propeller shaft bearings. The propeller would never turn again. Add to that the tons of water pouring into both the port and the starboard blast holes, and the *Independencia* was in very serious trouble.

Right after the fourth explosion, Rothweiler started the two Cummins V-12 diesels and began to move the yacht forward, steadily increasing speed. He was soon turning the yacht and heading it back toward the port side of the doomed *Independencia.* By then, McKenna, Jorges, Hoover, and Bilib had Ingram submachine guns in their hands and had put shoulder bags filled with ammo over their shoulders. In addition, the Ninja Master had thrown the Man Hugger (or the "Flying Porcupine," as John W. Hoover called the chain and ice picks) over his left shoulder and had three of the Nazi daggers in his belt. Ray Gordel carried a Colt CAR-15 SMG, and had his walkie-talkie in his hand. He was wait-

ing to give orders to Alfred Rothweiler, who had cut speed and
was moving the *Laughing Lady* very close to the port side of the
freighter.

   The dark forces of death were about to close in on the night.

CHAPTER 16

People who are busy rowing seldom rock the boat. Captain José Sanchez and Colonel Calixto Bernardo Hevia were good examples. Earlier in the evening, Major Calleja had sent a report that *Little Big Man* had been captured, that the *americano* crew were prisoners, and that the three leaders of the treasure-seeking expedition had been taken aboard the *Ernesto Guevara*. All that remained to be done was for the treasure to be placed aboard the *Independencia*.

Colonel Hevia had been especially relieved when Calleja had made the report. A week previously, General Rolando Ramiro Dorticos had informed him that he had made arrangements to have a special unit of the Cuban navy take him to the *Independencia*. "They will take you in a small, fast yacht," El Tiburón had said. "I want you to personally supervise the transfer of the gold and silver and other valuable items. After the treasure is on board the *Independencia*, I want you to list every item. Do you understand?"

The clever Hevia certainly did understand. "The Shark" didn't trust Major Emilio Calleja. "*Sí, yó comprendo.* However, I should like to point out that Major Calleja is a loyal Cuban and an honest man," Hevia had defended Calleja.

"Of course he is," Dorticos had replied in an oily voice. "Nevertheless, I want to be positive that all will be well. For that reason, you will itemize the treasure. Furthermore, Colonel, you will not let Major Calleja and Captain Penzula know you are aboard the freighter. They will learn of your presence when the *Independencia* arrives to transfer the gold and silver and other valuable items from the American ship. Do you have any questions?"

"No, sir."

Dorticos had smiled, and his little eyes had narrowed. "Le
me give you some advice, Colonel. Great wealth often turns the
head and the morals of the best man. Make sure that does no
happen to you. You may go, Colonel. . . ."

Only a few hours away from *Laughing Lady,* the submarine
and the *americano* ship, Colonel Hevia and Captain Sanchez were
in the steering compartment on the bridge, with the helmsman and
First Mate Alejo Castilla, enjoying what they considered victory
when radar and sonar detected the fast approach of a vessel—yach
size—coming straight at the freighter from the northeast. Not too
concerned, they waited until they saw the dark form of the ship
coming at high speed toward the port bow of *Independencia.* Suddenly, the newcomer veered off and moved down the port side. She
crossed the stern, and a few minutes later charged up the starboard
side, continuing straight ahead.

Hevia and Sanchez watched the vessel through night binoculars, each with an uneasy feeling, each suspecting that something
was wrong.

"I'm not sure, but—I think it's the *Laughing Lady!*" Sanchez
said at length in an odd voice.

It was then that the first report from the deck came in over the
ship's intercom system, with one of the deck watch reporting that
the smaller vessel had stopped briefly by the stern, on the starboard
side, and that one of the men in the stern of the yacht had placed
something against the hull. By then, *Laughing Lady* had turned
and was moving in very close to the port side of *Independencia.*

"Fire on her!" Captain Sanchez had ordered, his voice rising
in panic. His eyes wide, he stared at Hevia. "A mine! They've
placed a mine against the hull!"

Hevia's lower jaw fell. For a moment he gaped at José Sanchez, who was forty-two years old, lived to eat, and had a paunch
that made one think he was trying to conceal a football under his
pants and shirt.

Recovering from shock instantly, Hevia deduced what had
happened.

"It's the Americans," he said, his voice raspy. "They've escaped and captured the *Laughing Lady.* Major Calleja and his men
are no doubt dead. In all probability, they also killed the crew of
the *Ernesto Guevara.* No other explanation is possible!"

Even the helmsman, a young Cuban not more than twenty-two, had turned and gaped at Hevia as though he had lost his mind and was wandering in a forest of madness.

"Colonel, that is impossible!" raged Sanchez angrily. "Only hours ago, Major Calleja said everything had gone according to plan! Why, they didn't even have to fire a shot. And how could three men take over a submarine? Why—".

"Where else could the damned Americans have obtained magnetic mines?" growled Hevia, cutting off Sanchez with savage vehemence, "if not from the submarine? Do you think magnetic mines are a part of equipment needed to search for sunken treasure?"

It was then that they heard the roaring of automatic weapons firing from the port side of the freighter and from the attacking yacht. Several minutes later, they learned that six deckhands had been cut to pieces by slugs and that the Americans had placed mines against both cargo doors and against the port hull close to the stern.

Sanchez almost screamed orders at Alejo Castilla. "Close all bulkheads and get the men out of the boiler room. We might be able to stay afloat. I—I d-don't know."

Hevia's eyes widened and a deep frown creased his forehead. His feeling of deep dread increased. "Captain, can the seawater flow through the opening when the cargo doors in the hull are open, or torn off by an explosion?"

"No. The opening is too high above the waterline." Sanchez looked puzzled. "Why do you ask?"

"Issue weapons to the men," Hevia said quickly. "Those maniacs are going to try to board us. That is why they placed mines against the cargo doors."

They heard the first explosion at the stern on the starboard side. The blast did more than make the *Independencia* tremble. It conveyed to Colonel Hevia and Captain Sanchez that their mission had been reduced to total failure. . . .

Scott McKenna and the other four men who would board the freighter kept down and watched as Rothweiler maneuvered *Laughing Lady* into position. The three other men kept their M16's trained upward on the port-side railing. Bilib and Hoover, however, kept watch over the blasted opening where the two cargo doors had been. By now the Cubans realized they were under attack and would have prepared a slug-filled reception.

Gordel spoke into the walkie-talkie in his left hand: "Come to a full stop and glide in. You have only another thirty feet. That's it! That's it! Get in as close as you can."

Thinder, Glazier, and Kling suddenly opened fire with their M16's, streams of 556 X 45mm projectiles streaming upward toward the port-side railing where they had spotted several Cubans about to lean down and fire. One Cuban was lucky; he pulled back in time. The other was unlucky and too slow. He was knocked back from the railing by a dozen slugs, his AKS 74 assault rifle dropping over the side and splashing into the water.

The hulls of the two vessels came together slightly, then separated a foot.

"Get set," McKenna said casually when he saw that the stern of the yacht was rapidly approaching the cargo opening of the freighter. The others had seen the distance narrowing, and the Ninja Master had only spoken to make sure every man was on full alert. He picked up the Man Hugger and placed it over his left shoulder.

Gordel yelled at Thinder, who had taken out his Tracer-1 walkie-talkie: "Ellery, the instant you see that all of us are inside the freighter, tell Rothweiler to shove off."

The stern came to the blasted opening, whose sides and some of the bottom were twisted hull plates. The two explosions had torn off the bottom inside hinges and had so weakened the curved braces inside the double hull that the top hinges, on each side, would not support what was left of the doors. The majority of each door had fallen into the water and was now at the bottom of the Gulf of Mexico. Even so, a thousand pounds of twisted steel sheeting—part of the top of one door—hung precariously from the top hinge closest to the bow.

This was it! The cargo opening into number two hold of the *Independencia* was directly across the stern of the yacht. McKenna, Gordel, Jorges, and the two other attackers first raked the opening with short bursts of slugs, after which they rushed across the stern, climbed up on the railing, and jumped across the foot of open space into the inside of the hold, again triggering off short bursts as they dived for any kind of cover they could find. What they found were crates of coconuts, just as they had been cut from the trees, most of the crates the size of a refrigerator. Hundreds of stacked steel drums—one on top of the other—contained copra, the dried meat of the coconut that is turned into oil. Smaller wooden crates were filled with *coco* cake, the mealy material left over after the oil has been pressed from the copra. The *coco* cake would be used as cattle feed.

The two explosions that had destroyed the port-side cargo doors had toppled many of the drums and had torn open several dozen of the crates so that hundreds of coconuts were scattered all over the floor. They looked like some kind of alien life form in the dim glow of the half-dozen wire-shielded ceiling lights that had not been broken and shaken loose by the terrific concussions.

Not one shot had been fired at the attackers from inside the hold. Either the hold was empty or else the Cubans were attempting to ". . . sucker us into some kind of an ambush," whispered Jerry Bilib, who, with the Ninja Master and Jorges, was huddled beside a crate. Across from them, to their right, were Gordel and John Hoover. "What the hell are we going to do, Scott?"

By then, Alfred Rothweiler had pulled *Laughing Lady* away form the port side of the freighter. Very quickly, she was gone and the sound of her engines were fading in the distance. McKenna and his four companions were now very much alone, and to a man they felt it.

Ray Gordel and John Hoover dashed across the six-foot space, and Ray offered the same question as Bilib. "We can't stay here, and we can't just run forward and take the chance of being wasted. The only thing we can be sure of is that all the bulkheads will be closed because of the explosions on both sides of the stern." He glanced again at McKenna, making it clear that he was depending on the judgment of the Ninja Master.

"We'll move to the left, to the wall between this hold and number one hold," McKenna said, his voice low and steady. "We'll then go along the wall to the starboard side. From the starboard wall, we'll come up between this hold and number three hold. We'll be able to reach the bulkhead. Once we're in number three hold, we'll be able to get to the deck and the center superstructure. Ray, John, watch our rear. Cotton, Jerry, keep your eyes—"

The roaring of submachine guns and assault rifles stifled the Ninja Master. What had happened was that John Hoover had looked out to the side of a crate and had been in time to see two Cubans, thirty feet ahead, staring out at him from behind several other crates. The two crewmen, realizing they had been seen, opened fire along with several other crewmen, two using AK-47 assault rifles and two triggering Soviet PPS submachine guns (or machine pistols, as the Russians referred to SMG's). A barrage of

7.62 X 25 Tokarev projectiles chopped through the pine boards of the crates and made a lot of *thud thud thud thudding* sounds as they buried themselves in coconuts, which were very effective in stopping slugs. Five of the semispitzer-shaped 7.62mm projectiles stabbed into the side of the crate, not far from where Hoover's head had been, causing hundreds of splinters to fly outward.

"The bastards were waiting to ambush us," Jorges growled. "Damn it! They could keep us pinned down here indefinitely!"

McKenna's computerlike mind did some rapid calculating. Several hours earlier, while *Laughing Lady* was still moving toward the *Independencia,* he had mentioned to Ray and Cotton that the six packets of C-3, equalling ten pounds, were too powerful. Why not cut them into smaller packages—"Or don't we have enough timer-detonators?"

They had twenty T-detonators. The result was twenty small packages, each one weighing eight ounces, give or take an ounce, meaning some weighed slightly more than others.

McKenna did not have time to tell either Ray or Cotton to throw one of the packets forward. The eighteen Cubans on the starboard side of the hold did the dumbest thing possible: they charged, firing AK-47 AR's and PPS SMG's, a hundred or more projectiles stabbing into the sides of the five crates, on the other sides of which were the Ninja Master and his attack force of four. What saved the Americans was that the inexperienced Cubans had not used selective fire, but instead were keeping their fingers down on the triggers. The cyclic rate of an AK-47 is six hundred rounds per minute. Within seconds, the thirty-round box-magazines were empty.

The Castro goons with the Soviet subguns had the same problem, even though they couldn't have used selective fire even if they had wanted to. A PPS SMG could only be fired on full automatic. At 650 rpm, the magazines of the chatterboxes were soon empty. Before the Cuban sailors could duck for cover and reload, McKenna and his men leaned out from behind their protective crates and began firing their Ingram M10's, single rounds, very fast, the big .45 H.P. Silvertip slugs stabbing into the Cubans. The "brave protectors" of Communism screamed and went down, blood dripping from bullet holes. Gordel's CAR-15 and its 5.56mm projectiles also did plenty of damage, the slugs sending two Cubans into hell in only seconds. . . .

The turkey shoot took only nine seconds, during which time

twelve Cubans—with hopes, dreams, and ambitions—were turned into Mute People of that Dark Land ruled by the Pale Priest. Six of the attackers had managed to duck behind crates. After reloading, they debated whether to retreat or continue the attack, the decision resting with Enrique Roto, a machinist's mate.

McKenna whispered to Ray and Cotton, "I'm going to the left. When I reach the wall, I'll work my way over to the starboard side. I'm going to try to come in behind them."

John Hoover, frowning when he saw McKenna pick up the Man Hugger, said in a merciless tone, "You're going to get your arse shot off if you try to use that damn contraption."

Ray and Cotton, who knew better than to try to move Gibraltar with their bare hands, merely nodded. Gordel said, "Good luck."

McKenna moved rapidly to his left, the Ingram SMG in his left hand, the Man Hugger lying over his right shoulder. The cork in the points of the ice picks made the weapon safe for him to carry. He quickly reached the wall between number one and number two holds, then began to move between crates toward the starboard side. He had a strong sense of evil about the interior of the ship—he was certain that people had suffered and slowly died in this hold. A Castro prison ship. The *Independencia* had once been a prison ship.

He soon saw the bulkhead between number one hold and number two hold. It was closed. Carefully he moved forward between "islands" of crates held down by steel strapping bands. He soon saw that directly ahead was a six-foot-wide aisle extending from the bulkhead to his left to the bulkhead between this hold and number three hold. He hesitated; he hadn't counted on the passage. The Cubans also knew the aisle was there. It would be ideal for an ambush should the enemy be clever enough to deduce that one of the Americans might try to cross the open space as part of a plan to come in behind them. One thing a ninja never did was underestimate an enemy, even an enemy of an inferior nation.

McKenna changed course and began to creep to his right, the aisle only ten feet in front of him, to starboard. He had moved twenty-five feet and was between two large crates filled with coconuts when he heard whispered voices on the other side of crates in front of him. Three or four men were whispering in Spanish. McKenna did not understand Spanish. But in any language, he knew he was almost on top of the Cubans. Unless they moved to their right, they would have to cross the aisle, or go to their left to reach the other bulkhead. But why do that when there was a bulkhead to their right—McKenna assumed.

The Will of the Will of the Will of the Tao. . . .

McKenna looked all around, then placed the Ingram on the floor, took the Man Hugger from his shoulder, and very quickly pulled the square pieces of cork from the points of the ice picks, all the while being very careful not to let the links of steel chain and the blades clink-clank-clink. He picked up the Ingram SMG with his right hand and, holding one end of the Man Hugger in his left, moved the ten feet to the edge of the aisle. He waited, every cell in his body on full alert. In less than a minute, he heard the same voices whispering in Spanish. He didn't become excited. Death was part of life. He waited patiently, knowing that the Cubans, only seven feet to his right, were as good as dead.

"*¡Adelante—de prisa!*" Enrique Roto whispered. McKenna heard the words but didn't know what they meant. From the tone, he assumed it was some kind of order. A few moments later, he did know that the Cubans were moving to the right. In spite of their trying to move quietly, he could hear their feet coming down on the wooden slats covering the steel floor. The Cubans had to be headed toward the bulkhead between number two hold and number three hold.

McKenna almost felt ashamed of himself. It was too easy. He raised the Ingram, stepped out into the aisle, and moving his left arm upward and out, began twirling the Man Hugger above his head at the same time he began to work the trigger of the deadly little chatterbox.

One-two-three! Three of the Cubans went down, two with bullet holes in the back of their necks, the third—turning around to look behind him—taking a 9mm hollow point through the left rib cage. He let out a strong, querulous scream and started to fall to the right, stumbling against a fourth man. The fifth and sixth men began to spin around to face McKenna and get off rounds with their PPS machine pistols; however, the sudden attack had given the Ninja Master the advantage.

Enrique Roto was trying to raise his PPS when McKenna pulled the trigger of the Ingram and let fly with the Man Hugger. Roto gasped, dropped the PPS, looked down at the bullet hole in his chest, and crashed to the floor on his back. Within the same few seconds, Jesús Presendis—he had almost been knocked off his feet by the Cuban who had taken a slug through the left side—started to swing his AK-47 assault rifle toward McKenna.

Carlos Fisternos let out a high-pitched but very short scream when the Man Hugger wrapped itself around his neck and the short lengths of four ice picks buried themselves in the sides, the back, and the front of his neck. Three more ice picks had stabbed him high in the chest, but two had been stopped by ribs. The high scream became a low bubbling gurgle, accompanied by a tidal wave of blood that began to rush from his mouth and the front and the sides of his neck. Blood also began to seep from around the three ice picks in his chest. Looking like the victim of some strange species of metal snake that had wrapped itself around him, Fisternos went down in a spray of blood.

In the meanwhile, McKenna had seen Presendis swing the AK-47 toward him. Happy that he had balanced the Man Hugger properly, Scott jerked to his left and twice pulled the trigger of the Ingram, the two cracks of the small SMG lost in the louder roaring of the Soviet assault rifle. McKenna had been very fast. Jesús Presendis had been slower, and not as lucky. His stream of 7.62 X 39mm projectiles cut by McKenna's right side, one bullet missing him by an eighth of an inch. The entire swarm of slugs kept right on going and set up a screaming chorus as they ricocheted from the bulkhead door at the bow side of the passage. McKenna did not miss. His two 9mm H.P.'s chopped Presendis in the chest, the second one hitting and going through the heart. Stone dead, the dummy dropped.

McKenna looked sternward and saw that the bulkhead between numbers two and three was closed. He darted back to the side of the same crate from which he had attacked and broke the eerie silence by calling out, "THEY'RE ALL DEAD. COME AHEAD!"

"OKAY! WATCH FOR US!" Ray Gordel yelled back.

It was then that McKenna and his men and every Cuban felt a great shudder ripple through the *Independencia,* and the deck tilt ever so slightly to stern. They knew why. Tons of water were pouring through the blasted holes on the port and the starboard sides.

Colonel Calixto Hevia and Captain José Sanchez, each armed with a Soviet Vitmorkin machine pistol, had left the wheelhouse and were on the upper deck, standing in front of the midships superstructure and waiting for the first mate and a group of sailors to arm themselves and report back to them.

"I'm positive she won't sink," Sanchez said truculently. "The water won't even be able to reach the boilers. The bulkhead to stern in the engine space will hold." He paused, then added, as if to reassure himself, "I'm positive. The *Independencia* will not sink."

Hevia, who considered Sanchez an unrealistic fool, gave him a long, reproachful look. They had both gone to the railings on each side of the ship and had looked down to see the amount of damage that had been done by the explosions. They had not been able to see much. But they had stared fearfully at the fins cutting back and forth through the water on both sides of the vessel—scores of great whites patiently waiting. The rain had stopped, but the thunder in the distance was becoming louder and the wind had quickened.

The *Laughing Lady* was 155 meters to port, and she, too, was waiting; but it wasn't likely that she would pick up any survivors who escaped the sharks. A logical man, Colonel Hevia considered himself as good as dead. He might as well be! Even if he survived, even if he and some of the others were picked up by passing ships or—*Madre de Dios!*—by the American navy or Coast Guard and he managed to get back to Cuba, he would probably be shot. The structural order of command demanded that someone always had to take the blame for failure. In this case, General Dorticos would blame him in his report to Castro, and Castro was known for demanding revenge against those who failed.

As if needing conversation, Sanchez continued in a nervous voice, "It was bad enough when the *americanos* planted mines against the hull. But to actually come aboard us! What do they want? I tell you, Colonel, it is like our *Líder Máximo* has always said. The *americanos* are crazy. They are unpredictable!"

Hevia almost said it was Fidel Castro who was crazy. It was very dangerous to send men to Nicaragua. However, years of extreme caution made Hevia think better of saying what he really thought. By God! Sanchez was half right. These Americans were crazy. If they had acted like normal men, they would have sailed away after they had freed themselves and recaptured their ship with its hundreds of millions of dollars in treasure. Instead, like a group of commandos, they had come after the *Independencia* and had actually come aboard the vessel. Why, there couldn't be more than ten of them!

"The Americans want to reach this control center," Hevia

said, glancing back toward the superstructure. "But I intend to stop them on the second deck."

It was then that Alejo Castilla, the giant of a first mate, and Sergei Mikhaylovich Kudryatsev, the bosun and the only Russian on board—everyone knew he was a KGB watchdog—and forty men came around from the starboard side. Thirty-four of the men were armed with either PPS machine guns or AK-47 assault rifles —the last of the AR's and SMG's on board. The rest of the group were armed with old fashioned Soviet Tokarev autopistols.

"Roto and his group have not reported back to us," Hevia said brusquely to Castilla, who was six feet tall and had 243 pounds of solid muscle attached to his large bones. "All of you heard the firing from number two hold. The Americans must have killed every single one of them."

An angry look crossed Castilla's broad face. The other men appeared unsettled, the way one looks when told there's been a death in his family.

"*Mi Colonel,* the *americanos* can't get through the bulkhead door into number three, unless Enrique and his men forgot to lock —" The first mate caught his mistake. "They couldn't lock the bulkhead from number three hold if they died in the second hold," he said sheepishly. "But they still cannot get past the bulkhead at the top of the stairs to the second deck. It's locked from the second deck."

An explosion from deep inside the vessel, from the area of the second hold, made the deck shake.

"There's your answer," Hevia said obdurately. "The *americanos* came aboard with explosives. Come, we'll use the hatch to the stern of the superstructure. When we get to the second deck, we'll make it easy for the bastards. We'll open the bulkhead for them."

Captain Sanchez watched Colonel Hevia and the men rush to the hatch, wondering how killing the *americanos* would help the *Independencia* survive. The deck was already slanting noticeably to aft. The water couldn't get past the stern bulkhead in the engine space, Sanchez told himself in desperation. But if the double wall between the engine space and the shaft tunnel escape trunk couldn't support the dead weight of thousands of tons of water. . . .

The Ninja Master and his four men moved with great speed. After pushing open the thick and heavy bulkhead door between the number two hold and the third hold, McKenna and his tiny group tossed a packet of C-3 through the bulkhead opening to rattle any Cubans who might be waiting and to keep them down. They had timed the package for only one minute, and as soon as the package exploded, they had charged through the opening, firing short bursts and taking positions between crates of coconuts.

They soon discovered they were alone in number three hold, in which there were two sets of steel stairs and two landings, the first landing halfway up, the second at the top of the second flight of steps.

The Ninja Master and the other four men studied the bulkhead at the end of the second landing, twenty-nine feet above them. They knew why the other bulkhead had been open: because dead Cubans can't close and lock doors.

"We can blast it open with the C-3 we have," Gordel said thoughtfully, staring upward at the bulkhead that opened to the second deck. "But the explosion will probably destroy the top landing. It's a ten-foot area up there. With the landing gone, we'd have no way to get to the opening."

The Ninja Master asked in a quiet tone, "How long will this freighter stay afloat?"

"I think we should get the hell off this damned ship," muttered Jerry Bilib. "What we're doing is just plain nuts."

He knew his words were as useless as drifting smoke, when Ray glanced speculatively at Jorges. "Cotton, you know freighters better than any of us. Will the bulkheads hold?"

Jorges shrugged and scratched the right side of his face. "It depends on how well this tub is built. The stern bulkheads will hold if they're as large as the ones forward. Whether or not she floats depends on the strength of the retainer walls, the walls across the ship from port to starboard. They're not like the pressure hull of a submarine. If one compartment fills completely with water, then you have a tremendous amount of pressure—or push." He cleared his throat and glanced from Ray to Scott. "It's a calculated risk."

"I'll go up the steps and check the bulkhead door," McKenna said before anyone else could say anything. "Should it be locked, we'll call *Laughing Lady* and have her pick us up."

"I hope to God the damned door is locked!" muttered John W. Hoover, watching the Ninja Master run toward the steps.

No one commented. Gordel, Jorges, and Bilib, within their

own minds, agreed with Hoover. Yet it was their "manly" sense of bravery that prevented them from putting their true feelings into words. To do so would not only have been a kind of disloyalty to McKenna, but also an admission that they were stupid for placing themselves in such a precarious position.

Ray Gordel thought he understood why Scott had wanted to go aboard the *Independencia*. It was because he was a Ninja Master. In one respect, the ninja were like Adolf Hitler's elite Schutzstaffel, or "Defense Echelons"—the infamous SS. The SS had subscribed to the doctrine of total annihilation. So did the ninja. So did Scott McKenna.

McKenna reached the top landing at the top of the second flight of steps, walked over the the bulkhead, and pressed down on the lever handle. He then pushed against the door with his left knee. He and the men below saw the round door swing inward, toward the second deck, a few inches.

"Well, shit!" muttered Bilib as McKenna motioned for them to come up the steps. The four men started toward the bottom steps.

Once they had reached the landing, it was Jorges who whispered to everyone, but particularly to the Ninja Master, "This is too much of a coincidence. Why wasn't this bulkhead locked from the other side? I suppose you'll tell us it's just chance."

"The laws of chance do not cause coincidences," McKenna said perfunctorily. "They only impel them. I'm going out there to look around."

He opened the bulkhead door a few feet, stepped through the opening, and, with his Ingram ready to fire, looked up and down the second deck. He found that he was in a very wide passage. In the direction of the bow, twelve feet away, was one of the end walls of the clean-and-soiled-linen room, its front ending toward the port side, leaving a seven-foot space in front of the port hull. This space formed a narrow passage the length of the linen compartment.

It was the same to aft, to McKenna's left. There was another wall, it and the front of the vegetable room ending toward port, creating another seven-foot-wide passage. McKenna reasoned that the steps to the superstructure amidships had to be sternward—to his left as he faced the port side.

He turned, pulled open the bulkhead door, and motioned with his hand. The deck had ceased tilting toward the stern, indicating that the water had filled the compartments aft of the engine space and that it had nowhere else to go. The *Independencia* was help-less, dead in the water and without power. She would, however, keep afloat and could drift.

The Ninja Master and the four men moved sternward, con-stantly turning and watching all avenues of approach, especially the two narrow passageways in front of the linen room and the vegetable storage compartment. They moved quickly through the seven-foot passage to stern and, twenty feet later, found themselves in another large area similar to the one fronting the bulkhead. The only difference was that this area had a telephone and a rolled-up fire-hose on the stern wall. Again, there was a long wall on the bow side. This was the other end of the fresh-vegetable room. The wall to aft was one end of the refrigerated meat-and-fish compartment. They could hear its refrigeration units running.

The tiny attack force considered its position. Hoover quickly took a position from which he could watch the length of the nar-row passage aft. Bilib appointed himself guard of the corridor on the bow side.

"The steps to the main deck have to be close by," Gordel said in a tight voice filled with tension. He stared at McKenna. "We'll run into most of the crew up there unless they've abandoned ship."

From ten feet to the left, Hoover snorted. "Those spics would have had to patch up hundreds of holes in the bottoms of the lifeboats if they did. We turned their keels into screens!"

"Scott, we've come far enough." Jorges sounded determined. "We've sunk their sub. If we get out of here alive, we'll sink the *Laughing Lady.* Even if we die in here, the other men will send her to the bottom—and we've wrecked this freighter."

"And have snuffed a helluva lot of Cubans!" Gordel inserted quickly. "Even your ninja code should be satisfied."

"It is and you're both right," agreed Scott. "Let's get back to number two hold and contact the boys on *Laughing La—*"

"WATCH IT!" yelled Hoover. It was he who had first spotted the attackers pouring into the opposite end of the narrow corridor he was watching. He jerked back in time to avoid a dozen 7.62mm PPS subgun slugs that stabbed into the end of the passage wall where he had been standing. Other slugs stabbed into the wall of the opposite passage, many of them narrowly missing Jerry Bilib. He jerked back at the same time that McKenna, Jorges, and Gordel raced forward and the quick-thinking J. W. Hoover dropped to his knees, thrust his Ingram around the corner, and fired a long raking horizontal burst upward, his rain of 9mm metal ripping across four Cubans who were almost to the end of the passage. Jorges—cursing in Spanish—got between Hoover and the corner of the wall, shoved his I-M10 around the edge, and triggered off another raking burst on full auto, the sixteen big .45 Silvertip hollow points killing more of the Cubans. Dropping their weapons, they went down screaming in a flurry of arms and legs and bodies crashing together.

Across from Jorges and Hoover, McKenna and Bilib—holding the 11.5-inch-long Ingram-like pistols—were firing from around the corner of the wall into the other passage, the floor of which was already carpeted with dead and dying Cubans. And still the chili peppers stormed forward, all the while firing their AK-47's and their PPS machine pistols, the roaring pounding on the ears of McKenna and his crew.

Two semispitzer 7.62mm Tokarev projectiles struck the left side of McKenna's Ingram. Clang! Clang! The wrecked SMG was almost jerked from his hand, one slug glancing from the side of the barrel with a loud scream and narrowly missing the left shoulder of Bilib, who had exhausted the ammo in his Ingram and was firing his .357 magnum Colt Python ("his" only because the revolver was in his possession. The weapon had formerly belonged to "Sally the Sheik" Samenta).

Ray Gordel didn't even have the time to think *We're as good as dead!* He was too busy firing the Colt CAR-15, which was the loudest weapon of all and had the largest muzzle flash. Ray cried out when a stream of slugs skimmed by his right side and one of them cut across the inside of his right arm, leaving a short but not-too-deep cut in his biceps. The stream of slugs continued and, narrowly missing McKenna, chopped into the wall of the vegetable room.

The Ninja Master, mentally conditioned to ignore all except the worst pain, hardly noticed when a 7.62mm projectile found the outside of his left leg, six inches above the knee. The trench it left behind was deep but not at all dangerous. The Ninja Master had received deeper wounds in Japan, while training with the *tachi, katana, wakizashi,* and other kinds of Japanese swords. Another bullet missed the right side of his neck by only a third of an inch.

For McKenna and his four men to pause to reload was out of the question. Nor did the Cuban attackers have time to shove full magazines into the AK-47's and machine pistols. The charge lasted only fifty-seven seconds. During that time, McKenna and his group had emptied their weapons, although Hoover had two rounds left in his 9mm large-frame Llama autoloader, and Gordel had three in his Hi-Power Browning. The attacking Cubans— those who had not been gunned down—had also exhausted their ammo, so that in another few moments the Ninja Master and his men were face to face with twenty-two Cubans, including a bull-angry Calixto Bernardo Hevia determined to kill the *americanos* who had wrecked the mission and destroyed his life. Yelling and screaming obscenities, the Cubans came straight at the five Americans, determined to beat them to death on the spot.

Bilib ducked very fast when Diego Manrique swung an empty AK-47 at his head, swinging the empty assault rifle the way one would swing a baseball bat. Bilib may have flopped as a professional wrestler because he couldn't act, but this was murderous reality and he didn't have to fake his blows. He didn't. He let the Cuban have such a powerful kick in the stomach that his foot came close to touching the inner side of Manrique's spine. With his stomach, spleen, and pancreas mashed together in one soggy mess, Manrique let out a short cry of supreme agony and fell back into three other sailors who were doing their best to reach Gordel. José de Unzaga did manage to reach the beefy ex-wrestler. A big man himself, he tried to slam a left fist into Bilib's stomach, in conjunction with a right edge-of-the-hand chop to the left side of his neck. Bilib stepped back and de Unzaga connected only with air. Quick and agile for a big man, Jerry Joe stepped forward and tried to slam de Unzaga over the head with the barrel of his empty Colt Python. But José de Unzaga was also fast. He ducked, but in so doing stumbled against several other men, lost his balance, and staggered within reach of the deadly hands of McKenna. Mc-Kenna didn't waste any time. A lightning-quick left *oyayubi* thumb stab to de Unzaga's throat and a *haishu* backhand to the bridge of the Cuban's nose started the goon on his way to oblivion. Choking, de Unzaga began to go down, hideous sounds escaping from his throat.

Three other Cubans felt they would be luckier than de Unzaga. While José Musalitore and Domingo Cabella rushed at him from the front, Juan Mura Casas came at him from the rear. His intention was to break the Ninja Master's spine by slamming him across the small of the back with the wooden stock of his AK-47.

McKenna, sensing that Mura Casas was streaking in to his

rear, did the last thing his attackers expected. He had Stroked the Death Bird, and his sense of Jin, which was only a tiny part of Hsi Men Jitsu—the Way of the Mind Gate—was hyperactive, so that he knew almost to the second when the three Cubans would reach him.

At the last moment, McKenna took several fast steps forward, and sprang high into the air, both legs shooting outward, one to the left, one to the right. His right foot slammed Domingo Cabella in the left temple, the heel crushing the sphenoid bone, the small, thin bone about an inch to the rear of the eye. His left foot acted as a battering ram that snapped every bone in José Musalitore's face. Teeth snapped, blood spurted, and the agonized man started to sink into unconsciousness.

Even before the two pieces of commie trash had begun to fall, the Ninja Master executed a high backward somersault—his legs pulled up, his hands locked below his knees—that took him six feet to the rear of the astonished and heavily bearded Juan Mura Casas, who had always wanted to imitate the *Líder Máximo* as much as possible.

McKenna landed lightly on his feet while the confused Mura Casas was still trying to figure out what was going on. He spun around, had a very brief glimpse of a smiling *americano,* and instantly started to die, the result of a kick delivered so fast he never saw it coming. But he felt it as he began to choke to death. Scott had used a high roundhouse kick to tie a bloody knot, around his Adam's apple, with the top of his trachea and esophagus.

As an expert in Japanese Shotokan, Ray Gordel believed that, under prevailing conditions, the best defense was to attack. He had taken out the first two Cubans who had come at him with a *koshi* ball-of-the-foot kick to the stomach and a *mawashi geri* circular kick to the solar plexus of the second man.

Salvadore Fuegastes was much more difficult. He charged with a seaman's knife in his left hand, holding the four-inch blade low and close to him as he raised his right hand, as if preparing to deliver a ridge-hand chop. Instinct told Gordel that the man had been trained in some school of karate and knew how to use a knife. Even so, Ray was determined to lure the dummy into a trap.

Gordel feinted with a right *yoko geri kekomi* side kick at the same time that Fuegastes tried to employ a right-handed chop to the side of Ray's neck. Gordel ducked and pretended to stumble. Thinking he had the *americano* off balance, Fuegastes came in fast with the knife, using a quick inward and upward thrust. Gordel jerked back—and had him!

His left hand shot out and grabbed Fuegastes around the left wrist. Instantly, Ray twisted the arm, very quickly stepped to the side of the man, and, before the surprised Fuegastes could make any countermoves, hooked his right arm over the Cuban's left arm. Ray tightened his right arm, "locking" Fuegastes's elbow, all the while twisting Fuegastes's left wrist with his left hand. The man's fingers opened; the seaman's knife fell to the deck. Gordel tightened his right arm even more in the crook of the Cuban's left arm. Another twist of the wrist and Fuegastes howled in agony. Gordel had dislocated his elbow. A *shuto* chop to the side of Fuegastes's neck ended the conflict. Ray didn't even see the man fall to the deck. His attention was focused on other Cubans charging toward him—so fast and so close he didn't have time to repull his Hi-Power Browning pistol.

Victor Cotton Jorges and John W. Hoover were equally as busy, their clothes soggy with sweat and, in some places, with blood. Jorges stabbed Nicolás Vives in the face with the empty Ingram M10, the end of the short barrel punching out Vives's right eyeball. Vives screamed, staggered back, tripped over a corpse, and fell.

Then Jorges got unlucky. A big fist thrown by Mariano Tacón, one of the engine-room officers, caught Jorges in the left rib cage. While staggering him, it only increased his rage. All this time, Cotton had been fighting with a special hatred, a burning loathing for any Cuban who subjected himself to the will of Fidel Castro. Castro! That *minga,* that *bufo,* that *cabrón*! He was a traitor to Cuba, an Adolf Hitler to the people, and an abomination in the eyes of God.

With a bellow of rage that would have made a crocodile shiver, Jorges used his left foot and with all his power stomped on Tacón's left instep. When the man howled with pain, Jorges punched him violently in the solar plexus with the barrel of the Ingram submachine gun. The stab brought so much agony to Tacón that he was unable to scream. All he could do was bend reflexively forward and feel his strength dwindling to zero.

"*¡Coño de la madre!*" snarled Jorges. He raised his right knee, grabbed Tacón by his long hair, and jerked his head down. The raised knee caught Tacón in the nose and mouth, the big slam breaking the maxilla and the mandible—the upper and the lower jaws—and splintering teeth. Out cold, Tacón sagged.

Turning his attention to J. W. Hoover, Jorges saw that the ex-Marine was in serious trouble. Francisco Trosco, behind Hoover, had almost succeeded in applying a stranglehold. Two more spicballs were trying to get at the struggling Hoover from the front but were afraid of his legs. Then Pedro Girona got lucky and managed to grab Hoover's left ankle. In an instant, Hoover was off balance and Trosco and Girona were pulling him to the deck. Principe Angloco, the other Cuban who had been in front of Hoover, now advanced and started to raise one foot, his mouth fixed in a snarl.

Jorges knew that if he did not help J.W., no one else could. McKenna was headed toward Jerry Bilib, who had killed one man by breaking his neck in an underarm headlock, but now was surrounded by three more Cubans who were about to rush him. Gordel was struggling with two Cubans and apparently winning the battle. As Jorges rushed toward Hoover, Ray used a *hiji* elbow strike against the joker coming at him from the rear, broke up the attack of the man in front of him with a right *morote uke* forearm block, and countered with a rapid series of left and right *shuto* strikes that forced the man in front of him to retreat.

McKenna attacked like a whirlwind. Cándido Zilbidaz, one of the sailors in front of Bilib, felt his face explode with an H-bomb of agony. In a microsecond, a cloudburst of blackness was raining over his consciousness and his legs were turning to water. He would never know it, but the Ninja Master had killed him with a powerhouse kick to the glabella, often called—and mistakenly—the "bridge of the nose." While the bridge of the nose is directly between the eyes,, the glabella is half an inch higher or directly between the eyebrows. McKenna's kick had caused such a serious concussion in the front lobes of Zilbidaz's brain that he would never again regain consciousness and would be dead in thirty minutes.

McKenna executed a fast pivot on his right foot and blasted Estrada Menocal with a left-legged *yoko geri kekomi* side thrust kick, the heel and sole—they were all one on the canvas deck shoe—of his foot smashing into Menocal's groin. The savage ram knocked him in the direction of Ray Gordel, who had just knocked his opponent unconscious with a leaping Shotokan *tobi yoko geri* kick that caved in the man's breastbone. In an instant, Ray had

pulled his Browning Hi-Power pistol and was ducking to avoid a
tall Cuban advancing on him with a Vitmorkin machine pistol.
Under different circumstances, the Cuban would have been a good-
looking man. But now his face was a mask of hate, his mouth
pulled back over his teeth. At any moment he would fire.

As McKenna killed the third Cuban to the right of Jerry Bilib
—the Ninja Master used a *tae kwon do* front snap-kick to the solar
plexus—Cotton Jorges reached Principe Angloco, who was only
half a blink away from caving in Hoover's intestines with a right
foot stamp. At the last instant, Angloco turned and threw up his
left arm in an effort to block Cotton's incoming right fist. The
Cuban failed. Cotton's fist crashed squarely into Angloco's upper
lip and nose, the grand slam making the Cuban see any number of
planets and exploding suns. Cotton next let him have such a terrific
left uppercut that the top of Angloco's spine almost snapped as
Angloco's head was forced back. He didn't make a sound as he
dropped.

Now uncertain of their success, Francisco Trosco and Pedro
Girona jumped to their feet to meet the new threat, for the moment
forgetting John W. Hoover, who, although flat on his back, did not
forget them. He sat up, reached out, grabbed Girona by the left
foot, and twisted with all his might as Girona started to take a step
in an effort to get to one side of Cotton Jorges. Girona yelled from
the quick pain that shot from his hip, from the area where the ball
at the upper end of the femur rested in the socket of the hipbone.
Hoover's twisting of the foot forced Girona to turn all the way
around to his left so that for an instant he faced Hoover before he
had to reverse his body again to face Jorges.

At the same time that Francisco Trosco rushed Jorges, Cotton
kicked Girona in the testicles, and Ray Gordel moved quickly to
his right to avoid Estrada Menocal, who was in agony and stumbling backward past him.

A big man, Trosco extended his arms, intending to grab
Jorges in a bear hug and squeeze the life out of him. Even Jorges
and Hoover—scrambling to his feet—were surprised when Trosco
uttered a loud "OHH!" and stopped as though someone had jerked
on an invisible chain. Then Jorges and Hoover saw the reason for
the Cuban's abrupt halt. The hilt of a Nazi dagger was protruding
from his right side, three inches below his armpit. Blood began to
flow from the Cuban's mouth; his eyes rolled back in his head and
he fell forward to the floor on his face.

Jorges and Hoover turned and saw McKenna pulling the second Nazi dress dagger from his belt as he sprinted forward. . . .

All this time, Colonel Calixto Hevia and Alejo Castilla, the first mate, had hung back, logically concluding that it would be foolish for them to risk their lives when so many common sailors were available. After the two forces had charged down the short, narrow corridors, Hevia and Castilla had waited, confident that, in spite of the loses suffered during the charge, the survivors would make short work of the *americanos*. The *americanos* were outnumbered almost five to one!

The head of the Cuban Department of State Security and the first mate of the *Independencia* could not have been more wrong. In not quite five minutes, Scott McKenna and his miniature force had demolished all but six Cubans. The six included Colonel Hevia and Alejo Castilla, both of whom soon realized they had to take an active hand or suffer total defeat. It was when Ray Gordel pulled his Browning autopistol that Hevia, advancing, raised his Vitmorkin machine pistol, and Castilla charged into the area ahead to help Sergei Kudryatsev, the bosun, and the three other crewmen.

A lot of things happened at the same time. The Ninja Master sprinted straight toward Sergei Kudryatsev, who was frantically shoving a full magazine into a PPS machine pistol. Hoover, Jorges, and Bilib closed with the last three Cubans. Hevia pulled the trigger of his Vitmorkin, which he had set to fire single rounds.

Gordel moved to his right just in time. Havia's 9mm flat-nose bullet cut by the left side of his neck. Angrily, Hevia moved the Vitmorkin again, but he couldn't shoot. Castilla, charging straight at Gordel, was in the line of fire. He swung the barrel toward the other Americans, but he couldn't fire at them either. Having closed with the crewmen, they were moving first one way, then another. Yet Hevia knew that if he waited several moments, he would be able to kill the three Americans the farthest away from him. The tall American, the one charging Kudryatsev, was only ten feet away. Hevia raised the Vitmorkin and pulled the trigger.

Gordel was not worried about the big Cuban charging toward him. The mean-faced chili dog might have a chest as wide as a tank, but a 9mm hollow-point slug would put an end to all his ambitions.

Castilla was only seven feet away when Gordel's finger started to tighten on the trigger. At exactly the same instant there was a deep, rolling rumble, and the deck suddenly tilted sharply to stern. The pressure of the water had crushed the retainer wall of the engine space, and hundreds of tons of water had poured in.

Everyone was thrown off balance—except Scott McKenna, who had been in the middle of a leap toward Sergei Kudryatsev. Gordel had also stumbled and his right hand had been jerked upward. His 9mm projectile missed the first mate by three feet and struck the ceiling.

Colonel Hevia's bullet also missed the Ninja Master, the slug zipping by his right side and narrowly missing Cotton Jorges, who had (just before the deck tilted) hammered Cepero Bonilla to the deck with a series of blows to the head.

Sergei Kudryatsev didn't stand a chance against Scott McKenna. The Russian was pulling back the cocking knob of the PPS machine pistol when McKenna's right foot stabbed into the front of his neck and made mush of his Adam's apple and his windpipe. He would be brain dead within minutes.

The sudden tilt of the deck to stern had also caused Colonel Hevia to lose his equilibrium. In panic, seeing McKenna coming straight in, he fired blindly, and during that single shave of a second wondered how any human being could move with such astonishing speed! McKenna had jerked to the left and the bullet had gone by his right arm, straight into the right hip of Arsenio Salamanco. It didn't make all that much difference to Salamanco. J. W. Hoover had been about to pick him up and break his back over a knee. Salamanco jerked, made an "Uuuullll" sound, and collapsed to the floor.

McKenna grabbed Hevia's right wrist and twisted, forcing the Cuban officer to drop the Vitmorkin. He then broke his lower jaw with a straight-in *seiken* fist blow. A right *shuto* chop to the neck! A left *shuto* to the side of the neck. Then a right *nukite* strike to the solar plexus! Calixto Hevia gurgled, dropped, and began to die, the last lines of a song racing through his mind. . . . *Los caminos de me Cuba/Nunca van a donde deben.* . . . "The roads of my Cuba never lead where they should."

Sabas Jovellar also started his journey into the Ultimate Elsewhere. Jerry Bilib had succeeded in throwing him over his shoulder and then had kicked him in the face. When Jovellar collapsed, Bilib had kicked him in the neck.

Alejo Castilla was next to die. He had come in fast and had

succeeded in getting his hands around Gordel's throat. Bringing up his arms inside Castilla's massive arms, Ray had thrown his arms outward and broken the choke hold. Rapidly, Ray had then slapped Castilla's ears with the palms of both hands, the burst of pressure in the Cuban's eardrums slowing the man. Jumping back, Gordel let him have it—a hard snap-kick to the stomach. Another snap-kick to the balls. Finally a *tobi yoko geri* flying kick to the chest. Unconscious and dying from a ruptured artery in his stomach, Castilla sank unconscious to the floor.

The Ninja Master and the four other men looked briefly at the bodies on the floor. All five were bloody from wounds; yet none of the cuts were serious. No one said anything as Ray Gordel walked over to Sabas Jovellar. Ray had seen the bowl of a pipe sticking up from one side of his shirt pocket.

"Ray, what are you doing?" asked Jerry Bilib, wiping his face with a handkerchief. He glanced at McKenna, who was standing straight and taking deep, measured breaths. Then he looked at Jorges. Cotton had pulled his Tracer-1 walkie-talkie from its case on his belt and was turning it on.

Gordel stooped down over the dead man and began patting his pockets. He soon found what he wanted: a package of pipe tobacco. The heavy paper was green with a red border. In the center was the picture of a smiling señorita.

Gordel put the package of tobacco in his shirt pocket, stood up and saw that Cotton had made contact with *Laughing Lady* and was telling Gene Sisney to "pick us up fast. The freighter is about to sink."

It was McKenna who said, "Let's get to the number two hold —fast!"

Twenty-two minutes later, the *Laughing Lady* bobbed gently 870 feet to the starboard side of the *Independencia*. By the time the men had reached the second hold and the *Laughing Lady* had pulled alongside the blasted opening, the deck of the vessel had tilted another two feet to stern. Due to the slant, they had some difficulty jumping to the aft deck of *Laughing Lady*.

Alfred Rothweiler then took the yacht to a position from which they could see the freighter die. They watched from the large wheelhouse, with the bow of the yacht pointed at the starboard side of the freighter. Because of the black night, the only way they could see the *Independencia* was to use the large search-

light on top of the superstructure. Jorges moved the wide beam
back and forth over the dying vessel.

"I wonder why it's taking her so long to go down?" John W
Hoover asked as he bandaged a deep bullet groove on Gordel's le
side. "Man, I thought she was going to sink right out from under
neath us! Yet she's still afloat!"

"Some of the retainer walls are stronger than others," ex
plained Jorges, who was working the control of the searchlight o
the hardtop. "When enough compartments are filled with water
she'll take the final plunge. Did you hear that? It sounded like
shot."

"I thought I heard it," said Will Glazier.

Scott McKenna inclined his head forward. "I heard it. I'r
certain it was a shot."

The sound in the distance had been the report of a Vitmorki
machine pistol. Captain José Sanchez had pressed the muzzle o
the barrel against the roof of his mouth and pulled the trigger. Th
top of his head and part of his brain had been blown all over th
deck.

"Hey, look!" exclaimed Jerry Bilib excitedly. "She's goin
down."

The men pressed against the glass of the windows as Jorge
made another sweep of the vessel with the beam of the searchlight
The bow of the *Independencia,* already at a twenty-degree angle
lifted high out of the water. Just another thirteen degrees and, lik
a monstrous metal finger, the entire forward end of the ship
pointed straight up at the black sky. There were loud crashing
sounds as the derrick hooks tore loose from their foundations and
crashed into the water in which scores of great whites, in a feeding
frenzy, were tearing into screaming Cuban sailors who had either
jumped or fallen from the deck of the dying freighter.

"Those poor bastards," murmured Gene Sisney. "Not even
commie son of a bitches deserve to die like that."

Thinking otherwise, Jorges frowned but remained silent. Un
less you were Cuban, you could not understand a Cuban-Ameri
can's hatred of Castro and his dictatorship.

There were loud rumblings and crashes from within the
freighter as crates of coconuts and *coco* cake, drums of copra, ma
chinery, and equipment smashed through walls toward the stern.

All at once the bow jerked. Then the entire upper half of the
vessel moved backward so that the foredeck and part of the mid

ship superstructure were upside down. The freighter remained at this angle and quickly slid beneath the surface of the Gulf of Mexico. The water churned. There were a lot of bubbles. The water became calm, and all that remained were hundreds of items too light to sink. There were still Cuban sailors desperate for life, frantically trying to crawl onto anything large enough to protect them from the great whites.

"Al, get us out of here," McKenna said in an even voice to Alfred Rothweiler, who was still at the wheel, contentedly smoking his pipe. "All we have to do is get aboard *Little Big Man,* sink this yacht, and go home."

"Right!" Ray Gordel said amicably. "While we're at it, we can also hope that the U.S. Coast Guard doesn't stop and ask us questions, or if it does . . . that we have the right answers. Some ship passing in the distance must have heard those explosions and reported them by radio."

"Possibly," McKenna agreed. "What we have going for us is that we did not break any laws of the United States. We were on the high seas. All we did was protect ourselves against pirates."

The Ninja Master didn't add that he was almost certain they would return safely to home port without being questioned by the Coast Guard or anyone else. He was positive. His sense of Jin told him so. How do you explain Hsi Men Jitsu to men—even intelligent men—who thought of a ninja as something you see in motion pictures?

Behind McKenna and to his left, Motor Mouth Kling was saying to John W. Hoover, "I had an uncle in Kansas who raised chickens. One time they ate a lot of sawdust by accident. You know what happened? All the chickens laid wooden eggs. Except for one hen. She laid an ordinary egg—but hatched a woodpecker!"

The

DEATH MERCHANT

by Joseph Rosenberger

S E R I E S

He's the world's fiercest dealer in death—but only if the cause is right, and the danger is deadly. Go with the Death Merchant on his lethal missions with these action-packed adventures that span the globe:

☐ **THE HINDU TRINITY CAPER (#68)** 13607-5 $2.75

☐ **THE MIRACLE MISSION (#69)** 15571-1 $2.75

☐ **APOCALYPSE (Super Death Merchant)** .. 10160-3 $3.50

At your local bookstore or use this handy coupon for ordering:

DELL READERS SERVICE, DEPT. DJR
P.O. Box 5057, Des Plaines, IL . 60017-5057

Please send me the above title(s). I am enclosing $_____.
(Please add $2.00 per order to cover shipping and handling.) Send
check or money order—no cash or C.O.D.s please.

Ms./Mrs./Mr._____

Address_____

City/State _____ Zip_____

DJR—8/88

Prices and availability subject to change without notice. Please allow four to six
weeks for delivery. This offer expires 2/89.